Yolo 4

Diary of a Mad Woman
A Novel by
Sa'id Salaam

Prologue

"Shyne, wake up!"

"I'm not sleep!" Shyne shot back. She was slightly perturbed at the interruption. She quickly realized who she was speaking to and softened her tone accordingly. "I was reading, Bae."

"Huh?" Asad asked with his face twisted into a question mark. "I didn't say anything."

"You didn't just tell me... Never mind," the fussy little diva shot back and went back to reading.

The small book had become a big distraction from the huge problems her family faced. Her beloved father was still in a bullet-induced coma up in Baltimore. The doctors said he had a fifty-fifty chance of survival. So did they because Shyne had vowed to kill each and every doctor, nurse and candy striper at the hospital if he died. No, it wouldn't be their faults, but they would get the blame.

The diary gave Shyne a chance to finally get to know her long lost mother better. What better way to get to know a person than through their own thoughts written in their own words? She traced her mother's words with her finger before starting to read. When she started to read, it was like she could her hear mother's voice ringing clearly in her mind.

"Dear Diary, I just killed someone..."

"Dang, Ma!" Shyne exclaimed and giggled at the end of reading about how a seven-year-old Yolo had strangled her playmate. She'd obviously forgotten about setting a fire that had killed four people when she was just nine herself.

"Dear Diary, I've been molested..."

Shyne was cheering and clapping at her mother cutting Larry Brown into pieces for molesting her when it dawned on her why Yolo had taken her and Sun to witness the execution that time. She was growling from anger by the time she finished reading about the brutal beating that had followed and her foster mother's plan to rent her

1

out to grown men. Shyne swore an oath to track down this She-Ra Brown, wherever she was, and murder her.

"Aww man," she pouted when she reached the part about Yolo killing the woman. Now she was all worked up with no one to kill.

Luckily for her, the world was full of people who needed dead.

Chapter 1

"You guys go on and eat. We're about to go look at some um... lawn, barbeque, um... Okay, bye," Sun stammered and took off with Asad right behind him.

"They going straight to the game store to buy games," Shyne snitched.

"Mmhm. I already know!" Bryonna laughed. They'd all grown up together so knew each other well. Just like they knew where they were going, their husbands knew that the future fat girls were headed to stuff stuffed crust pizza into their faces. Shyne and Bryonna took their babies to the food court and did just that.

"How's my P-M-B niece?" Shyne cooed to Little Yolo as she sat in her carrier. The baby smiled her little gummy smile and kicked her chubby baby legs at the attention.

"P-M-B?" Bryonna wondered. Knowing Shyne, it was something crazy so she made sure to swallow so she wouldn't choke upon hearing her response.

"Puppy, Monkey, Baby. That's what she looks like. Like she can swing from a tree," Shyne cracked and cracked up.

"I know you not talking when Malik look like an insect!" Bryonna shot back. The two went back and forth snapping on one another's children until someone ambled by and volunteered to be talked about instead.

"Bitch! Um..." the young, flashy guy screeched in a high-pitched voice. Physically, he looked to be about twenty, but was dressed like a throwback pimp from a 70s Blaxploitation movie. Pimpy Pimp did indeed model himself after pimps from that era. The young pimp idolized Suga Fly and the like.

His vocabulary only consisted of a couple hundred words so he inserted pregnant pauses between them whenever he spoke. It appeared as if he was deep in thought, but the truth of the matter was that he was just a dumb ass. His whore knew it, too, so she tried to help him out.

"Better have my money?" she asked, even though it didn't make sense since she'd just handed over her trap money. The upscale mall was a good place to turn quick tricks. A quick blowjob in a bathroom while shopping was a win/win.

"Hell yeah! I told you fifty dollars and you brang me...?"

"Fifty dollars! See?" she said and helped him count it.

Bryonna and Shyne wore wide smiles as they watched the comedy show a few feet away. Pimpy Pimp saw their smiles and stepped straight to them.

"What y'all bitches... um... names?" he inquired, looking back. Both Shyne and Bryonna were too stunned for words, so he kept right on talking. "Y'all bitches look nice and clean. Y'all wanna sell some pussy fo' me?"

"Nigga, I'll..." Bryonna growled as she tried to climb over the table and get to him.

"Chill, B," Shyne urged as she pulled her back down. She then turned back to the pimp with a smile, "Sure! Give me your number. I'll hit you later."

"Um..." Pimpy Pimp replied since he didn't know his own number.

"4-0-4-5-5-5..." his whore recited and saved the day. Saved the day but not his ass.

"I'm telling, Sun!" Bryonna huffed, looking around for her husband.

"Nah, just let it go. He's already dealing with enough with our dad in the hospital," Shyne said. It was true but the absolute truth was that she wanted the pimp all to herself.

"Oh, okay," she relented since Sun was heading to Baltimore in a couple of days to check on him. No sense in adding more onto his already full plate.

What she didn't know was that the pimp was dead either way. Pimpy Pimp would have made out better getting killed by Sun. Sun doesn't set people on fire.

****

"Um..." Pimpy Pimp said when he took the call from the unknown number on his screen.

"Hello," his bottom bitch helped. She was his English-to-dumb ass translator.

"Yeah, hello," he smiled and nodded at the assist. "Who dis?"

"Dis um... Shyne," Shyne said. She didn't mind using her real name on the 'burn-out' phone since it would get burned up, too. "I met you at the mall?"

"Oh yeah, pretty lil bitch with the babies!" he exclaimed, adding fuel to the fire literally since Shyne was calling from a gas station.

"Mmhm," she agreed with her lips pressed tightly together. If they parted, all types of curses and threats would have spewed out. This may be an age where some woman enjoyed being called bitches, but not Shyne. She was raised better than that.

"So you ready to slang some ass fo' ol' Pimpy Pimp?" the pimp pimped.

"Un huh!" she cheered eagerly. "But... don't you wanna hit it yourself first?"

"Um..." he said, actually having to give it some thought. He was a pimp for real and preferred cash to ass any day. In the end, Shyne was cute so he decided on a sample before putting her on the stroll. "Okay, sure!"

"Great! Meet me in Mosely Park," she said as she finished filling her Super Soaker water gun with gas. "I'm burning, though."

Shyne had called from the west side of Atlanta so she made it to the park first. The park was dangerous at night but so was she. Not only was she packing a disposable flame thrower but she had a .40

cal as well. Any normal woman would be afraid to walk through the
dark park alone, but Shyne wasn't exactly normal and the gun meant
she wasn't actually alone, either.

"We're at" Pimpy Pimp texted when he pulled his pimped out
ride into the park.

Shyne stared at the phrase for a full minute trying to decipher it.
"Oh!" she giggled when she got it and texted back. *"Last pavilion"*

"Um..." he reiterated, trying to sound out 'pavilion'. He would
have never gotten it. Luckily for him, Shyne waved her phone so he
could see her.

At night, the park was transformed into a free motel. Various
free as well as per-pay...screw sex acts were being performed in parked
cars and under the pavilions. Pimpy Pimp caught a glimpse of back
shots and blowjobs as he drove to the rear of the park. Seeing the action, he decided he wanted both before setting Shyne out.

"Hey," Shyne giggled with her hands behind her back when the
pimp rolled up and parked. Visions of him dancing around in flames
spread a wide smile on her face.

"Hey, yaself," he greeted as he approached. "We gotta fuck quick
cuz I gots hoes to pimp." He unbuckled his pants as he approached
her. Guys are always happy and yes a little proud to show off their
penis to a new girl. He snatched his pants open, like a curtain on a
Broadway stage on opening day. Out came the dick and out came
the water gun. Perhaps it shouldn't be called a water gun since it was
filled with premium unleaded gasoline.

"Mmhmm," Shyne laughed and squirted him.

Pimpy Pimp's dense patch of pubic hair soaked up the gas like a
sponge. Pimpy Pimp's slow brain processed the information as slow
as an old computer. He blinked and frowned as he put it all together. First, there was the water gun. Then, the smell of gas followed by
the burning on his balls. Then there was the pretty girl, a lighter and
a spark followed by fire and pain.

"Bitch, you set my balls on fiyah!" he screamed. It was the most complete sentence he'd ever uttered in his life. It would also be his last, too, considering that Shyne had sprayed him from head to toe.

"Told you I was burning," Shyne laughed as she walked away from the inferno. No one stopped fucking or sucking to watch the flaming man do his last dance before death finally got the best of him and pulled him to the ground.

Chapter 2

"Dear Diary, I want to thank God for Mr. Grimsly. Not only did he save my cherry but he takes good care of me too. He taught me how to fight! Now, no one will ever hurt me again. Oh, he taught me a move called 'The Bitch in You'. He claims it'll bring out the bitch in any man. I can't wait to use it. He also taught me how to make a weapon out of almost anything..."

"Oh wow!" Shyne exclaimed. As she read, she recalled her mom teaching her and her twin most of the same lessons. 'The Bitch in You' was 'The Opera Singer'. Shyne had once used the brutal arm bar on a guy and he'd hit all kinds of high notes. Just like an opera singer.

Poor Asad and the kids got slightly neglected as she became captivated by the pages of the diary. Page by page, she bonded with her mysterious mother. It was like having a long talk with her as she heard her mother speak the words as she read.

"Dear Diary, Guess what? Mr. Grimsly said yes! I can go to school! I start high school on Monday..."

Mr. Grimsly reluctantly agreed to let his prize student go to public school. In the end, he knew she needed the social interaction with people her own age. He just hoped she didn't kill anyone.

Since Yolo didn't have a birth certificate, Grimsly had to pull a few strings, teeth, actually, to get her some documentation for enrollment. The fake documents contained her real name along with the names of fictitious parents. Mr. Grimsly was listed as her guardian so he was able to enroll her in school.

That was the easy part. What to wear, however, was a bigger problem.

"Absolutely not!" Mr. Grimsly protested when Yolo came out in a short skirt.

"You no like?" she asked and did a twirl that made thing worse. The skirt flared out as she spun and showed off her red panties underneath.

"NO!!!" he shouted and pointed at the stairs. She pouted and stomped up the stairs to change. The process was repeated when she returned in a pair of skin tight jeans. Then again when she emerged in a pair of tiny shorts.

"How is this?" Yolo huffed as she appeared in a tasteful summer dress. "I borrowed it from Miss Celie."

"Well, tell her I said thank you," he said, missing the quip. "That is how a young lady should dress!"

"Anyway, I'll see you later," Yolo said and planted a parting kiss on his cheek, causing him to smile.

"I don't think you're quite ready for the school bus. I'll drive you for a while," he insisted.

They'd both seen how rowdy the school bus could be. They drove pass plenty of kids making out or fighting at their bus stops. Yolo was down for all of it, but Mr. Grimsly, on the other hand, wasn't trying to hear any of it.

If he had it his way, he'd go inside and sit next to her in each class. He couldn't, so he let out a sigh as she walked into the school. She turned at the last second and waved goodbye before blowing him a kiss and then turning away quickly just in case he didn't return it. He did but it hit her back as she departed.

"What a sweet, obedient girl," he mused as he pulled off.

Yolo was sweet back then, but obedient, not so much.

Yolo hit the first bathroom she found and pulled the frumpy dress from over her curly pigtails. Underneath she had on the same short skirt she'd started with and under it, the same red panties she'd shown off earlier. She blended in well with the rest of the scantily clad teen girls. The school looked like the set of a rap music video since that's who the kids mimicked. Makes you wonder how things would be if rappers rapped about good morals and manners and dignity and respect. Now that's unrealistic.

"A-yo, Ma," a teen called out as Yolo traipsed by. Her name wasn't ma so she had no idea he meant her and so kept on walking. That is, until he grabbed her arm.

"Ha-ya!" Yolo grunted as she karate chopped him in his Adam's apple. She would have extracted the bitch in him with her 'Bitch in You,' but he collapsed to the floor gasping for air.

"Yo, that bitch is wild!" a teen named Rush gushed, talking about the pretty girl. He'd had his eye on her but waited to see how John made out first.

Yolo snapped her head into the direction of the insult whoever said it was getting fucked up. She locked eyes with the school's pretty boy and paused. He was pretty but was still getting fucked up for calling her a bitch.

The bell sounded, signaling the start of first period, so the ass whooping would have to wait. Those are the worst ones.

****

Yolo entered her first period English class and scanned the room. The good girls sat up front in their Color Purple dresses so they could hear and learn while a pack of ratchet girls cackled and cursed in the rear since they could give a fuck about English. Their speech consisted of broken English strung together with slang and curse words.

Poor Yolo was torn between good and evil. Curiosity got the best of her so she went to the back to sit in the ratchet sections. Being homeschooled put her far ahead of 9th grade English so she wouldn't miss anything. Being homeschooled also left her green to the things that were important to some kids.

"Bitch, that nigga Rush came to see a bitch last night," a girl named Andrea bragged.

"Un uh, bitch!" Carla shot back.

Yolo frowned curiously as she listened to the girls refer to themselves and each other as bitches. To her surprise, no one was offended. She wondered in what type of alternate universe did females embrace the word bitch. It must be a world where males and females equated to being niggas and bitches.

"I heard he got a big dick," Mandy said. It was a true lie since she'd heard herself say it while she herself had sex with the popular teen.

The next thing Yolo learned in the strange new world was that a big dick was coveted. The ratchet girls boasted and bragged about who had a big one but never mentioned any other qualities they sought. Bright futures and good jobs never came up; just who had a mean fuck game. It was no wonder that most of their dates ended with empty stomachs and sore vaginas.

Growing up in a brothel, Yolo had witnessed plenty of sex acts. She'd found them amusing rather than erotic, so she got a kick out of listening to the girls recount their sexapades in and around the school. It was all fun and games until someone saw her ear hustling.

"Un uh! This bitch been listening to us all period!" Carla announced. All heads turned to face Yolo.

"Sup, bitches," she greeted warmly and smiled.

"No this bitch didn't just call us bitches, bitches!" Andrea fussed.

"A bitch like me will fuck a bitch up!" Mandy declared. "Nosey bitch! I should beat that ass!"

"Oh shit!" Shyne shouted in excitement; a little too much excitement. So much so that she woke her husband. "My bad."

"Good timing," Asad said, hearing their baby daughter begin to whimper. "It's your turn."

"Okay, Babe. Don't go back to sleep, though," she said, shaking her ass as she went to heat a bottle for the baby.

"Good timing indeed!" Asad said, rubbing his hands together in anticipation of what was to come.

Chapter 3

"Phone, Mommy!" Little Malik announced when BIG began rapping on her cell phone.

She bit her tongue at the sarcastic remark fighting to come out of her mouth since she could hear the phone as well as he could. It was her brother's ringtone so she hurried to take the call. "Sup, Sun?" she asked, amused by the double meaning. "How's Daddy? He awake?"

"Nah," Sun sighed. "No change. Still sleep. Still got internal bleeding. They may have to operate again."

There was a long silence on the line as they both absorbed the heavy words. Neither could comprehend their superhero father being so vulnerable and helpless. To them, it was like Superman being crippled or Aquaman drowning.

Rico had practically moved down to Baltimore with his nurse friend. This gave him the inside scoop on their father, who was still being guarded by federal agents awaiting him to either wake up or die, with either being fine by them.

"Man," Shyne whined, sounding like a six-year-old. She wanted to be up there, too, but Asad had put his foot down about her traveling while pregnant so she was stuck in Atlanta. That sucked for the bad people of Atlanta because a bored Shyne is a dangerous Shyne.

"Yeah, I know," Sun said in reply to her sigh. He felt the same helplessness as she did. "Here go Rico."

"Sup, Sis," Rico said, taking the phone. He adored his scrappy little sister and it came through the line.

"Hey, Rico," Shyne said, feeling his smile loud and clear. She enjoyed chopping it up with him because he made the same corny jokes as their father. Same corny jokes she made, too, but would never admit it.

"Love you, too," Rico replied at the end of the conversation and hung up.

"You ready to get this money?" Sun asked when Rico passed him his phone back. It was purely rhetorical since he already knew the answer.

"Hell yeah!" Rico exclaimed just as he knew he would.

When Little Rock died, the resurgence of The Black Mob died with him. That meant the black market of drugs, pussy and the numbers game was once again a free for all. Industrious pimps, pushers and number runners were free to make as much money as they wanted.

Sun and Rico planned to rob them all.

****

Bonita lay flat on her stomach but arched her ass to accommodate the vigorous back shots Danny was delivering. She cursed in rapid fire Spanish from the thorough dicking she was receiving. The hot blooded Latina had some good, hot pussy that made the dealer want to feel it for real.

"Fuck this..." he announced as he snatched his dick out of her. He snatched off the condom before plunging back inside. "Shit! This shit is good!"

"Just don't cum in me, Papi," she warned as she rocked side to side to make him cum quicker.

"You got a fever or something?" he wondered because it was so hot. Two strokes later, he snatched out and skeeted on her light brown back.

"I'm not finished. I want some more!" Bonita protested as his dick began to deflate.

"Put it in yo' mouth and get it hard," he suggested, moving up to her face.

"Go wash it off first," she protested as if repulsed by the notion of tasting her own juices. In fact, the truth was she loved to but this was business, not pleasure.

"One sec!" Danny cheered and rushed to get a soapy washcloth. The second he cleared the room, she sprang into action.

Her big, brown Puerto Rican breasts bounced as she bounced down the steps. She quickly unlocked and opened the door to let the two masked men inside. Even behind their ski-masks she saw their eyes shoot to her big brown nipples before dropping to her hairy bush. One averted his eyes and turned away just as quickly. After all, he was married.

"Second room on the right," she whispered and rushed back upstairs.

Rico and Sun crept around downstairs for a minute before heading up. Once they were sure that the house was empty, they made their move. Even if Bonita hadn't told them what room they were in, they would have figured it out from the sounds of the loud blowjob in progress.

"Shit!" Danny said over the sounds of her slurping. His heart broke when the gunmen walked in.

"A-yo, you can keep going for all I care. Just tell us where the money at," Rico said. He knew firsthand how good Bonita's head game was. They'd gown up in the same projects and had been fucking since their teens. Now he used her as bait in armed robberies.

"Mmhmm," Bonita agreed and kept on blowing the man. It was meant to ease the sting of getting robbed; especially since she got an equal share.

"I'm good!" he said, shoving her away. "What if I don't give y'all shit?"

Sun racked the pump shotgun in reply. It didn't actually speak, but it made his point loud and clear.

The thug knew that it would cut him in half at that range. "Oh," he said since he understood. "Top drawer, black case."

Rico followed his directions like a driver followed GPS and found a cash case. It would have been fine if the brothers didn't know that he had a lot more.

"Bruh, we watched you hit five trap houses today. All them shits was booming! Nice try, but come off that dough!" Rico insisted.

"OR..." Sun said, leveling the gun at his genitals.

Money can buy a lot of things but it cannot grow a new dick.

"Jackpot!" Rico cheered when he found the cash. He actually grunted from the weight of it when he picked it up.

"Tie him up," Sun demanded as he passed Bonita some plastic ties.

"Don't look so sad, Papi," Bonita purred as she secured his hands behind his back. She tried to kiss him goodbye when she finished but he turned his head.

"'Preciate you taking it in stride," Rico said with a sarcastic salute. They would have murdered him for resisting if he hadn't.

"New York, huh?" the dealer nodded at the accent. "Which one of these Baltimore niggas put you on me?"

"Some nigga called DannyBoy88," Sun laughed.

Danny lowered his head in shame upon hearing his Instagram name. All that flossing had gotten him robbed.

"Yup, you should kill that nigga!" Rico laughed.

It didn't take long for Bonita to dress since Bonita didn't wear much clothing. Once she did, they left to split up the couple hundred grand they'd netted.

Chapter 4

"No, please don't beat my ass!" Yolo pleaded and cracked up. She laughed so hard tears streamed down her face and her stomach ached. She laughed so hard that she almost peed.

"This bitch thinks it's a game!" Andrea protested. "You think this a game?"

"Meet 'us' at lunch and 'we' gonna beat that ass!" Mandy dared. What she didn't and wouldn't do is dare to fight by herself. She would lag back and steal punches and kicks once the battle began, with her scary ass.

"We? What are you, French or just scared?" Yolo teased. She knew she could whip them all at once but it would be a lot more fun doing it one by one.

"Bitch, I'll give you a head up!" Carla volunteered. Her friends never said it out loud but they were eternally grateful for the beating she'd saved them from.

News of the impending battle had spread from class to class, period by period. Carla was a good fighter, but the girl was no match for the highly trained killer. While the former smoked weed and twerked, the latter could dismember a two-hundred-pound man in under an hour.

Rush heard about it, too, and was front and center when the two girls squared up at lunch time. Yolo's karate chop victim was also front and center rooting for Carla to get some get back on his behalf.

"'Bout to beat this bitch ass!" Carla vowed as she prepared for battle. She had a bunch of girls in her corner assisting and hyping her up like it was a prize fight. She took off her earrings as they slathered Vaseline on her face.

"Are you ready yet?" Yolo sighed impatiently.

"Bitch!" Carla shouted and rushed in. She threw a wide, looping haymaker that Yolo easily ducked. She leaned back, causing her to spin completely around when she missed.

Yolo passed on the opportunity to punish the girl and instead laughed along with the crowd. The laughter infuriated the bully just like Mr. Grimsly had taught her it would. The girl, now in a blind rage, released a flurry of punches, kicks and elbow. All hit nothing but air.

"Are you sure you want to fight?" Yolo inquired. "I mean, you can't really fight."

"Hell yeah, she wanna fight!" Mandy answered for her, except it wasn't the same answer Carla had in mind. She'd had enough already. Mandy was to blame for what happened next.

"Okay," Yolo shrugged. She became a cute blur as she sprang into action. She could have killed the girl a hundred different ways, but chose to simply humiliate her instead.

"Oh shit!" the crowd roared when Yolo slapped her so hard that it spun her like a top. She spun around and was met by another slap that sent her spinning back in the opposite direction.

Yolo hated her electric blue weave so snatched it out track by track. Carla's friends looked at each other to see if anyone was going to help. They all shook their heads like 'hell naw'. And who could blame them?

"A'ight, that's enough," Rush said and moved in to break it up. He wisely grabbed Carla because Yolo would have broken him up, too, had he touched her. He only did so because he saw the school's security guard approaching.

It was too late, though, because he'd seen the action. "Both of you to the principal's office!" he demanded until he got a look at Carla's face. "You, to the principal's. You, to the nurse's office!"

"She started it!" Yolo declared when an irate Mr. Grimsly entered the office. He was pissed but also glad that the girl had shown some restraint. He'd taught her how to gouge out eyeballs, so he was relieved to see the other girl's were only swollen shut.

"She's right," the principal co-signed. He had been dealing with the ninth-grader for three years so knew she was a bully.

"I see," Mr. Grimsly nodded. "Well, I'm going to take her home. We'll try again tomorrow."

"Is this issue resolved, ladies?" the principal wanted to know.

"Yes!" by both agreed in unison.

Yolo popped up and followed her guardian outside. She was relieved to not be in trouble. Or so she thought.

"And just what do you have on, young lady?" he demanded once they reached the car.

"Huh?" she wondered until she looked down and saw that she hadn't put her dress back on. "Oh."

"Dang, Mommy! The first day of school, though?" Shyne said, shaking her head. She'd obviously forgotten her own first day of high school.

****

"That must be really good," Bryonna said as she drove them to the zoo.

Shyne was curled up in the passenger's seat as they rode towards downtown. Their kids were strapped into seats and carriers in the backseat.

"Huh? What? Oh," she replied. "It is! My mom was a damn trip!"

"You gonna let Sun read it once you're finished?" she asked, thinking that if she did, she'd get to read it herself; with her nosey ass.

"NO!" Shyne reeled and snatched it protectively to her bosom.

"Okay, dang!" Bryonna said of the reaction. "Anyway, you like my new truck?"

"I do! I see my brother must have worked some overtime," Shyne said sarcastically. She knew good and well Bryonna had no idea what Sun actually did for a living.

All they ever told her was that it was family business. She was smart enough to know that whatever it was paid well since he always returned from his trips with gifts and their bank accounts swelled. She was also wise enough to know that whatever it was had left their dad in a coma from being shot.

"He sure has!" she shot back and placed a hand on her stomach.

Shyne twisted her lips dubiously at what the gesture could mean. "Nuh uh," she dared.

"Nuh huh! Just peed on the stick this morning. I'm right behind you."

"Biter!" Shyne spat back. The two had a standing bet to see who could have the most kids. Why not, since they could afford them and afford to stay home with them?

Shyne had fun with her sister-in-law and the kids at the zoo. They spent the entire day there enjoying the sights. Now she couldn't wait to get back to her mother's diary.

Chapter 5

"Dear Diary, I think a boy likes me! Guess what? I think I like him, too...

"I may have to skip this part," Shyne said, scrunching her face in disgust. She was Team Killa all the way and didn't want to hear about anyone else. She kept reading, though, because, like her father, she was nosey.

"He's tall and cute, and every time I look up, I see him looking back at me! Then, he got this deep voice and be like..."

"Sup, Ma," Rush said, catching Yolo off guard at her locker. He had no idea how close he'd come to getting karate chopped in his throat for surprising her.

"I don't know," Yolo responded since she wasn't quite sure what he meant. She didn't socialize much, so the slang was new to her.

"Well, I do. Me and you. Now, that's what's up," he cheered and nodded at the sound of it.

"Okay," Yolo agreed as well. She had no idea what she was signing up for, but would soon find out.

"Saturday night, me and you at The Point," he said and gave her his number.

"That's what's up!" she called his back, sounding corny with her new slang. Even she heard it in her voice and repeated it a few times to practice.

That wasn't the problem, though. The problem was figuring out how she was supposed to get permission from the overprotective Mr. Grimsly.

"Ooh, I know!" Young Yolo snapped her fingers at her bright idea. *The best way to get permission was to sneak out the window. Once her guardian retired for the evening, she made her escape.*

"Hmmm?" Casper uttered as he watched Yolo climb out her window on the security monitor. He debated for a moment whether or not he should wake Mr. Grimsly. In the end, he decided not to and followed

her himself instead. After all, she was supposed to be the future enforcer of his organization. He grew even more skeptical when he saw her jump into a waiting car. "She'll be a baby mama before she becomes a killer," he quipped sarcastically as he discretely followed Rush's mother's car in one of his own.

Despite being the boss of The Black Mob, white Casper didn't think much of black people. After all, he'd made a fortune off of blacks selling dope to other blacks. Not to mention that he'd been gang raped by some in prison. He let out an 'I knew it' sigh when the car pulled to a stop at the local make out spot dubbed The Point.

"What's here?" Yolo asked when Rush pulled up and parked. She'd expected movies and popcorn, but Rush just pulled out his dick.

"This..." he proclaimed proudly as he produced his penis. Yolo cocked her head curiously at the cock and watched it grow erect until it throbbed in his hand.

"Take me home!" Yolo whined and pouted. This was not what she'd expected or agreed to. She was nothing like the whores at She-Ra's house or the THOTS from school.

"Put out or get put out," Rush laughed. Yolo sucked her teeth and reached for the door handle. Rush then made the worst and the last mistake of his short life. In fact, it was the mistake that cut his life short. He grabbed her arm and pulled her back. "I didn't steal my mom's car for nothing! You gonna suck this dick!"

This was typical behavior for him and many other guys like him. Date rape is far more common than people believe. Most times, girls are so shocked and embarrassed that they just keep it to themselves. Some even blame themselves for putting themselves in a situation to be date raped. However, they shouldn't blame themselves for someone else's sickness.

Yolo didn't do that, either. She struck back.

"Typical," Casper said, shaking his head when the car began to rock. He assumed they were fucking but in fact, Rush was getting fucked up.

Yolo shot him a Three Stooges *eye poke that forced him to relax his grip. She swung over the backseat and put him in a chokehold. Rush kicked and clawed in an attempt to stay alive.*

"Hmmm?" Casper mumbled once more. The action in the car began to appear more violent than sexual. He pulled his gun and got out to investigate.

"Bitch!" Rush growled as he pulled Yolo's small arm from around his neck. She was still young and hadn't reached her full strength yet, so the athlete easily overpowered her. He then climbed over the backseat intent on raping her, but the battle for her vagina was cut short when the dome light came on from the door being open.

"Who the fuck is you?" Rush demanded as he looked up.

Looked up right into the huge barrel of a Desert Eagle. That's a helluva sight to take with you into the afterlife.

The cannon in Casper's hand replied by sending a massive .50 caliber slug through his head. The large hole in his forehead wasn't shit compared to the gaping hole in the back. The left half of his brain fell out and onto his back. Yolo was covered in blood and brain matter as she climbed from underneath the corpse.

"Thank you!" she cried like the terrified child that she really was. She rushed to him and hugged him tightly. So tightly that she squeezed some of the hate out of his black heart.

"You're um... welcome," he reluctantly replied. He remembered feeling the same gratitude when The Baron stopped him from being raped by his cellmate. He wrapped his arms around the trembling child and hugged her back. "Let's go before Mr. Grimsly wakes up."

"What about him?" Yolo asked about the dead teen.

"Fuck him!" he shrugged and led her to his car.

"Aww man!" Shyne pouted. "Y'all was supposed to set him on fire!"

Chapter 6

"Gay is the new straight!" Suga Britches proudly proclaimed in his first interview since officially 'coming out'.

Rumors had swirled about the platinum rapper, who often wore women's clothing and twerked in his videos, since shortly after he debuted. It was written off as swag by the new generation, but that shit was gay as fuck to the old heads. The capri pants, lip gloss and the fact that he was from Atlanta was all that needed to be said.

"Tell 'em, baby daddy!" his partner, west coast rapper Fuck-Man, co-signed.

The Bay Area rapper was once his bitter rival. Their social media beef, which stemmed from who could twerk the best, had blown up the internet. They settled their beef with a twerk off. It ended up in a tie and they ended up in a relationship. It's only right that if two 'men' engage in a twerk that they end up fucking. That shit is in-fuck-ing-evitable.

Both left their R&B baby mamas for one another, which wouldn't have been necessary if they'd kept it private, but once their sex tape got out, they came out. They then began to push their licentious lifestyle on the masses of young, impressionable kids who listened to their music.

Now, all across the country, little boys wanted to dress, act, talk and walk like Suga Britches and Fuck-Man. Parents were furious to find out that their sons were swiping their sister's *My Little Pony* panties.

To make matters worse, their R&B diva ex-girlfriends decided to cash in on the craze and became lesbian lovers as well. They quickly leaked a sex tape of their own and then hit the studio to record their debut album.

"I told you guys! Oh, and yeah, I want in on the action!" Shyne said when she showed her brothers the interview.

Sun and Rico watched in shock as the two homos pushed their twisted lifestyle. They were even more shocked when they found out the hit song 'Go Slow' was an ode to anal sex.

"Aww, man! I loved that song," Rico protested.

"Maybe you shouldn't tell anyone else about that," Sun suggested, cracking him and his sister up.

"That's funny, Sun! Ha-ha-ha," Shyne giggled. "Let me come with you guys!"

"With your belly poking way out? No way! Asad would kill me if anything happened to you," Sun protested.

"Blow all of us up," Rico added. "We got this, Sis. Maybe we can use bodycams like the police have to when they kill people."

"That's a good idea," Sun decided, "cuz you definitely ain't coming!"

"You guys suck!" Shyne pouted. The poor girl was bored out of her mind. She felt like a hen sitting on an egg. Actually, she was but still, a bored Shyne is a dangerous Shyne.

****

Suga Britches and Fuck-Man were known to put on an exhilarating show. There was lights, twerking, and fireworks. The two provided the whole nine yards when it came to entertaining. They would pop bottles and spray the crowd and each other with the liquor and champagne.

Rico and Sun flew out to Oakland to catch their next show. Actually, it would be their last show. The brothers arrived at the arena just after sound check. A few modifications to the fireworks ensured that there would be plenty of lights, cameras and action.

Since the rappers had decided to openly sin and spread corruption, they were going to die openly and extremely violently. Now their followers would see where they were leading them.

"Wanna smoke one?" Rico asked once they were settled back at their hotel. They still had a couple of hours to kill before they killed a couple of rappers.

"Nah, you know my wife doesn't like me smoking," Sun said. He'd actually quit on his own but blamed it on Bryonna.

Rico dropped down and looked under the sofa, behind the curtains and in the bathroom before responding. "Great news! She ain't here!" he laughed and lit the blunt. After a few tokes, he passed it to his brother. Soon, it was just like the old days with them laughing, joking and smoking. The munchies set in soon after, so they hit up a burger joint.

****

"Can you see?" Sun asked loudly, as if he was on a walkie-talkie instead of a cell phone as he turned his torso so that the bodycam he wore scanned the room.

"Yeah, and I can hear, too!" Shyne responded just as loudly. "Hey, Rico!"

"Sup, Shyne," he said, waving in front of the lens. "You ready to see the show?"

"Yes, I am! It's getting hot in here..." Shyne sang and giggled.

She continued to watch as they rode over to the arena. Once there, they used their backstage passes to get backstage while the warm up acts warmed up the stage.

"Ready to pop these bottles?" Sun exclaimed happily. His large bottle contained 190 proof moonshine while Rico had pure rubbing alcohol in his.

"Hell yeah!" Rico replied just as the little rappers came out of their dressing room smelling like ass and K-Y Jelly.

Both wore mini-skirts and football jerseys. Both wore eyeliner and lip gloss. And both were about to die.

"What's up, Oakland!" Fuck-Man screamed into the mic, causing his hometown to go wild. "This my baby daddy, Suga Britches!"

"Sup, Oakland!" he yelled and twerked a little. As if on cue the DJ threw on their new single 'We Don't Love Them Hoes'.

"I bet y'all don't," Rico laughed as they put on.

A few minutes into the act, they retrieved their bottles.

"Y'all bitches ready to pop some bottles?" Suga Britches wanted to know. He let out a little giggle when Fuck-Man grabbed his booty. "A'ight now! You finna bite off more than you can chew!"

"I don't chew, I swallow!" he replied and sprayed him with champagne.

The crowd followed suit and popped their bottles and sprayed around as well.

"Let's roll!" Sun said. He and Rico danced onto the stage and sprayed the rappers with the flammable liquids. Then they quickly exited the stage and waited for the fireworks.

The DJ threw on their song 'I Swallow' just as the fireworks began. The crowd went crazy when the two men caught fire, thinking that it was part of the show, while they twerked like never before, trying to put the fire out.

"Yay!" Shyne cheered and clapped as she watched them burn to death.

The show was over.

****

"Oh my God!" Suga Britches' baby mama, Perco-Sex, exclaimed as she read the urgent text.

"Mmhmm," Slut-Mouth mumbled from her muff. She assumed the outburst was from the way she was sucking on her pussy.

"Something happened to our baby daddies! They dead!"

"Mmhmm," she mumbled and kept right on sucking.

Whatever was going on could wait. It wouldn't have to wait long as Perco-Sex sat her phone down and began to thrash around in ecstasy as she arched her back off the bed and came in Slut-Mouth's mouth.

"Mmhmm."

"Okay, your turn," Perco-Sex said and took position between Slut-Mouth's legs.

Although their relationship was a spinoff of their gay baby daddies' hooking up, they both discovered that they enjoyed eating pussy. Now with their actions the two were corrupting young girls, turning them on to drugs and sex.

"I got a text, too," Slut-Mouth said as her partner began. She sat the phone back down to concentrate on a nut of her own. Once she got it, the two showered, dressed and headed for the airport.

A good show of grief could boost sales.

"'Bout damn time!" Slut-Mouth grumbled when a limo pulled up. The driver jumped out to open the door and got cursed out. "Ole nappy head bitch!"

"Bitch pregnant, too! Should've swallowed!" Perco-Sex teased as they got in.

The driver padlocked the back doors before getting back behind the wheel. "We have to stop for gas. Hope you guys don't mind," the driver asked sweetly and got cursed out again.

"Gas? Bitch, you shoulda got gas 'fo' you picked us up!"

"Make us miss our flight and we gon' whip that ass!"

"That would be a first," Shyne laughed and pulled into a gas station. She stuck the nozzle into the open sun roof and opened it full blast.

"Bitch, fuck wrong with you? I'ma fuck her up!" the dirty divas protested. They tried to exit, but the padlocks kept them stuck in place.

A line from her mother's diary popped in Shyne's head as she lit a book of matches. She tossed it into the opening and said, "Okay, bye-bye!"

Chapter 7

"Shit!" Rico fussed when he heard his phone. It was bad timing since Shonda was riding him backwards real slow like he was in his own porno movie. She kept having orgasms that left creamy goodness on his dick. The BIG ringtone said it was his brother so he took the call. "S-s-s-up, y-yo?"

"Chillin', B. I...yo, what you doing?" Sun asked, hearing the sounds of sex on the line.

"Who, m-m-m-me? N-n-nothin'," he lied, trying to sound normal. He almost pulled it off, too, until Shonda came again. Her already tight vagina contracted and squeezed his shaft, pushing him over the edge along with her. "Argh! Shit! Grrr!"

"Man, I wish I hadn't heard that," Sun laughed and shook his head. "Call me back once you're completely done. I got a lick for us."

"Round...four?" Shonda asked once they stopped shivering from round three.

"Raincheck? I gotta holla at lil' bro. Besides, don't you have to work?" Rico replied, rolling off the bed. He made sure not to look at her naked body because it would make his dick turn to stone and demand a round four.

"Yeah, yeah," she giggled as she looked at the clock. There was just enough time to wash all of his cum off and out of her and get to the hospital.

"Tell my pops I said hello," he said when she joined him in the shower. Again, he kept his back to her to avoid getting aroused.

Rico was naïve enough about love to believe that laying pipe was the key to keeping her on his team. In truth, good sex is rather low on the scale. Sure, every woman likes a dick slinger but that doesn't pay the bills. Just like eating a dick doesn't take the place of food or keep a roof overhead.

Shonda was falling in love with him and he was falling for her, too, but again was too naïve to know it. He thought it was just good pussy. After all, who doesn't love good pussy?

****

"Sup, yo?" Sun asked when his brother called back. "You ready to get this money?"

Sun could see Rico his lips like 'yeah right' when he didn't even bother responding to his question. Of course he was ready to get some money, so Sun went on and filled him in.

A drug ring down in Dallas, Texas was slinging heroin in ice-cream trucks. They'd given away free samples to thousands of kids, turning them into loyal customers. Those thousands meant million in sales. They also sent crime skyrocketing as a new breed of junkie, who did any and everything they could to get high, emerged.

"My people say if we catch 'em right, it could be worth a million or two," Sun relayed.

"Well, let's catch 'em right then. A mil apiece sounds good."

"Three-way split. Gotta cut Shyne in. You know she would be down if she wasn't pregnant. But since she is she gotta lay low and rest..."

"True. She probably on bedrest," Rico guessed, guessing wrong.

****

"I hereby sentence the defendant to..." the judge paused and looked down at the paper on his desk as if he was calculating years and years. The only thing on the paper the judge consulted was doodles of penises he'd drawn during the trial along with a six-digit number that he would receive for keeping the little bastard out of prison.

The rich teen in front of him had just been convicted of date rap-ing several classmates. His team of lawyers had argued that he was too rich and spoiled to understand right from wrong. The pretty little redhead boy would have a hard time if sent to prison. The rapist would definitely get raped himself. That's the law of the jungle and ain't nothing wrong with that.

"Taking into consideration the skimpy clothes of the so-called 'victims,'" the judge said, making sarcastic quotation marks with his fingers as he shifted the blame to the victims, "Billy Marks was enticed beyond reason. So I feel...five years of probation is more than fair."

The wails and sobs of the victims and their families filled the courtroom. They were so loud and heartbreaking that they drowned out the low growl coming from the back row.

"You woulda been better off in jail. Gonna see how you like getting raped!" Shyne vowed. She then stood up and left the courtroom.

There was no need for her to follow him since she'd already done that. It was the first thing she'd done when she began following his case. She now knew his every move, including where he would serve his community service hours.

He definitely would have been better off in jail. The judge, too, for that matter.

****

"The Big D," Sun announced as he and Rico walked through the Dallas airport. He loved his job because it not only paid well but it also allowed him to travel the country and kill bad people. Who wouldn't love it? Some people need dead.

"Yeah, we gotta hurry back cuz dad is having surgery next week," Rico sighed. He'd known for the last week, but hadn't found a way to tell his siblings.

"For what now?" Sun asked with the exact pain in his voice that Rico had tried to avoid causing by stalling.

"He's still bleeding internally. Shonda said he might lose a lung. And those fuck ass Feds are still hovering at his door, waiting on him to get better so they can kill him," he growled.

"Like they can't get killed," Sun threatened. Each one of Killa's kids entertained a plan of breaking their dad out of the hospital.

The rest of the trip to the hotel was made in silent contemplation of a rescue mission.

Their mood went from bad to worse when Rico's contact, Chavez, picked them up for a tour of the area. They saw kids barely in their teens propped up in dope fiend leans. Young girls, barely old enough to have pubic hair, stood on corners renting their puerile pussies to sick grown men who liked such things.

"My own daughter didn't make it," Chavez announced, breaking the silence. "These monsters make fruit flavored heroin to hook little kids. My baby OD'd off of tropical punch flavored dope!"

"A-yo, fuck that money!" Rico decided.

His brother immediately nodded his head in agreement. "Yeah, it's hammer time," Sun added.

Chavez looked back and forth between the brothers with a curious frown. "What is hammer time?" he finally asked.

"You'll see. Take us by a hardware store," Rico replied. He did and the brothers purchased a pair of sledge hammers.

"We'll need these, too, and these," Sun advised as he added goggles and painter coveralls to the shopping cart. "This is going to get messy."

Not as messy as Shyne was about to get.

Chapter 8

"Big Bubba?" Shyne asked as she pulled up to the large man standing where they'd agreed to meet. The man certainly fit the description from the ad.

"Nah, I'm just some random 6'5", three-hundred-fifty-pound man standing in the same spot you agreed to meet someone else named Big Bubba," he said as he climbed into Shyne's work vehicle.

It had a sharp charge in the passenger's headrest just in case he got wrong. If he did, he'd be riding around with his head in his lap. And what fun is that?

"And you're sarcastic! That's perfect!" Shyne cheered. She would've clapped if she wasn't driving. "So... I mean...your ad... Is there really a market for such a thing? I was really being facetious when I did the search, but... you popped up."

"You'd be surprised. I get booked all the time! It's good money, plus, I love what I do," he replied.

"I bet you do," Shyne laughed as she continued driving.

"What's that smell?" Big Bubba inquired and cracked the window to get some fresh air flowing.

"Napalm," she replied as if it were the most normal thing in the world.

Big Bubba certainly couldn't say anything with what he did for a living.

****

Billy Marks was ordered to perform eight-hundred-hours of community service as a part of his probation. He was sent to a Southside housing project to clean up. Instead of cleaning, he paid the maintenance supervisor to chill out in an empty unit. His parents decked it out with A/C, a fifty-five-inch TV and a video game system. His penance for raping three girls was drinking beer and playing games.

Probably would have been just fine if not for Shyne. The same supervisor he'd paid sold him out and gave her a key. Shyne and Big Bubba watched as Billy arrived in his fancy sports car. He carried a twelve-pack of beer to last his eight-hour shift inside.

"That's him," Shyne told her passenger as he walked towards the unit.

"Mph. Pretty lil' fella. Got a nasty walk on him, too!" Big Bubba cheered.

Shyne could find no words so she remained quiet. After an hour or so, it was time to move. "You don't have any supplies? A kit? Nothing?" Shyne asked as she grabbed her napalm from the back.

"Nah, I prefer rawhide," he replied, causing her to wince.

"I am so sorry I asked," she said with a grimace. She put her ear to the door and listened to him whoop and holler along with the game. He was talking to another gamer via the headset he wore, so he didn't even hear them ease inside.

"Hold on, Mike, some niggers just walked in," Billy said, pausing the game.

Shyne smiled brightly at being called a nigger. She knew he was about to eat those words. Literally.

"What do you guys want? I paid Johnnie for this place, so run along. No crack here!"

"Ha-ha, you sure told them!" his friend Mike laughed on the other end of the headset.

"I'm sure there's plenty of crack right here!" Big Bubba laughed.

Billy didn't get the joke but he did get the dick. The hired rapist moved across the room in a flash and attacked.

"Oh my!" Shyne swooned when Big Bubba prepared to sexually assault him. She'd thought that she wanted to see it until she saw it. "I'll...umm...be right outside. 'Bout twenty minutes?"

"Betta make it a half hour. I'll holla when I'm done," he replied to her back as she stepped outside.

Big Bubba said he would holla when he finished, but it was Billy who did the hollering. He hollered the whole time. And to add insult to injury, his friend Mike could hear him the whole time.

Now Billy got to experience an unwanted dick in him just like his victims had. Bubba flipped and tossed him like a rag doll for the next forty-five minutes, filling him with DNA. Luckily, his DNA wouldn't survive the fire.

"All done," Bubba said, sticking his big, sweaty head out the door.

"My tu-... Ewww! What's that smell?" Shyne reeled. Being pregnant always made her super sensitive to odors. Big Bubba just cocked his head at her as if to say 'really'. "Oh. Oh yeah."

"Guess it's my turn to go outside. You got a cigarette?" It was Shyne's turn to answer a stupid question with a gesture. She twisted her lips and looked down at her baby bump. "Oh yeah. Probably not."

"Probably not," she quipped to his back then turned to the victim. Billy was curled up in the fetal positon shocked by a mixture of shame and pain.

"Are you okay?"

"N-n-n-no. That m-m-ma-man r-raped me," he moaned. The sides of his mouth were ripped from too much Big Bubba. His anus didn't make out any better, as a trail of blood ran down his leg.

"Poor fella. Now you know how those girls felt!" she spat and tossed the contents of the jar on him.

"What's this?" Billy moaned as the jelly-like substance coated him. It was one of those questions that a person asked but really didn't want to hear the answer to.

"Napalm. I made it myself," Shyne cheered proudly. The blank look on his face said the he didn't share in her enthusiasm. Shyne shrugged her shoulders and lit a match.

Billy screamed louder than he did when Big Bubba was raping him as the flames spread. He took off out the door, running to escape the flames. The air, however, only added fuel to the fire. He dropped in the middle of the courtyard and burned.

"Where to now?" Big Bubba asked as they rode away. He had been hired for two gigs and hoped that the second one was also a sweet white boy. It wasn't.

"To see a judge," she told the rental rapist. "I still can't believe what you can find online!"

"Believe it! I've done parties, weddings, a Bar Mitzvah..."

****

Rico and Sun followed the ice-cream truck for two days figuring out its route and the best place to strike. When the time came, they made their move.

A Dallas apartment complex was the last sales stop of the day before the truck returned to the distribution center. There, they turned in the day's profits and picked up the drugs for the next day's run. This truck had the longest route, which meant it was also the last one in.

"Here you go," Jafe smiled as he served a young girl a dose of heroin. He'd watched her habit grow over the last few months so he knew that the hit wouldn't get her through the night. That meant he could slide by later and trade his dick for dope so that so she wouldn't get sick.

The girl didn't have time to smile back or say 'you're welcome' before she rushed off to get the drug into her system to ease the pain of withdrawals.

"Hol' up!" one final customer yelled as he approached the truck.

"Make him run," Jafe laughed. He always got a kick out of taunting the addicts, adding insult to the injury he'd caused.

"Ki-ki-ki," Manuel giggled as he pulled off. The customer jogged to catch up. When he did, the driver pulled off again.

YOLO 4   37

"Th-thank you," the customer huffed when he finally got to the window.

"Hurr' up!" Jafe snarled. "You're the last one of the day."

"Last customer ever!" Rico corrected before shooting him in his sarcastic smile. He literally wiped the smile off of his face. It landed right behind Manuel.

"What the fuck?!" the driver asked. He didn't like the answer because Rico shot him, too.

"Let's ride!" Sun suggested as he ran over to join him. He pushed the dead driver out of the seat and took his place.

"Yo, it's like... a hundred grand in here!" Rico said when he saw all the cash in the cooler.

"More fuel for the fire," Sun replied.

All money ain't good money and this money was especially dirty. It had too much blood, sweat and tears on it for them.

The mood grew tense as they reached the distribution center. The brothers looked around to make sure the coast was clear before pulling in. It wasn't, but they couldn't see the unseen eyes that were watching.

A set of eyes saw the van pull in and hit a button. On command, the large roll-up door rolled up, granting them access inside.

"Here we go," Sun said as he pulled in. Both men shot their eyes in all directions for any threats.

"Four ever there," Rico announced, pointing at the men standing at a table mixing heroin. "I got them, you take the office."

Sun nodded and came to a stop. They double checked their vests and weapons and then sprang into action.

"Late again, Jafe," a Latin man chided when the side door slid open. He looked up and saw Rico with a pump.

Sometimes, some things have a bark that's louder than its bite. However, this wasn't one of those times because the twelve gauge made him turn a full flip when it hit him. It looked like an acrobatic performance when he gunned the others down.

"What the hell is going on out here?" the man from in the office demanded when he came out to investigate the sounds of gunfire. He did not like the answer. In his defense, no one liked getting hit with an AR-15.

"Justice!" Sun replied and let him have it. A three shot burst shredded his chest and sent him back into the office. Sun followed him in and found him sprawled in front of a desk. On it were stacks of money totaling over a million dollars.

"You see this shit?!" an agent asked as they monitored the hidden cameras from an unmarked van nearby.

"Yeah, what is it, a stick up?" he asked. That theory quickly went out the window when Rico came in with a gas can.

"What the fuck?" the first agent asked. They watched in disbelief as he poured five gallons on the money and all around the room. He also rigged the gas tanks of all the vans parked inside.

"W-w-what do we do?" his partner asked. He picked up his radio to call in the cavalry if told to.

"Nothing. We need to find out who they are and who sent them," he replied as they snapped still pictures of both men's faces.

"This one is for Shyne!" Sun said as he lit a book of matches. The warehouse exploded as they made their way to the getaway vehicle parked nearby.

Unbeknownst to them, they drove back to their hotel with federal agents on their tails.

Chapter 9

"Dear Diary, guess what! Oh, you can't guess, so I'll just tell you. I'm in love! With a man named Killa. I don't know what his real name is but, shoot... I don't even know if he's real! Anyway, he's a real killer. He killed a hundred men before he turned twenty-one! He makes Mr. Grimsly seem like Mr. Rogers..."

"Ooh, mommy was a groupie!" Shyne chuckled and kept reading. Page after page was dedicated to proclaiming her love for her father.

"I got jumped today! By four girls who thought I wanted their men. What would I do with four dead men? That's what they are, too, because Mr. Grimsly gave me the green light to take the lead on my first hit!

Those bitches hit like bitches, too. It took everything I had not to murder them on the spot. I want to get them so badly, but Mr. Grimsly says it's personal and not business. Anyway, at least I get to kill Treble, Ray, Reggie and Ace."

Yolo easily lured Treble and company to their untimely deaths. The promise of new pussy had been getting dudes deaded since the caveman days. Cavemen following cave chicks into some cave in hopes of some hairy cave woman pussy and instead ended up with a busted head.

It was fairly simple to get them all to drink the poisoned champagne while waiting for some friends of Yolo to show up. Pretty simple until Treble slipped his hand under her skirt and began playing with her pussy.

"Oh my!" Yolo gasped when his finger reached her clit. It was silky, slippery and wet. She let out soft moans from the feel of the new sensation. She was delightedly curious, however, she drew the line when he tried to insert his finger inside of her. She protested vehemently on behalf of her intact hymen. "No!"

"Okay, chill, little ma," Treble said and went back to making circles on her love button.

Yolo was on the verge of a life changing orgasm when a deep yawn interrupted him. Like a game of 'Monkey See, Monkey Do', all the men followed their leader and yawned as well. And when he fell over dead, they did, too.

"Not yet!" *Yolo pouted at the interruption. She was far too curious to see what all that electricity would result in, so she put her finger where Treble's had been and did what he'd been doing.*

"Damn it, man!!!" *she exclaimed when her whole body shook from her first orgasm. She picked up the smoldering blunt from the ashtray and took a pull, hoping to come down from her cum high.*

Yolo cleaned her DNA from Treble's fingers before removing all other traces of her being there. Once she got home, she rushed into her room and masturbated again. Then again in the shower and once more when sh-

"Dang, Mommy! You all fast!" Shyne exclaimed like she didn't hump the air before she went straight up to her room and woke up Asad. "Asad, you sleep?"

"I was," he pouted as he prepared to roll out of bed. Pregnant Shyne often sent him to the store at all times of the night, so he was ready to go. "What do you need?"

"This," she replied.

Turns out, he didn't have to get out of the bed after all.

****

"Wake up, Shyne!"

"What, Malik?" Shyne fussed at her son. She instantly regretted it when his bottom lip poked out. "Mommy's sorry. What do you need, baby?"

"Your phone," he replied, pointing at her phone.

She let out a heavy sigh seeing several missed calls from her brothers. For both of them to be calling, it couldn't be good.

"Yeah," she said with a snarl when Sun took her call. "Sup with Daddy?"

"Nothing. Still sleep," he sighed, to her relief. It was only for a moment, though, because his next words broke her heart. "We gotta go to New York. Grandma died."

Shyne didn't recall anything that was said after those dreaded words. She didn't remember saying goodbye or hanging up. She had no recollection of packing her clothes or her kids for the trip to New York. Asad was halfway through South Carolina before she came back to reality.

"I didn't even get to say goodbye," she moaned. It had been her habit to chat with the wise old lady every Sunday, but she'd died on a Saturday.

Asad couldn't think of anything to say to comfort her so he reached across the SUV and took her hand instead. The squeeze he gave said what he couldn't.

Fourteen hours after leaving home, they crossed the 159th Street Bridge into The Bronx.

"Hmph?" Asad asked with a curious frown on his face as they rode up the hill on Ogden Ave.

The Bronx is like that for anyone who's never been there before.

"TV..." Shyne was cut off by the navigation system telling her husband to turn left. He did and they entered the projects a block later.

Shyne pointed at Rico's car and directed Asad to park next to it. She scooped her daughter up from her car seat and led the way up to her grandmother's apartment.

"Who?" Bryonna barked in response to the doorbell.

"Me," Shyne replied, posing in front of the peephole. The sound of multiple locks being unlocked echoed through the cinder hallway.

"I'm sorry about your grandma," Bryonna wailed and hugged her bestie. Once the greeting ended, they stepped inside.

"Where's my brothers?" Shyne asked. The question was barely out of her mouth before she heard Sun laughing in the courtyard. The nosey young lady looked out the window and saw her brothers down on the bench. "I'll be back."

"I wanna come," Malik protested. Shyne was not in the mood for one of his fits so took his hand. Her brothers were in the middle of an animated conversation with some of the projects hoods when she arrived.

"A-yo, y'all remember when I shot Reese in the ass in the lobby?" Marco laughed.

"Yeah, and Grandma whooped yo' ass right there!" Rico cracked up. "Then made you clean up the blood!"

"Got rid of that dirty gun, too!" he added. Saved him from being charged with the multiple murders on the gun.

"How 'bout when she caught us fucking in the staircase?" a pretty hood rat named Yvonne asked Rico. "Whooped my ass, too! Told me to respect myself better than that!"

"It didn't work. I just fucked you on the roof instead!" Rico laughed.

"Me, too. So did I. Hear-hear!" the other dudes co-signed since they'd all had a turn with her on the roof.

"But, I ain't do it in the staircase no more!" she laughed.

Shyne wore a proud smile as she listened to all the fond stories about her grandmother.

"Yo, someone needs to write a book about Grandma, Granddad and Uncle Cameron," Sun announced.

"I'm sure someone will," Rico replied. He was right, too, because Killa and Cam's fathers definitely needed their stories told as well.

One by one, the project people dispersed to go do project stuff, which included Marco taking the Yvonne up to the roof and rocking her for old time's sake. Meanwhile, the siblings were left alone on the project bench.

"Man, I'ma miss Grandma," Rico sighed. Sun and Shyne both felt a twinge of jealousy at him having a ten-year head start over them on getting to know the woman.

"Well, at least I was her favorite," Shyne announced.

"Says who?" Sun laughed. "Please! I was definitely her favorite. She said so all the time."

"That was only to make you feel better. Actually, she didn't even like you," Rico snickered. "You, either."

"Yeah, right!" Shyne cracked up.

Truth be told, their shared great-grandmother treated each of them like they were her favorite. She had the ability to make each one feel like they were the only one. She did have a favorite offspring, though. He was lying in a coma in a hospital in Baltimore.

"I should k-i-l-l the doctors for letting great-grandma die," Shyne spelled out so that her son wouldn't understand.

"Bruh, grandma was ninety!" Sun replied. "She had a good run."

"True, but we should fuck somebody up! It'll make us feel better," Rico added.

"Fuck!" Malik repeated and got popped in his mouth.

Rico laughed until he got popped, too. "My bad," he apologized. "Yo! Remember when we first met? We got into that big fight!"

"Hell yeah!" Sun laughed and got on his phone. He searched and found the footage of it that their father had uploaded to the internet.

The next day, they buried their beloved great-grandmother in a grave next to her husband and sons. While at the cemetery, they also visited the graves of their mothers and brother. The empty plot between Sincerity and Yolo drew their eyes like a flame does a moth. It belonged to their father.

****

"Yo, what happened?" Rico asked as when they returned to a flurry of activity in the projects. Neither Sun nor Shyne could answer since they'd been with him.

The question was rhetorical anyway since it was obvious that there'd been a shooting. Police milled about, collecting shell casings from several different automatic weapons. An ambulance rushed off with a victim inside while a bloody sheet covered another. The twins wanted no parts of whatever had just happened but when Rico went to investigate they followed.

"Yo, take Bryonna and the kids up to the apartment. I'll be up in a minute," Shyne told her husband.

"No, you take Bryonna and the kids up to the apartment and keep your ass there until I say so!" he shot back.

"Okaaaaay," Shyne giggled girlishly and followed his directions. Her first stop inside was to print him a coochie coupon because his attitude had turned her on.

"Yo, what the fuck, Marco?" Rico asked when he found his friend.

"Them niggas from Webster came over here and aired shit out," he explained.

The two projects had been beefing for generations. They'd been beefing for so long that this current generation had no idea what the feud was even about. All they knew was they'd been going back and forth shooting at each other for decades.

"Who that?" he asked, pointing to the corpse with his head.

"Yvonne," Marco replied, twisting his lips woefully.

They both lowered their heads in sorrow. Not just because of the warm memories of her hot vagina but because she was one of them. She was a true ride or die chick who was down for her hood. When dudes went to prison, it was Yvonne who wrote letters and took collect calls. It was her who demanded money from the hood to put on their books. And it was her who gave them some 'welcome home' pussy when they got home.

"Well, we said we wanted to fuck somebody up," Sun reminded.

"It would make us feel better," Rico agreed. "Let's go see Sarge."

****

Sarge was a highly decorated ex-Marine who lived in the projects. He had a silver star, a bronze star, a purple heart and he was completely out of his mind. He lived on the top floor of his building in a virtual fortress.

"Don't stand in front of the door," Rico warned when they reached Sarge's apartment.

"Why?" Sun asked as his brother knocked on the heavy steel door.

"Who?" Came the reply from the other side.

"Rico Forrest," he said from the side. The locks click clacked for a full minute before the door eased open.

"Come in," Sarge ordered. Rico stepped inside followed by his brother. Sun got the answer to his question when he saw a bazooka aimed at the door.

"Who is he? Killa's Sun," Sarge asked and answered when he saw the unmistakable family resemblance. "Sarge."

"Sun," Sun greeted, shaking the outstretched hand.

"I been waiting on you," Sarge told Rico. He knew they'd strike back for the recent assault. And that meant they'd need guns. Sarge had guns.

"I see!" Rico cheered, seeing MP-5 machine guns on the coffee table. Both brothers rushed over to fondle the hardware.

"Nine millimeter, semi or fully auto..." Sarge said, rattling off the guns' specifications.

"We'll take 'em!" they both announced happily. Rico produced a pound of weed and handed it over as payment.

"Hmmm?" Sarge said as he inspected the herbs. He opened the bag and stuck his face in to inhale. He nodded in agreement with the fruity aroma and sat down to roll one. "Smoke one."

Sun opened his mouth to say no but his brother quickly cut him off. If a man trades you machine guns for weed then invites you to smoke, you smoke.

****

"I wanna come," Shyne pouted when she caught her brothers sneaking out later that night.

"We're just going to the store," Sun said, causing her to twist her lips dubiously.

The brothers were both dressed to kill in all black everything. Shyne reached up and pulled Rico's hat down on his face into a ski mask.

"What, y'all gonna rob the store?" she asked sarcastically.

"Where is Asad? Didn't he tell you to keep your ass inside?" Sun teased.

"I put him to sleep, if you know what I'm saying," she giggled and humped the air. That's just how her brothers left her...humping the air

"Sup, yo," Marco greeted when Killa's sons met him and two other men out in the courtyard.

"Let's do this," Rico announced. "Me and Bruh gonna come from MLK side and flush them your way."

"And we gonna air that shit out!" one of the men cheered.

They took separate cars over to Webster Projects and returned the favor. In the end, four people lay dead and another five ended up in area hospitals.

Chapter 10

"Dear Diary, today is a sad day. Mr. Grimsly died. Actually, he was put to sleep after having a stroke. I put the doctor to sleep for putting him to sleep. Oh, and the other doctor, too, cuz he had a smart mouth. Casper said we're running out of doctors.

I'll never get to see Mr. Grimsly again... The worst part is that we didn't even get have a funeral. The cleaner came and took him away instead.

"Aww, Mommy," Shyne sobbed. She knew that the blurred ink on the pages were from her mother's tears and shed some of her own.

"You okay?" Asad asked as they rode south on I-75. They were headed home, but had a stop to make in Baltimore first.

"Huh? Oh, yeah," she replied and went back inside the book.

"So... Casper showed me a video of those girls jumping me. I know Mr. Grimsly said that I couldn't get any get back, but...he's not here anymore and Casper gave me the green light, so I'm going to kill all of them..."

Yolo set out to track down and murder each of the girls who'd jumped her. By the time she finished her murder spree, she had nineteen notches on her belt, but she still had a long way to go to reach a hundred. Luckily, niggas kept fucking up and volunteering to get added to her twisted tally.

"Yolo!" Casper screeched in that high-pitched voice that usually resulted in someone in getting killed.

"Yes, boss?" Yolo answered with her hand behind her back with its fingers crossed hopefully.

"I need you to go to Newark and deliver a message," he said.

Yolo was elated as she rode the Long Island Railroad into New York City. She transferred to the New Jersey trains from Manhattan.

She looked just like all the other school girls in her school clothes with her book bag on her back. However, unlike any of the other school girls, she had a gun and a grenade in her book bag. None of the other girls took that class.

Boobie Johnson ran The Black Mob's operation across the bridge in The Brick City. His bustling blocks sold tons of weed, coke, heroin and pussy. Things were all good until he started abusing all of them. He'd violated the fourth crack commandment by getting high off his own supply.

Boobie would get up in the morning, smoke a blunt, shoot a speed ball and fuck a couple of the Mob's prostitutes. Not only had he knocked a few of them up, but his money also wasn't adding up. He'd began to turn in less and less every week. He'd also started dodging Casper's calls, so he sent a messenger with a message.

"You must be the new bitch," Boobie said as he pulled up to a young Yolo standing in front of Newark's Penn Station.

"I guess," she said as she hopped into the front seat. She didn't like being called a bitch but since she was going to kill him anyway, she let it slide.

"Pretty little bitch," he said to her exposed thigh before giving it a squeeze. He then slid his hand up her leg and under her short skirt. "I gotta hit that first before you hit the block."

"Sounds good to me. Let's go to your house," Yolo agreed and parted her legs, granting him access to her slippery vagina. When he tried to push a finger inside, she replied with the usual, "Chill."

"Damn, Ma!" he reacted to having his hand slapped away. "You act like you a damn virgin or something."

"Actually, I am," she shrugged since it was no big deal to her. Being only seventeen and unmarried, she felt that she was supposed to still be one.

Mr. Grimsly didn't just teach her how to be a killer. He taught her to be a lady as well. He taught her to respect herself so that others would, too. She'd taken his advice, for the most part. She still liked dressing sexy, though.

"Yeah, right!" Boobie laughed. He hadn't seen a virgin over the age of thirteen in his life. Hell, he had some that age selling pussy at that exact second. "Anyway, what's this important message Casper's bitch ass got for me?"

"Tell you once we get to your house," she replied and parted her legs again. Boobie took the bait and played in her pussy until he pulled up to his house. Another block and she would've busted a nut.

Boobie made a big deal out of sucking her juices off his fingers. "Follow me."

Boobie led the way up the steps and unlocked the door. He didn't have a shred of chivalry in him so he walked in first without holding the door open for her. As soon as they were inside, she pulled her gun and lifted it to the back of his fitted cap. The cap did a flip when the bullet passed through it. Boobie took two more steps after being shot before death set in.

Yolo dug in his pocket and retrieved his car keys. She'd reached the front door when she remembered she was supposed to give him a message.

"Oh yeah, Casper said to tell you hello," she happily told his corpse before skipping out of the house.

Yolo was pretty sure Boobie wouldn't object to her using his car, so she drove it back to the train station.

****

"Dear Diary, Okay, so Pastor ate my pussy. I almost felt bad, but it felt soooo good. I almost hated having to shove explosives up his ass and blowing him up.

I'm already eighteen and he's only number thirty. I might not make it. How can I impress Killa if I can't kill a hundred people by twenty-one..."

Yolo contemplated blowing up a bus or some other act of mass murder, but quickly discarded them. She knew that Killa wouldn't respect it. *As a matter of fact, with his reputation for killing bad people, that might just get her put on his list.*

Besides, unauthorized killings were frowned upon by Casper. Quite a few of the thirty notches on her belt were violators of that very rule.

Luckily for her, Casper sicced her on his old crew from Brooklyn. One shotgun and eight shells brought her tally to thirty-six.

"What?" Casper asked when he saw her lip poked out after the Bar Murders.

"That's still only thirty-six," she pouted, about to cry.

"Well, why don't you blow up their funeral? That should get your numbers up a bit," he offered in consolation.

Truth be told, the funeral would host more of the people who'd sold him out and turned their backs on him. He'd done his entire bid without snitching on anyone and got fucked for it. Literally. So, now it was time to fuck back.

****

"Okay, red to red. Green to green. My hip bone is connected to my pelvis bone and my pelvis bone is connected to my... Mmmm," Yolo sang as she paused putting the bomb together to masturbate.

"Oooh, Mommy! Just nasty!" Shyne shrieked. She shook her head, laughed and got back to reading.

Yolo planned to blow up a funeral just like her idol had once done. However, instead of sending it inside with a family member like he'd done, she snuck in and planted them in the caskets. She also set up a camera so she and Casper could watch the fun.

"That's my Aunt Rosa. Fuckin' cunt!" Casper growled when he saw his Cousin Guido's mom enter.

She put on a good show, wailing and flailing her arms.

"And the Oscar goes to..." Yolo cracked as she passed out in front of the casket. Her husband had to pick her three-hundred-pound ass up and sit it in a chair.

The mothers of the other deceased men refused to be outdone by Rosa's grief show. Vito's mom climbed into the casket with her son and pulled the top down while Joey's mom fell out every few feet until she reached her seat.

The actresses were all seated front and center when Yolo pressed the button.

"Yay!" she cheered as the blast literally knocked a few heads clean off. The shrapnel tore through the funeral home, taking twenty-five lives in the process.

She was now at sixty-one kills. Not bad for a nineteen-year-old.

Chapter 11

Yolo had a headful of natural spiral curls that were in a big wild afro and because of it, it was getting harder and harder to fit her array of wigs over it. The young girl loved to change her appearance with different colored and length wigs. She especially loved the bulletproof dreadlock wig created for her by Mr. Grimsly.

Since ponytails and stocking caps no longer worked to confine her own thick crop of hair, she decided it was time for a haircut.

"Dominican Republic," Yolo read aloud from the sign above the beauty salon. A drove of pretty women flowed in and out so she figured this was as good a spot as any. She parked her car and went inside.

Yolo was awed by the gorgeous Latinas of all different shades gossiping in rapid fire Spanish with sprinkles of English. She'd taken enough Spanish in school to ride along with most of the conversation.

"My husband is so cheap! He makes me spend my own money to get my hair fixed," a dark-skinned Dominican lady grumbled.

"You don't suck his dick enough," a woman who was a shade lighter offered. "Suck his dick and then ask for whatever it is you want."

"Before... he cums, though!" a white Dominican hairdresser added. She was right, too, because after a man busted, it was naptime.

Yolo smiled as she followed the back and forth volley like a tennis match. In an hour, she was schooled on the powerfully persuasive power of the P. However, she still planned on saving it for her mysterious Killa. Until then, she'd just play in it daily.

"Hola, mamacita!" a hairdresser called out to Yolo as she waved her hand to get her attention. Her seat had just become empty so she could take her.

"Thank you," Yolo smiled as she took a seat. "I like to wear wigs, so I need this cut down."

"Cut?!" the woman reeled as she fondled Yolo's thick spiral of curls. "Girl, a good relaxer is all you need."

"A perm! No, I don't want a perm. Plus, my scalp is too sensitive. Just cut it, please," Yolo replied.

"Okay, let me wash and condition it first," the lady said and got to work. Yolo relaxed and continued listening to the sexually charged stories floating around the salon.

"So, my husband just bought us a chalet on the Island," Blanca bragged. The Island she was referring to was their homeland of the Dominican Republic. Most of the women dreamed of striking it rich so that they could return to the beautiful Caribbean island and ball the fuck out.

"Guillermo is doing it big!" another woman cheered.

The familiar name really caught Yolo's attention. She recalled a man with that same name explaining to Casper why his receipts were so low. If this was the same man, then he was a liar and a thief. And in this world, snitches get stitches and thieves get chopped up and fed to pigs.

"Yes, yes, he is," Blanca said, waving a diamond laden hand to prove it.

"Ouch! Hey..." Yolo whined as her scalp began to burn. "What did you do?"

"Oh, stop whining and come to the sink," the hairdresser demanded. She positioned Yolo under the water to rinse the perm from her hair. "Uh oh!"

"Uh oh, what?" Yolo screeched in feared. The cool water provided some relief until she saw clumps of curls landing in the sink. "What did you do?"

"It'll be okay. You wanted it cut, anyway," the woman chided as she finished rinsing her hair. She wrapped her head in a towel and blotted it dry. When Yolo looked in the mirror, she saw bald spots all over her head. She reached up to touch it and more fell out.

"What did you do?" she whimpered with tears streaming down her face.

"Stop whining and let me fix it," the woman fussed and knocked Yolo's hand away from her head.

"Remember those words!" Yolo dared as she stood from the chair. She marched out to her car and grabbed her gun to murder everyone in the shop, but she remembered Casper's rule about unauthorized killings and went home instead.

****

"Hey, Casper, remember the Dominican dude, Guillermo?" she asked offhandedly. *"The one who hit a string of bad luck?"*

"Yes, his spots been raided, stash houses robbed, fire, plagued, floods..." Casper said, recounting all the excused he'd recently been given. The man had done well for so long, which was why he tried to give him the benefit of the doubt. He'd even doubled his dope shipment to help him work off his debt.

Guillermo, however, had other plans. Retirement plans. And he planned to steal as much of Casper's money as possible to pay for them. He'd already purchased a villa in the Dominican Republic and filled several bank accounts. Once he flipped his last shipment, he would be in the wind.

"Does he have a wife name Blanca? Pretty little thing with outrageously large breasts?"

"Yes, her tits weren't that big when he met her but... Why?" Casper asked, scrunching his brow curiously.

"Oh, okay. No. Yeah. So...I met her in the beauty salon today and she told me that her husband just paid 1.8 million for a house in the Dominican Republic," she said as if she didn't know she was getting him in trouble.

"Kill him! And her! And bring me those titties I paid for! NO! Bring her to me!" he screamed ferociously.

"Okay," she agreed eagerly since she needed the bodies. Her baseball cap flipped off her head as she jumped for joy.

"What in the hell did you do to your hair?" he asked with a grimace.

"I told her to cut it down so I could wear my wigs but she put a perm in it instead. Now it's fried, dyed and laid to the side."

"No, it's fried, dyed and bald on the sides!" he corrected. "What did you do about it?"

"Nothing. You said no unauthorized killings. Business, never personal," she pouted.

"Well, make it your business to murder that bitch for doing that to your hair!"

"Wake up, Shyne! We're here," Asad announced.

"I'm not sleep!" she insisted, unaware that she had indeed dozed off. She wiped a line of slobber from her face as she looked around. They were in Baltimore at the hospital. It was time to visit their dad.

Chapter 12

"Is that the guy from Dallas?" the federal agent asked despite the warning on his screen.

Sun's face had been put into a facial recognition program that sounded an alert every time it was picked up.

"Gotta be his son," another agent guessed correctly. Even with Killa's slight face lift and thirty-plus years on him, he and his sons still looked alike. "The plot thickens..."

It got even thicker when Rico showed up and rang the alarm with his own handsome face. They both could have been arrested on the spot and charged with the multiple murders in Dallas, however, the agent in charge knew there was more to the story so fell back. He would give the brothers just enough rope to hang themselves and then kick away the chair from under them.

Shyne left her husband and children along with Bryonna and her niece in the waiting room. Because the patient was in such bad shape, security had been reduced to one city cop and a few cameras. It was doubtful that Killa would survive surgery so the agents were ready to move on to their next targets. Rico and Sun.

"Sup, yo," Shyne greeted as she entered the hospital room. The cop had orders not to let anyone in, but he was about his money so instead, he charged one hundred bucks a head like the VIP line at the club.

"Chillin'," Rico said as he and Sun stepped back from Killa's bedside to give her some space.

"Hey, Daddy," she beamed with the same enthusiasm she used when he was awake. Now, instead of snapping on her big head, he just lay there silently. That didn't stop Shyne from carrying on a conversation with him.

"Okay, guys, time to let the patient get some rest. He has a big day tomorrow," a pretty nurse said as she breezed in.

Sun checked her out for half a second before turning his head away. He was so happily married that he didn't feel the need to look at other women. He looked to his older brother waiting to see him bag her up, but he didn't even notice her.

"Okay," Shyne said before leaning over and giving her father a kiss on the cheek before leaving the room.

"You and ol' Shonda must be getting pretty serious," Sun asked knowingly once the siblings were inside the elevator.

"Huh?" Rico asked, meaning yes. They were but he hadn't really thought about it. They'd made no formal plans or agreement to be a couple. They just were.

"I'll take that as a yes!" Shyne cheered. "That's cool, though. She seems like good people."

"Yeah, she cool," Rico downplayed it. He had to admit it was now more than having someone on the inside to keep tabs on their father. He may have selected her for her big ass but it was her big heart that had reeled him in.

"How is he?" Bryonna asked when the trio reached the waiting room.

"He has surgery tomorrow. In sha Allah he'll wake up," Shyne pouted.

Asad came over and put an arm around her to her outside. The twins and their families went to a nearby hotel while Rico went home to Shonda.

After Shyne rocked Malik and Amina to sleep, she did the same to her husband. Asad had a peaceful smile on his face when she got out of the bed. She took a quick shower to rinse off their relations and settled on the sofa with her favorite book.

****

"Dear Diary, I got the green light on old Guillermo. Looks like he won't get to retire in the Caribbean after all. Oh, and the bitch who balded me, too..."

Yolo used a pair of trimmers to shave her head. Her scalp had pink spots from the chemical burns, but would heal in time. In the meanwhile, she donned a cute, short wig that framed her pretty face. The shiny black bob fit her disguise perfectly

"Who?" the security guard barked into the intercom. He asked again when he didn't get a reply. Still no answer, so he snatched the door open with gun in hand. His tone softened when he saw the pretty girl at the door.

"Hey, I'm the new masseuse," Yolo greeted with a smile. She contemplated shooting him when his eyes dropped to her exposed cleavage. 'Some security" she thought to herself. It was a lesson she'd learn from the Dominican ladies at the salon. Men who think with their dicks are easy to trick.

"Where's the other girl?" he asked, looking down the driveway. Guillermo usually tipped the usual girl to give his security guards dick a massage. There would be no happy ending today.

"She's tied up right now, so I came in her place," she said truthfully. The regular girl was indeed tied up in her house, allowing Yolo to take her place.

"Well, did she tell you the arrangement?" he asked, grabbing his dick through his slacks to explain.

"Uh, yeah," she smiled, catching on. "As soon as I take care of the boss, you're next."

"Okay, well, you better get started. Miss Blanca returns soon."

"I would love to do her, too," Yolo smiled as she followed him inside. They arrived at the indoor pool where Guillermo was sipping cognac and watching a homemade porn.

"Oh my!" Yolo blushed at Blanca on the wide screen with her mouth stretched wide from a thick dick. She glanced over at Guillermo and saw that same dick in his hand.

"Who are you? Where is Tonya?" he demanded to both.

"Tied up," they replied in unison. The security guard backed away from the exposed dick. He went back to his station to await his hand job.

"Well, I hope..." Guillermo said while switching scenes on the DVD player. Yolo instantly recognized the girl she'd tied up on the screen. She was vigorously riding Guillermo's big dick backwards. "...you can ride like she does."

"Umm..." Yolo said as he lay back ready to be mounted. She cocked her head curiously at the cock. The victim closed his eyes when she took it into her hand. Yolo ran her finger down a thick vein while reaching in Tonya's bag. She ignored the gels, flavored creams and anal lubes and pulled out her knife.

"What the..." Guillermo said when he felt a sharp pain form the sharp knife on his dick. It was so hard that the knife only cut through the skin and veins.

"Casper and his money is what!" Yolo replied.

Guillermo instinctively grabbed his manhood, leaving his throat free to be cut.

"I should have used She-Ra's knife," she complained as she cut his jugular. Her old knife would have cut down to his spine.

Guillermo hopped up and took off trying to escape death. The thing about death, though, is that there is no escaping it; especially when you run the wrong way and land in the pool.

He fought for a full minute before going still and floating face down.

Yolo washed the blood from her hand and went looking for the bodyguard.

"Pst...in here," the man called from a cracked bedroom door. Yolo smiled and followed him inside. He was hard and ready for his hand job.

"Oh, why not?" Yolo mused and dug in the bag once again. Right next to her pistol with silencer, she found a small tube of lubricant. She squeezed some into her palm and grabbed his dick.

"I can feel your heartbeat."

"Mmhmm," he happily agreed as she began to slow stroke his shaft.

Yolo curiously worked him up and down, amused by his moans and groans. She'd learned that the head was the most sensitive part.

The man's feet kicked whenever she rubbed it. His moans and breathing grew deeper as she stroked. She'd watched more than enough porn to know what would happen next.

"Arg!" he grunted as he sent a blast of semen high into the air. Yolo whipped out her gun and shot him before it landed. He came and went at the same time.

"Guillermo! Why did no one meet me at the door?" Blanca bitched as she stormed inside. "Where is every one? Who will get my bags? Who are you?"

"Yolo," Yolo replied and shot her, too. That made a total of ninety. The hairdresser made the total ninety-one.

Chapter 13

"Have you been up all night?" Asad asked when he found his wife on the sofa with the diary.

"No, I..." Shyne said but got cut off by the dawn outside of the window. It was proof that she had, indeed, been awake all night. Her husband shrugged his shoulders and laid out his rug for his morning prayer.

Shyne smiled and sat up to watch him pray. She loved nothing more than to hear him recite the Qur'an in his deep, melodious voice. By now, she even knew all the words to the first chapter which is recited in every cycle of prayer.

"In the name of Allah. All praise is for God, Lord of everything in existence. Most Gracious, Most Merciful..." until he ended with "Ameen."

Asad stifled a smile when he heard his wife's 'Ameen' along with his own. He never pushed religion on her but appreciated the fact that she prayed with him, even if it was from the sidelines. Shyne also dressed modestly, except for in their bedroom once the kids were asleep. No wonder she stayed pregnant.

"You ready to go to the hospital?" Asad asked. Killa was scheduled for surgery in a couple of hour so his children planned to hold a vigil in the waiting room.

"Nah, I'll wait until it's over. He'll be okay," she said hopefully.

"In sha Allah," he added since it was up to the will of God.

"In sha Allah," she agreed. "I need to get some sleep, so take your kids with you."

"I'll take them to the zoo. No sense in sitting around a hospital with them," he said. He fed and clothed the kids while Shyne finally got in the bed. The moment her family departed, she picked up the diary once more.

****

"Dear Diary, so I sucked a guy's dick today..."

"Ewww!" Shyne reeled in disgust. She almost put the book down but she was nosey, like her daddy, so kept reading.

"Then I cut the shit off! This country bumpkin named Playa D kept fuckin' up his money. He thinks with, wait, that should be 'he thought with' since I past tensed his ass.

Anyway, I only did it for a distraction. Plus, I needed the practice for whenever I meet my boo, Killa. The women in the hair salon all said that's what men like and if you don't, someone else will. I don't want no one else doing that to my man! Okay, so let me tell you about my day..."

Yolo began the day by thanking God the second her eyes opened. It was something Mr. Grimsly had taught her and she continued to do it every day. Then she masturbated. That was something else she did every day. She'd come across a grainy picture of Killa on the internet and jacked off to it like a boy does a porn magazine.

It was a Sunday, which meant the hair salon would be closed. That meant the hairdresser who fucked her head up would be home. Luckily for her boyfriend, she was on her period so he wasn't there when death came knocking. Actually, ringing the bell.

"Who?" Esmeralda demanded at the incessant ringing of her doorbell.

No matter how many times she'd asked, the ringer wouldn't respond. She finally snatched the door open to give the ringer a piece of her mind. Funny, because that's exactly what she'd come for.

"Argh!" Yolo grunted as she punched her with all she had while wearing a pair of brass knuckles. The girl staggered a few feet before falling sound asleep.

"Wha-, who, wha-?" Esmeralda stammered when she awoke several minutes later. She was stripped, gagged and bound in her bathtub.

"Did you know perm contains lye?" Yolo asked from behind goggles and a surgical mask.

"Wha-?" she tried to ask, trying to make sense of her predicament. She strained her memory to remember who the girl was as she watched her mix up the solution.

"Lye. It's a strong alkaline solution," she said, repeating what she'd recently learned. *"Why would anyone want to put this in their hair? A better question is why did you put it in my hair? Especially after I asked you not to, too!"*

Esmeralda now remembered who she was. Not that it would help her now, anyway. She was helpless as Yolo took a gloved hand and scooped out a glob of the lye solution. The woman lifted her leg to keep her at bay but only made it worse. Yolo slapped the lye between her legs, then smoothed some on her thick, lustrous hair and sat down.

"Mm-mm-mph!" Esmeralda mumbled urgently when she began to burn. That translated to 'this shit burns' in gagged language.

"I bet," Yolo agreed and pulled off her wig to show her her damaged scalp. *"I know it burns."*

And burn it did until her head and vagina were bloody and raw. It would have been payback enough but Yolo wasn't satisfied. She turned on the hot water full stream to add injury to injury while hurling insults.

Drowning would be a relief for Esmeralda so she stopped trying to fight it. Once the tub filled, so did her lungs.

She became kill number ninety-one. Nine to go.

****

Playa D thought with his dick most of the time so it was only fitting that Yolo cut it off. She gave him a little head to distract him long enough to pull out her knife. It came off in with one swipe of the super sharp blade. Yolo hummed the music form the Benny Hill Show as he chased her around the room trying to get his dick back.

Yolo took a shower to rinse the blood off before joining the meeting once again. She eagerly awaited the order to lead someone else off to slaughter.

Big Rock from Baltimore blamed his problems on some out-of-towners so she got the nod to go down and body them.

****

"Mmm, you feel soooo good!" Yolo told Killa as she felt an orgasm edging closer. Actually, she told his picture as she played in her pussy. She was almost there until she heard Casper yell her name from downstairs. "Shit!" she fussed at the lost orgasm, delayed that is, because she would make up for it later.

She'd heard murder in the boss' tone so she didn't waste any time going to see what he wanted. "Sup, boss?"

"Is this live?" Casper asked as he and Nut viewed footage on a security monitor. They were watching so intently that neither had noticed her arrival.

"No, from a couple of hours ago," he replied

Curiosity got the best of Yolo so she peeked over their shoulders to see what they were looking at. "Killa! Urg!" she cheered then grunted as she came instantly.

"Really?" Casper chuckled when he saw her reaction to the man. He knew right then that he had to poison her mind against him. If the two dangerous killers ever joined forces, they would be unstoppable.

The three watched as Killa robbed and murdered one of their associates down in Atlanta. Yolo sucked her teeth loudly when the woman on the screen loudly sucked Killa off. She did it to save her life, keep some of the cash and to spite her boyfriend.

"Go kill them both!" Casper ordered as Killa left the house with a duffle bag full of his cash. It was bad enough that his associate had been skimming off the top, but now Killa had swooped in and taken it all.

"*Both?!*" *Yolo screeched at the thought of killing her idol. Thoughts of killing everyone present and running away with Killa ran through her mind.*

"*Not him. The woman and the baby," he replied. "No, not him. I have plans for Mr. Killa. He's going to work for me!*"

"*Yeesssss!" Yolo cheered and pumped her fist triumphantly at the prospect of working side-by-side with Killa. She rushed out to go get dressed for the trip. A last second question turned her back around.*

"*Boss, we can't have two killers in the house," Nut warned. It was scary enough having Yolo around all the time.*

"*We won't. All I need is one," Casper replied with Yolo listening at the door.*

She twisted her lips ruefully and walked away. This was a world of cross and double cross, so what did she expect?

Chapter 14

When Casper put the squeeze on Killa, he had no choice but to comply. The man knew everything about him and his family, yet no one knew much about The Mob. All that they knew was that they were extremely strong, extremely dangerous and everywhere at the same time.

Killa would play ball for now. For as just as long as it took to find and kill them all. Threats against his family took it from business to personal.

The Black Mob furnished their new hired gun with a fully furnished condo in downtown Atlanta, as well as a luxury whip. The car and crib were loaded with all the bells and whistles, including GPS tracking and cameras.

Killa knew the condo was tapped and bugged with cameras and listening devices when he entered it. That's why he'd brought his girl, Kitty, with him. They wanted to see something, so he was going to give them something to see.

"Who is that?" Yolo demanded when she saw Kitty walk in behind Killa. She pouted and crossed arms defiantly as the couple began to strip. She turned her head but not her eyes when Kitty dropped and gave him some head. She sucked his dick while Yolo sucked her teeth.

Yolo watched as Killa returned the favor. He buried his face between the girl's thick thighs and lapped Kitty's kitty. Meanwhile, nine-hundred miles away, Yolo slid her hand down her own wet panties. She and Kitty came at the same time.

"Get a room," Casper teased as he walked in on her orgasm. "As soon as you get done, get dressed. Your flight leaves in an hour."

"O-kay," Yolo said, going for round two once Casper left the room. She made circles on her clit while Killa pounded Kitty's size sixteen booty doggy style. She busted another nut and got up.

She printed a still picture from the camera for round three. Now she had someone to talk to when she got lonely.

****

Yolo was pleased to see that she would be seated next to a woman on the flight. She usually got seated next to some player who offered nothing more than some dick. As soon as the plane was airborne, she pulled out the picture for a chat.

"So... you liked when that girl went down on you? I know you did. Blanca said guys like that. I don't mind doing it for you, you know. I..."

"Aww, how sweet! Is that your boyfriend? He's a cutie!" the woman next to her cooed affectionately.

"Yes, we just started dating, but..." Yolo smiled as she turned. The smile vanished when she saw the woman was a man dressed like a woman. They were headed to Atlanta, after all. Still, Yolo didn't appreciate his/her flirting with her man. She was crazy, after all. "So, you think my man is cute?"

"Mmhmm," he/she squealed and snatched the picture from her hand for a closer look. If he or she was a cat, that would have cost it another life. It lost another life for kissing the picture, then another when it said, "We need to have us a threesome!"

"We can!" Yolo lied. She looked around the plane to see if she could get away with killing it real quick. She shook her head at the packed plane. "Can we go to your place?"

"Mmhmm! Chile, I can't wait to get some man-meat in me!"

"Remember you said that," Yolo giggled without a trace of the extreme violence that came along with it.

"Mmhmm," it agreed happily.

Once they landed in Atlanta, he/she took Yolo to its mid-town condo.

"This is bad!" Yolo cheered, admiring the well-appointed unit. A pair of Samurai swords on the wall really caught her attention. She rushed over for a closer look. "Are these real?"

"Girl, yes! Be careful," it suggested as its guest removed one from its perch.

Yolo expertly wielded the weapon executing strikes and jabs.

"I see you know what you're doing, huh?"

"Yup!" she replied and lopped off an arm. It's been said that a person shouldn't complain about losing a limb when they have another. Yolo cut off the other, giving it a reason to complain.

"Yeeoooww!" it yelled until the next swipe took its head clean off. Its wig came off as the head flipped in the air before landing.

"Okay, remember you said you wanted some man-meat in your mouth?" Yolo asked the head. It didn't reply but she understood.

She removed its panties and cut its dick off. Now he was a she. A she with a dick in her mouth because that's exactly how Yolo left her.

****

Candy had sweet talked Killa out of some of the robbery money with sweet talk and good head. That's a winning combination in any language. Probably other planets, too, but I'm just speculating. Anyway, she could have taken the money and run but instead, she got greedy and decided to stay in the plush house with the hot wheels in the garage. She'd called the police to report the robbery and murder. Once the crime scene was cleared, she poured herself a glass of wine and lit a blunt. Her toddler was sleeping soundly when the doorbell rang.

"Who?" she yelled, hoping that it was one of Dallas's cute friends. She could use a good nut after the day she'd had. It would be great if the handsome robber had come back to lay some pipe. No such luck. It was death ringing the bell.

"Me!!" Yolo called through the door, as if she knew who she was. It did the trick because the door came open.

"Me, who?" Candy barked then softened her tone when she saw the pretty, young girl on the step. She like pretty, young girls so she invited her in. This was Atlanta, after all. "How can I help you?"

"It would have been helpful if you had taken that money and ran," Yolo said with a sigh as she pulled her gun. She had no problem killing grown-ups, but the kids were giving her nightmares.

"I..." Candy began but got cut off by untimely death. Yolo shot into her open mouth and blew the rest of the statement right out the back of her head. She set out for the child and found her sleeping soundly in a pink bedroom. Yolo never got her powder puff bedroom and felt it.

"Pow," Yolo whispered, aiming her finger at the sleeping child. She then turned and walked away with plans to call the police once she got back downtown.

"Did you see that?" Nut demanded as he and Casper watched what was supposed to be a double murder.

"Wow," was all Casper could muster when he didn't see what he'd ordered. He said wow once more in reply to Yolo's text that the deed was done. "Who do we have in Atlanta?"

"To kill her?" Nut asked hopefully. He was skimming money as well and didn't want to have Yolo visit him, too.

"No! Just a spanking. Parents sometimes have to spank their children."

****

"Whew!" Yolo shouted as she busted a nut courtesy of the handheld showerhead. The wonderful wand had five settings and they all made her cum.

She remembered the child at home alone with her dead mother as she toweled off. Before she could reach a phone, there was a knock on the door.

"Room service!" a voice called. Yolo grabbed a gun since she hadn't ordered any food yet. She snatched the door open ready to shoot, but no one was there. The hall was empty save for the room service cart outside her room. She shrugged her shoulders and dragged it inside.

The Black Mob phone rang so she quickly answered it. She had murdered a couple of people who'd sent Casper to voicemail.

"Open it," Casper said with a sarcastic smile that could be heard through the line.

"Wh—" Yolo almost asked until she realized that he meant the stainless steel dome on the cart. She let out a sigh at whatever bullshit was yet to come. The sight of the little girl's head sent her reeling backwards.

"Do we understand each other?" he wanted to know.

"Yes!" she grunted through clenched teeth. "It won't happen again."

"It better not! You know Killa is on my team now..." Casper said as if that meant something. "Speaking of Killa, I have a job for you. I need you to just babysit until our boy arrives."

****

Assistant District Attorney Stathum and Public Defender Queen tagged team countless innocent black men into the state's prisons. They forged documents, lied to juries and hid evidence to get men convicted. Once such man had been executed and his family wanted revenge so they'd contracted a hit through The Black Mob and they put their newest addition on the job.

The crooked lawyers liked to hire prostitutes for their celebrations. Since The Black Mob controlled the flow of pussy in Atlanta, they'd put themselves in harm's way. The two called for a black girl to tag team them just like they did black men in court.

"She's here!" Queen cheered in response to the knock on the hotel room's door. He jumped up and rushed to open it with his partner's eyes glued to his ass.

"Someone ordered some pussy?" Yolo asked as she entered the room.

"Yes!" the both replied with raised hands like first graders.

She knew then that they were both gay. "You faggots strip!" she shouted, causing them to jump. As soon as they landed, they complied by coming out of their clothes. "Now kiss!"

"Huh? Us? Each other?" they asked, batting their eyes coyly. They were both fronting, though. They knew they'd been wanting to kiss each other for the longest. She would have had them fuck each other if the guest of honor hadn't knocked.

"Who could that be?" the ADA asked.

"A hired killer coming to kill you both," Yolo laughed.

They assumed she was joking and laughed along with her. This time Stathum answered the door. He pulled it open and came face to face with a pistol so big, it looked like he was staring down a tunnel.

"Told you," Yolo snickered. Then she saw him. 'OMG!' she shouted in her head as her crush walked in. She expected a warm welcome but instead, he barely looked at her when he spoke.

"Get out!" Killa demanded without taking his eyes off of his victims. As much as he hated working for The Mob, or anyone for that matter, he was going to enjoy killing these two. They definitely needed dead.

Yolo pouted at the snub and climbed off the bed. She didn't know that he wouldn't look at her so that she wouldn't get a good look at him. He didn't usually leave witnesses, but he'd been ordered to spare the girl.

"Don't look so tough to me," she huffed in a fit of professional jealousy.

Casper had succeeded in sowing seeds of dissention.

"Shyne! Don't you hear me?" Asad repeated. "Your dad is out of surgery. You need to get to the hospital."

Chapter 15

Luckily, breathing is an involuntary action because Shyne was too worried about her father to concentrate on anything else. The cab driver rambled on about something as he drove her to the hospital, but she didn't catch a word of it.

"Keep the change!" Shyne demanded once they arrived. It was way too much for a tip, but she didn't have time to wait for change.

"You want me to wait?" he called out after her as she rushed inside. She didn't have time to reply, so she didn't.

Her brothers were seated in the waiting room when she arrived. "How is he?"

"Dunno yet," Sun shrugged helplessly.

"Waiting on the doctor to come out now," Rico added.

As if on cue, the doctor came out of the double doors. He looked around and saw the Forrest family and headed over. "Well…" he began with a heavy sigh. He had no idea that Shyne was ready to pounce if he said the wrong thing. "He's in recovery now. I think we stopped the bleeding. At this point, it could go either way."

"It better not go the other way or you going…"

"Thanks, Doc!" Rico cut in to cut off his sister's threat. No sense in biting the hand that feeds you; especially when you're still eating.

"Thanks, Doc," Sun agreed while Shyne glared at the man. "Can we see him?"

"Yes, but he's still unconscious, so only for a few minutes. I…um… don't know if or who you pray to, but…" he said and turned to walk away.

"You can go first," Sun told his sister. She hopped up and rushed in to see her dear dad.

"Hey, Daddy," she said softly as if she might wake him. "I've been reading Mom's diary. Man, she loved you! You want me to read some to you? Okay…"

"*Dear Diary, I only have six more to go to catch my boo. He'll have to want me then. Only problem is hating ass Casper is cock blocking! Every time someone fucks up, he sends Killa to handle it...*"

Then, to add insult to injury, Killa would take Kitty to the condo and fuck her brains out. Yolo would masturbate along with the action but she hated Kitty for sexing her man. Yes, her man. Although, he didn't know she existed, in her demented mind, they were a couple and Kitty was the side chick.

"*In the mall, church, Chuck E. Cheese's, anywhere. If I ever catch you anywhere, I'm going to kill you,*" Yolo vowed as she watched her ride Killa backwards.

A news report of multiple murders in The Bronx caught her attention. While homicides in the projects weren't new, ten at once had Killa's name written all over them. When she heard the name University Projects, she got dressed and sped to New York City.

The projects were usually bustling with activity, however, they were eerily quiet when Yolo arrived. There were no dealers, users, kids playing or teens fighting. There weren't even any squirrels or pigeons anywhere to be seen. Yet, Yolo could feel Killa's presence.

"*Damn, my baby aired this shit out!*" she cheered as the bags starting coming out of each building. Her panties got wet so quickly that they squished between her legs.

The projects slowly came back to life once the dead were carted away. Yolo felt close to Killa as she sat on the bench he'd once sat on. She had no idea just how close she really was as she watched a pretty, elderly lady and her teen granddaughter walk by. Had she known that it was Deidra and Cameisha, she would have introduced herself, as Killa's girlfriend, no less.

"*Xavier, if you behave yourself, you can get a toy. One toy,*" Sincerity stressed as she led her son through the courtyard. Yolo snapped her head their direction when she heard Killa's born name.

A mask of murder spread on her face as she slipped into a rage. The pretty girl was pregnant but that wouldn't have stopped her from gunning both her and her son down. Their lives were spared only because she saw no resemblance between the child and her boo. People always named their children after great men. That's why there are so many Muhammads in the world.

Yolo basked in Killa's world for a few more hours before heading back to Long Island. When she arrived back home, she found Casper chewing out her boo for the project murders. She was hot about the way he was talking to him, but he was the boss. For now, anyway.

"What's wrong?" she asked when he rudely hung up the phone.

"Your boyfriend went on an unauthorized killing spree," he replied.

"You want me to fly to Atlanta and kill his girlfriend?" she pleaded.

"No, I have something else for you to do. Get the DC 2000."

"Dang, Mommy, you cooked a baby! Cooked it and fed it to its parents!" Shyne exclaimed and put the book down. She picked it right back up again and continued to read as her mother got to a hundred kills. A couple of weeks shy of her twenty-first birthday. "Yay, Mommy!"

****

"Got a lick for us!" Rico announced when Sun took his call.

"When, where and how much?" he replied, ready to put his shoes on if the price was right. Bryonna side-eyed him as she listened to his half of the conversation.

"Whenever. Down your way. A ring of pimps with a bunch of young girls. Not sure what they holding, but if we get five bucks, I'll be happy. Shit, you can have it."

"Nah, you keep it," Sun declined. Like their father, he would murder a pimp just for the fun of it. Those lowlifes definitely needed dead.

"Bet. I'm on my way down," Rico said. He was about to fill him in on the details but Shonda emerged from the shower. When he saw her tight body wrapped in a towel, he decided to fill her in instead.

"Hello...? No, he didn't," Sun laughed when he realized he was alone on the line.

"What?" Bryonna asked and awaited half the story. She knew enough bits and pieces to know that her husband wasn't using the degree he'd earned in college. Whatever it was paid well, but it also made her fear for his safety.

Two weeks had passed since Killa's surgery and he still hadn't woken up.

"Nothing, babe. Rico coming down for some business," he said as he wrapped her in his arms. Their baby began to kick when he placed his hand on her belly.

Meanwhile, back in Baltimore, Rico was giving and getting a going away present. He and Shonda cut their sixty-nine off just short of cumming in each other's mouths. They now traded kisses as she slid slowly down his pole.

"I love you, you know?" Shonda assured him as she rocked her hips and squeezed her vaginal muscles to prove it. "Don't you?"

"Mmhmm," he agreed. It wasn't the right answer, so she squeezed again. She squeezed her vagina so tight that it forced the words right out of his mouth. "I love you, too."

She knew he loved her, which was why she'd stopped taking her birth control pills, but she wanted to hear him say it. Shonda grunted as the words made her cum instantly. Her intense orgasm pushed Rico over the edge as well. He let out a grunt of his own and became a baby daddy.

****

"Pimpin' ain't easy," Pimp Meech told Pimpin' Ken with a weary sigh. Both men were dipped in bright suits and cloudy diamonds as they lounged in the Pimps Up, Hoes Down Lounge on Atlanta's Metropolitan Ave.

"Shole ain't," Ken agreed, taking a sip from his diamond encrusted pimp cup. They both then cracked up at the false statement. Pimping was the easiest thing in the world.

How hard is it to trick little girls or grown women with no self-respect and no self-worth into selling their bodies? Not very hard at all in a society full of fatherless children. Abandoned daughters make the easiest prey. They work extra hard to please the first daddy image in their lives. Yeah, it's fucked up and they were about to get fucked up for it.

"Full house," Rico admired as he and Sun staked out the club from a safe distance while two federal agents staked them out from a block away.

"I hope you did that shit right," Sun said, wishing that he could have done it.

"I did exactly what she told me to do," he replied. Indeed, he had since Shyne had been on the line to walk him through the task. Earlier in the day, he'd gained entry as an HVAC guy to tune up the system. Shyne had instructed him on how to hook the gas line up to the air conditioning system, then hook it up to a remote switch so she could do the honors.

"Aight," he said, hitting Shyne on speed dial. "Okay, hit it."

"Already did!" Shyne giggled. "That juke joint should be about halfway filled up by now. Y'all better be ready!"

"Crazy girl," Sun said, shaking his head. He cocked a silenced MP-5 and got out. Rico did the same and followed. They posted up at each end of the block and waited for the lights to scatter the roaches.

"You passed gas?" Pimpin' Ken asked, sniffing deeply as if he wanted to inhale more of the smell of flatulence. Most pimps are faggots and like the smell of shit.

"Thought that was you," Meech replied, inhaling the natural gas seeping through the club.

The gas was heavier than air so it settled to the floor and built up. It was up to their knees when Ken decided to light one of those long as lady menthols. He flicked his Bic and ignited the gas.

"What the..." an agent shouted as the explosion rocked the earth. Orange flames blew out all the windows, along with a few body parts.

"Here they come!" Sun called out as pimps and hoes came running out burnt or burning. He and his brother opened fire and silently mowed them all down.

"Yay!" Shyne cheered as she watched a split screen from both of her brothers' bodycams. The Feds had cameras, too, and were recording all the action. Shyne planned to use the footage for entertainment, but the cops planned to use it in a court of law.

Chapter 16

"Dear Diary, so my baby had a baby and to top it off, it's by the same chick I saw in the projects. Knew I shoulda killed them! I couldn't help myself and went to see them. Saw Killa, too. We stared into each other's eyes for an eternity. I knew he wanted to just scoop me into his arms and whisk me away but..."

"Yo, but you sounding real crazy right now, Ma," Shyne chided. She shook her head at her love-struck mother and continued reading.

"He has so many distractions. A son in Philadelphia and now one in New York. Then the thick girl down south. I need to help him by eliminating some of the distractions..."

Yolo started when she got the nod to kill Kitty. It was supposed to be business to teach Killa a lesson after he killed a hundred pedophiles at a convention. Casper sent her to The Bronx to murder his family first, but they were already in hiding.

She wasn't sure where to find Kitty in Atlanta so she went to the condo The Black Mob had provided. Killa would often bring Kitty by to sex her in front of the cameras. The memories of watching him in action made Yolo wet. She dropped her jeans and got herself off. Kitty and her mom came in shortly after.

Yolo was indeed a lunatic but even she knew she'd gone too far when she saw the carnage she'd created. In a fit of jealous rage, she'd cut Kitty and her mother into pieces then put them back together again, mismatching their body parts. She'd used their blood to scribble Yolo and Killa all over the walls.

"Uh oh!" *Yolo exclaimed when she snapped out of her zone.* "He's going to fuckin' kill me!"

Yolo called Casper, who demanded she stay on sight. She used Kitty's phone to lure him home and took position on a nearby rooftop. When Killa arrived, she watched him through the scope of a high powered rifle.

"Let me end this," she said. Her panties become soaked at the sight of him but she was ready to fire. Then she would put the gun into her mouth and join him. If they couldn't be together in this life, then she would try the next. It doesn't work like that but she was a lunatic, after all.

"No! Not yet! He has to make penance first," Casper whined. It's a mystery why he thought he could play with the man. A murder mystery.

Yolo just shook her head at what she knew was coming. Killa. And he was coming to kill them all.

****

"Oh-my-God!" Shyne reeled as she read about the consensual rape that had conceived her and her brother. Yolo wrote in detail about her and Killa's first sexual encounter. From the searing pain to the orgasm in spite of it. Then the lights went out from being shot in the head. The bulletproof wig had saved three lives that day.

"Dang!" Shyne exclaimed when she got turned on by the sex. She marched right upstairs and woke her husband.

"Again?" Asad asked in surprise. "Most pregnant women want ice-cream and pickles."

"Well, I ain't most women, am I?" she insisted.

"No, you most certainly aren't," he laughed and then complied with her late night craving. Once they'd finished, they cuddled and watched the late night news.

"In breaking news from Jackson, Mississippi, a gang war between the Demons and the Devils resulted in four children being killed in the crossfire. The two groups met in Panola Park where a gun battle erupted. None of the gang members were hit, but five children playing on the monkey bars and swings were shot. Again, four have died and one is in critical cond-... wait! This latest update just the fifth child has died while in surgery...."

"Someone needs to kill those gang members!" Asad growled.

"Someone will!" Shyne assured him as she reached for her phone. She found the story online and texted the link to her brothers. She'd just made sure that someone would.

****

"Sun, look at all these fine motherfuckers!" Rico exclaimed as they walked through the airport in Jackson. The fresh air and down home soul food had grown some big fat booties on the country girls.

"No, thank you," his brother replied, lowering his gaze to the floor. He wouldn't want his wife checking out other men so he didn't do it to her with other women. Respect is a key element in any relationship.

"How is it being married? I mean, the same person err' day. That don't get old?" his brother wondered.

"Spending err' day with your best friend never gets old. B is as close to me as you and Shyne. I trust her more than I trust me," he replied.

Rico had no more questions since he was feeling the same way about Shonda. "I see," he said, nodding in agreement.

They stepped outside of the terminal and into a taxi. The federal agents behind them took the next taxi and followed them to the hotel.

The brothers had done their homework on both of the gangs. They knew all about them and none of it made any sense. The Demons were from the north side of town while the Devils were from the south side. Both gangs had cousins on the other side of the tracks that were their sworn enemies.

The Demons rocked the color gold while the Devils repped orange. They'd considered a color change when a Devil washed his shirt in the wrong temperature. It had faded enough to look gold and he'd been gunned down by one of his own. The shooting left him paralyzed but at least he learned to read the care label on his clothes before washing.

The brothers knew they couldn't bring guns on the plane so they had their father's friend Big Shawn hook them up with one of his contacts. Sun texted the number he'd been given once they reached the room. An hour later, they heard a knock on their door.

"Bobby Cox!" a cheerful older black man greeted with an out-stretched hand when Rico pulled the door open.

"Cocks?" Sun snickered like a child as his brother shook the man's free hand. The other hand held a large heavy looking tote bag.

"Cocks with a 'ck', huh? Very funny. Son, I'm sixty years old and been hearing that lame ass joke for fifty-five of them."

"My bad," Sun said, lowering his head in humility.

"Shole is. I knowed yo' daddy, you know?" Cox said. He left out the part about how Killa using the same joke about his name.

"You knew our father?" Rico asked in awe. He heard his past tense usage and quickly corrected it with, "Know our father?"

"Hell yeah! That's why I came out of retirement when Bigs told me who y'all was. Especially since y'all come to help with our rodent problem!" Cox cheered.

"Well, let's see what you got to kill rats," Sun said, rubbing his hands together eagerly.

"When in Rome..." the elder said, pulling two pump shotguns out of the bag first. This was the south and they shot buckshot. He could tell that they weren't feeling the scatter guns and went back in the bag. "'S'pose this mo' to y'all's liking?"

"Hells yeah!" Sun said, grabbing the Mac-10 from his hand. "My favorite!"

"Mine, too!" Rico cheered as he took the other. Cox produced a couple of Glocks with extended clips and a shit load of ammo.

"Want me to send a couple of big booty gals over here?" the gracious host inquired. After all, they were in the south and their father had always accepted a couple when he came to town.

"Nah, we both married," Rico beat his brother to saying.

"What we owe you?" Sun asked since Rico had stolen his line.

"Owe me? Shit, what I owe you? You boys doing us a big favor. One of them kids got kilt was my great-grand," he explained.

"Say no more," Sun sighed. He would be honored to murder these scum bags. As soon as Mr. Cox departed, Sun pulled a coin and told his brother to call it in the air. Heads equaled gold and tails orange.

"Heads!" he called as the quarter tumbled up and then down. It landed head side up, meaning Rico got to kill the Demons. That made Sun cheese brightly since everyone wants to kill the Devil.

****

"They're splitting up," one agent said to the other when Sun and Rico got in separate cars provided to them by Mr. Cox. The agents only had one car and had to make a quick decision.

"Follow...orange!" the other threw out. He liked orange better than gold so she made the call. It turned out to be a pretty good call, too, since they got to watch Sun gun down Devils all over the Southside.

"What should we do?" the first agent asked as Sun pumped his pump and sprayed a basketball court full of gangbangers.

"Nothing," his partner laughed. "Sit back and enjoy the show."

Meanwhile, Rico was busy mowing down Demons on the Northside. He was dressed in a gold shirt, which allowed him to get up close and personal to his victims. He hit their park, barbershop and the rest of their hangout spots. By the next day, they had eliminated both gangs. The ones who didn't get shot didn't want to get shot and vowed to quit gangbanging.

"Well done," the agent said once he figured out what they were up to. Now he wasn't so sure if they were the good guys or the bad guys. It seemed like they only killed people who really needed dead.

Chapter 17

"Dear Diary, I'm pregnant. Nurse Marquita, no, Mom. My mom took me to take a pregnancy test and I'm knocked up. At least I don't have to go on one of those shows to find out who my baby daddy is. OMG, me and Killa are going to have a baby. Now, I definitely have to get all those other people out of his life. That way it'll just be me, him and our child..."

"Ooh, Mommy! Please tell me you weren't that naïve!" Shyne interrupted. It was beyond belief that the woman who'd raised her so well could have been so gullible. She had been but she'd learned from her mistakes so she could teacher children better. Isn't that what being a parent is all about?

Yolo's piss poor upbringing, violent nature and twisted mind convinced her that it was a good idea to kill Killa's children. If he only had one, by her, then they would have his full attention. The decision was a prime example of the devil making evil deeds seem fair.

She knew he had a son in Philly so that's where she started. Once she had a head start halfway through Jersey, she gave him a call. Killa rushed down to Philly as well, hoping to save his firstborn.

"School's almost out," Yolo sang as she watched the school from the scope of the high powered gun. She'd arrived too early and ended up having to wait almost an hour. "And there's little Xavier Forrest."

Killa pulled up and jumped out to find his son. He had kept his distance from the boy for his own safety. Now his safety depended on him.

Yolo smiled widely when her bae appeared in the scope. She had already picked out a teacher to kill as a sacrificial lamb. She put the scope back on the boy's handsome face. Yolo had a change of heart about shooting the child, but the devil shouted its insidious whisper in her ear. "Do it!" it suggested as she squeezed the trigger.

"One down, one to go," she said proudly. Her satisfaction was short lived when she heard the father's wail of sorrow. "What did I do? Oh no!"

Yolo sobbed the whole way back to New York. The devil always withdraws after his whispers, so she was on her own. Nurse Marquita could do nothing to console her. It wasn't until she warned her that grief might affect her own unborn child that she got it together.

"Oh...wow," Shyne said in disbelief at what she'd just read. Heard, actually, because she'd heard her mother's voice narrating the story as she read along. Even now the grief and remorse came through loud and clear.

Shyne curled up in a fetal position and hugged her baby. Her son found her like that and joined her. The two spent the night right there curled up on the sofa.

****

"Wake up, Shyne!"

"Huh?" Shyne asked, looking around. She was alone in the room so she blamed her ringing phone for waking her up. "Damn it, Sun... what?"

"Good morning to you, too, dear sister," Sun replied, smiling through the line. "Did you catch the news last night?"

"No, I was talking to Mommy last ni-..." Shyne began then paused when she heard how it sounded. There was a brief silence on the line in memory of their mother.

"I need to read that book next," Sun suggested. He missed his mom just as much as Shyne did and wanted to talk to her also.

"No, you really don't. I kinda wish that I'd never started it. Now, I can't put it down. Mommy was..." Shyne had to pause again to choose one of the words swirling in her mind. Amazing was the first thing that popped up but it was closely followed by crazy, complex, complicated, capricious and conflicted. She was a leader, a follower, a lover and a fighter. She was a lot of things, but most of all, she was hopelessly, head over heels in love with their father.

"Um...okay," he replied to the silence that came next. "Anyway, I need to borrow that flame thrower."

"Where you headed?" she asked eagerly. As badly as she wanted to go wherever to kill whoever, she knew not to ask. She was in the waddling stage now and could barely make it up the stairs. Can't exactly go on a killing spree if you gotta pee every few minutes.

"To a *White Lives Matter* rally out in Kansas," he replied with glee. The racist group was holding a fundraiser and rally to collect legal fees for yet another racist cop who'd killed yet another unarmed black kid.

"Have fun and burn one for me!" Shyne cheered. "I got the flame thrower over here. It's in the garage."

"Your gara-... Yo, what does Asad say when he sees shit like that?" he wondered.

"Nothing. Just shakes his head, but doesn't say anything," she shrugged. "He uses my DC 2000 to cut watermelons for the kids."

"Um..." Sun said, since what can be said to that. "I'm on my way."

"Bring your wife," Shyne blurted before he hung up. She'd realized that she had been neglecting her friend in favor of reading her mother's diary. Who could blame her, though? That shit was good!

****

"Dear Diary, I got my pussy ate today. Actually, he licked and sucked it. That's what they should call it because eating pussy sounds kinda gross. So, anyway, I came so hard, I almost didn't want to shoot him..."

But shoot him she did. Shot the fuck out of the pervert who'd posed as an OB/GYN nurse and stole pictures of her pretty little kitty. Yolo felt relief from busting a nut and the murder, but it was short-lived.

"I need my Killa," she moaned in response to her baby moving around inside of her. Little did she know, there were actually two babies inside of her. Sun and Shyne were pushing each other trying to get more space.

Yolo packed her sniper rifle and waited on her adopted mom to run an errand. Once she left, she headed into the city and up to The Bronx. No one really noticed her since the guys snapped their heads away once they saw her baby bump. She entered a building and held her breath for the pissy elevator ride to the top floor. One flight of steps later, she was on the roof.

Yolo assembled her rifle and got in a comfortable perch to keep vigil for her boo. The door swung open urgently as a janitor burst through. He almost got shot until a crack whore followed him out. They both looked at her for a second then turned back to what they'd come for.

"Ten bucks," the whore said with an open palm. Her mouth opened wide like at the dentist once the money touched her hand. "Aaaah!"

"Y'all nasty," Yolo giggled as she watched the man fuck her face. His heavy tool belt forced his pants down to his ankles as he humped away. The whore gagged loudly every time he touched her tonsils. He came, she swallowed and they were on their way. "Just nasty."

Yolo really thought it was nasty when the same addict sucked three more men's dicks over the next hour. She had a semen casserole in her belly by the time she went to spend her money on rocks. One dealer got the same ten dollar bill he'd given her for head.

At least the money circulated through the hood. The weed man would get it next and trade it for a hero and soda at the bodega, Papi behind the counter would give it to his wife who'd give it back to the weed man for weed, the weed man would get his dick sucked by a crack whore, and then the crack dealer would get it back. Hood economics.

"Is that...that son of a bitch!" Yolo said with a snarl as she watched Doc amble through the projects. Her boo Killa was in this mess for not killing him in the first place. She took aim at his medulla oblongata and started to squeeze. Curiosity got the best of her so she let off the pressure to see what he was up to.

A few minutes later, he came out of Killa's building with his grandmother in tow. She saw he had a bootleg DC 2000 around her neck.

She didn't know what made her madder, the kidnapping or the biting of her device.

"Knew I shoulda got a patent!" she fumed and aimed her rifle at the base of his skull. She wasn't sure if he would trigger the device if she shot, so she didn't. Instead, she quickly packed her gear to follow them.

"Excuse us," the same crack whore, with yet another man in tow, said as they passed each other in the doorway.

"Aren't you full by now?" Yolo wondered. She didn't stick around for an answer because Doc was getting away.

"Save Grandma, Mommy!" Shyne cheered. She looked up and saw her husband and kids staring back. She sat the book down to spend some time with them.

Chapter 18

"White lives matter! White power! White lives matter!" came the thunderous chant of hundreds of hooded men. They weren't the KKK, but they'd donned the hoods to conceal their identities nonetheless, just like they concealed their racist beliefs from the public. They had to since they were teachers, preachers, doctors and lawyers. There were also some cops, robbers, judges and jury members amongst them. Not to mention several had black wives or girlfriends. For those, black vaginas matter, but not black men. That's why they were here yelling, "White lives matter and white power!"

"White power! White lives matter!" Sun and Rico giggled form under their masks as they blended in with the rest. Both had lumps and humps under their robes. That's because Rico had to AR-15s while Sun had a flame thrower.

"White lives matter! White power!" the shouted ferociously to the throngs of blacks on the sidelines.

Police worked hard to keep the two groups separated.

After a few circuits around the courthouse, the protestors mounted their pickup trucks to ride out to the night rally. There they had beer, food, a white supremacy rock group and a large cross to burn. Good fun for the racist, hillbilly fucks.

Sun and Rico trailed along to fuck it up.

Quite a few men removed their hoods once they hit the campsite. An equal amount left theirs on, which allowed Killa's kids to blend in. Which was great because the chicken smelled delicious.

"Yo, chill, Sun. You keep smashing that chicken like that and they're gonna know you black!" Rico chided.

"Shit, white people like chicken, too!" Sun said and kept right on smashing. His robe was now red from BBQ sauce. Not as red as the rest theirs were about to be, though.

"White live matter!" a man said into the microphone when the band cut the music. All eyes and ears were now on him as he took the stage. As he spoke, a large wooden cross was erected.

"Why the cross, though? What that do?" Sun whispered to his brother.

"Beats me," Rico shrugged. In his mind, the cross was a symbol of Jesus. Surely they didn't attribute their racist ideas to Jesus who'd taught that all lives matter.

The spokesman rambled off his disgusting dogma to the delight of his disciples. They threw in a 'white power' every now and then, like parishioners 'amened' when the preacher said something fly.

"Bruh, can I just shoot him now?" Rico asked wearily as the bullshit wore him down.

"You could but it would fuck up the grand finale," he advised. Rico twisted his lips but waited. They stood through another half hour of how black people came from apes and monkeys. That's about as stupid as black people saying whites are the devil. God created all people equally. He gave us different colors and languages so we could know each other.

Only the devil wants us to hate each other.

"And now, we're gonna burn this cross as a symbol of...of...as a symbol of um..." he stammered since he didn't know either.

"White power!" Sun shouted to move things along. The crowd agreed and chanted it once more.

"That's right! White...power!" he said and dug in his pockets. "Anybody got a match?"

"I do!" Sun announced and flipped his robe and hood off. The crowd stared in stunned silence at his black skin more than the flame thrower he held. The orange flames got their attention and they scrambled for safety.

There would be no safety today, though, because Rico flipped off and opened fire. He sprayed the machine gun knee high to maim, not kill. That's what the flame thrower was for.

Sun ignored their pleas, cries and begging for mercy as he burned them alive until they were dead. Just like they'd ignored the wails of the murdered black, teens and boys. He burned them for the Latinos and even for the white men who'd gotten killed for no reason.

"Should we call for help?" one agent asked the other as they watched the carnage through binoculars.

The other looked at the cross and lifted the one hanging from his neck as he contemplated. His head began to shake when he decided, "Nah. Let 'em burn."

Sun and Rico collected the almost a million dollars the rally had collected. Most times, the split their licks fifty-fifty but this time, they decided to set up a fund to help the families left behind.

Dear old Dad would be proud. If he ever woke up, that is.

****

"Nothing yet?" the doctor asked as he walked in on Shonda at Killa's bedside. She had been having a private chat with him as she took his vitals.

"Nothing," she replied sadly and poked her lip out.

It was now a month after surgery and still nothing. In fact, he was still bleeding internally. The doctor checked his vitals and signed the chart. It was still just a waiting game. As soon as he left, Shonda picked up where she'd left off.

"Okay, as I was swaying. Rico and I are getting very close. I haven't told him yet, but I'm pregnant. He shouldn't be surprised, though, from the way he be... Well, you probably don't need to hear all that," she giggled.

"Hear all of what?" Rico asked as he walked in. He'd just returned from Kansas and came straight to the hospital.

"Baby!" Shonda shrieked and ran to him. Ran into him, actually, and almost knocked him down. She planted wet smooches all over his face and lips.

"I guess you missed me, huh?" he said before turning to Killa. "How is he?"

"No worse," she said since it sounded better than no better. Both were true and neither was good news.

"Can he hear?" Rico wondered since he'd walked in on her having a one-sided yet animated conversation with him.

"I'm sure he can," she said, although she had no scientific proof to support it. She hoped he could since she confided in him every day she worked. "And, he was the first to know."

Rico opened his mouth to ask 'know what' when Shonda placed his hand on her belly to answer. It was still flat but he got the gist of what she meant. All his life he'd pulled out, but with her, he'd pushed in so deep that it was no shock.

Shonda wasn't sure how he felt about becoming a dad until a slow smile began to spread on his face. First it turned the corners of his mouth upward then it stretched them it until it almost touched his lashes.

"Say word!" he demanded like a typical New Yorker.

"Word!" she laughed and assumed a b-boy stance to remind him why he loved her.

"Guess we gotta get married, too, then," he announced since he was too cool for the whole down on one knee thing. Shonda was smart enough to catch the *too*, which she knew meant like his brother and sister.

"I guess so!" she agreed happily. They shared a few kisses before Shonda departed so that Rico could spend a few minutes alone with his dad.

"Sup, Pops. Guess what? I'm getting married. Yeah, I know, not the playa. I'm not a playa no more. See how all that playing turned out? Ma dead. Sun and Shyne's mom dead. The cycle ends now. I'm going to be a husband and full-time father."

Rico was too cool to cry in front of his father so his only choice was to leave the room. He certainly couldn't prevent the pent up tears from falling. Once they started, they didn't stop until they were depleted. Once they were, he felt a lot better. Nothing clears the mind like a good cry; especially for men.

Chapter 19

"Dear Diary, I've really messed up now. I can't believe I did that..."

The next few lines were smudged and unreadable from her tears. She cried the whole time she followed Doc and Killa's grandmother. The thought of almost killing the woman at Casper's command made her cringe. It was now her mission to save her. This would be her redemption. Or so she hoped.

"Why the airport? I can't bring in a gun to kill you," she asked and answered as she watched the kidnapper escort his victim into the terminal. *Gun or no gun, she was going to redeem herself and save the day. She grabbed her Black Mob phone and hit the first number on speed dial.*

"Where...is...she?" Killa growled, slow and deliberately. He skipped the threats since it was a given he was going to kill her.

"Damn, you got a sexy voice! You made my maternity panties all wet!" Yolo gushed when she heard that sexy voice on the line. She'd momentarily forgotten why she called. *"Oh! No, I didn't take her but I know where she is..."*

Killa twisted his lips dubiously as he listened. It made absolutely no sense and he couldn't for the life of him figure out what white man would kidnap his grandmother. The crazy white man he knew was Doc, and Doc was a dead man. Or so he thought

"What your lil' girlfriend want?" Sincerity spat sarcastically.

"She claims some white dude took grandma. They're at JFK." A second call a few seconds later confirmed her claims. Deidra gave him the gate number before the call went dead.

Meanwhile, the lovely little lunatic carjacked an old lady for her wheelchair. She took her wig, dress and oxygen tank, too. Not that the woman needed any of them since she'd strangled her and rolled her under her car.

Yolo made a makeshift blow gun out of the oxygen tank and a knitting needle. She wheeled herself in past the long ass TSA line and caught up with Doc and Deidra at gate 10. Her baby kicked, triggering her nesting instinct which causing her to try to knit. She couldn't knit for shit, but she tried.

"I'm gonna have to start bringing a change of panties cuz every time I see this man!" Yolo mumbled when Killa marched into view. He was sexy on a regular day, but today, he had murder written all over his face and was extra sexy.

"How are you even alive? Why won't anyone stay dead?" Killa asked in astonishment. The DC 2000 around his beloved grandmother's neck cause him to sink into a chair across from them.

"Chief Flores stayed dead when I cut his head off. I'm pretty sure she will too when I cut hers off, too!" the crazed doctor hissed.

"Then what? You just walk away?" Killa frowned, trying to make sense of why they were here.

"No, then we fight to the death…" Doc said as Yolo armed the makeshift gun. She turned the oxygen tank dangerously high with a knitting needle stuffed in its tube.

"We uh…" Killa said, recognizing Yolo despite the disguise she wore. He wondered what she was doing until she did it. Rolled right behind the doctor and fired the needle into the base of his skull. He died instantly, right in the middle of a dumb ass statement.

"Even Steven?" Yolo asked as Grandma Deidra snatched the deadly device from her neck.

"Not even close! We ain't even until you ain't breathing!" Killa growled. "You killed my son. First chance I get, I'm going to kill you."

"Or me you," Yolo giggled. "I would be honored to die by your hand. Either way, it'll be a beautiful death."

"Bitch!" Killa mumbled under his breath as she rolled away. Yolo stole one last loving glance, in which he stuck his middle finger up at her. Of course, she found that funny and giggled once more.

"Awww, Daddy, she saved grandma! You should forgi— Well, I mean… umm…" Shyne rambled. She was rooting for her parents to team up. She got her wish a few pages later when Big Rock and The Black Mob blew up both her parents' homes.

She cried along with her mother at the loss of her adopted mother, Nurse Marquita. Then she cheered when Killa and Yolo were forced to join forces. "Oh shit! Killa and Yolo! It's about to be on!"

****

"Dear Diary, Killa won't give me no dick! We slept in the same bed and everything. I woke up with a hard dick on my ass so I grinded against it. He was moaning until he looked at me. Then he got up and went into the bathroom..."

Went right into the bathroom to jack off. Killa knew she was right about them needing each other to defeat The Black Mob, but that didn't mean he had to fuck her. Even if he did want to, really bad.

"Look," Killa began as he returned. He could think clearly now that he had bust a nut. *"We have no choice but to stay together, but we are NOT together."*

"Okay," Yolo laughed. If this was day one, it was only a matter of time.

"Ooh, Daddy! You know you need to break mommy off with some dick!"

"Really Shyne?" Asad asked with his *really Shyne* look on his face and in his *really Shyne* voice.

"My bad," she giggled then went back to reading. Asad was on his own with the kids for the next two days as she read about her parents crisscrossing the country to wipe out The Black Mob. Then she gave birth...

"Dear Diary, Sun and Shyne have arrived. You should have seen Killa's face when she came out after him. God is The Greatest. He wanted a boy and I wanted a girl so He gave us both what we wanted. I guess I owe..."

Yolo vowed to never harm another child. No matter what their parents may have done, she would never cook another baby. How could she after being blessed with not one, but two beautiful babies of her own?

Shyne felt the same apprehension her mother had as she and Killa neared the end of their journey.

Only Big Rock and his bodyguard Bull remained. Yolo was sly enough to cut a deal with the underling to get at the boss. Every crew has a Judas ready to sell them out.

Yolo still didn't know if Killa planned to kill her after the last hit. He still wouldn't fuck her, no matter what she tried. Finally, she decided to kill two birds with one stone and took matters into her own hands.

Shyne covered her face with her hand as she read her mother's account of raping her father. It wasn't really rape since he was with it. She cracked her fingers and kept right on reading.

"So, now what?" Killa asked once Yolo recovered from yet another orgasm. He was pretty sure she wouldn't kill him. Actually, he was hoping she'd get back on top and ride him again.

"Now, I go kill Big Rock and finish this," she said. "Then, off to Cali to get my, our babies. We have plenty of money so you don't have to worry about me putting you on child support or nothing."

"I wasn't," he laughed. "But look, you can't leave me tied up. Besides, you'll need me to help with Big Rock. That bull is a dangerous man!"

"I know, that's why I paid him off. Once Big Rock meets his maker, Bull will take over, and since he was already fucking his wife, he had no problem getting him out of the way."

"Smart girl. Now, let me up so we can..." Killa was cut off by Yolo planting a parting kiss on the head of his dick. His lips got one, too, before she giggled and left.

"I wonder if they ever saw each other again," Shyne asked herself as she got up. In her defense, she had been up reading for two days.

Chapter 20

"Dear Diary, I bought She-Ra's old house and completely renovated it...."

A hundred grand later, the house was now a home. She moved in with her twins. Yolo found out really quick that being a single mom is no joke. It's double the work when you have twins. Still, she doted over her babies like any loving mother would.

Shyne smiled brightly when she read about Christi coming into all their lives. She and Sun had always accepted her as a sister even though they knew that they weren't blood related. Shyne now had the full story, including the part about her mom killing Christi's mother and boyfriend.

"Gotta tell Sun about this part!" Shyne exclaimed and called her brother.

"You just missed him," Bryonna said, taking her call. Sun leaving his personal phone at home meant he was away on a business trip. They would both have to wait until he called them.

****

"Welcome to Nashville," Sun read aloud as they passed the sign welcoming them. Ironically, the agents in the car following them did the same thing.

"My guess is the Williams Clan," the passenger's seat agent guessed when it became obvious that this was their destination.

"Yeah, I bet," his partner agreed since the Williams Clan had the meth trade on smash here. They made millions spreading the death and destruction that came along with the dangerous drug.

The local dentist saw an uptick in business from mouths rotted out from habitual meth use. The tricks who visited the toothless whores were grateful, but not the orphans and families. Even with all the money they made, The Williams Family still ran their operation in a rundown trailer park on the Northside of town. Say what you want about the inner city projects, but they ain't got shit on a trailer park full of meth addicts.

"Yo, this some *Walking Dead* type shit right here!" Rico exclaimed as they made a pass through the dilapidated park.

"And it's the middle of the day!" Sun replied as he swerved to avoid an addict giving head in the middle of the road. "My dude tells me it's the last trailer on the left."

"You getting to be like Pops," his brother noticed. He had been networking and was developing contacts in every city, just like their father. The only difference being that their father would have noticed the federal agents trailing them.

"Hell yeah! And I got us some heat lined up, too!" Sun nodded proudly. "My man Bishop gonna meet us at the hotel!"

****

Sun wisely set up a meeting for later in the evening so he and his jet-lagged brother could get some rest. The alarm woke him up in time to get down to business. He grabbed his disposable phone to handle the first order of business.

"Hey, baby," Bryonna sang when she answered the phone. The private number on the screen told her that it was her husband calling.

"Hey, yourself. How are you guys?" he asked, matching her smile.

"Missing you. Come home. Me and your daughter want you to come home. Now," she pouted.

"I can't, not tonight. I'll be home in a day or two. I'll take you guys shopping for whatever you want when I get back."

Ironically, Rico was making the same promise to Shonda of a brighter tomorrow. Except tomorrow isn't promised.

"I got it," Rico announced in reply to the knock on the door. He crossed the hotel room and pulled open the door.

"Sun?" the man asked, extending his hand as he entered the room. The tote bag clinked from the hardware inside, causing the brothers to smile.

"Nah, I'm... Rocky," Rico decided as he shook his hand. He hooked his head towards his brother and said, "*He's* Sun."

"Sup, yo," Sun greeted. The gun dealer was supposed to be a friend of a friend so neither knew the other. "What you got for us?"

"A couple of these... and... these. Oh, and these. You'll need one of these," he said, removing the guns from the bag.

"Well, we'll take two of these, one of those and a couple of these," he replied as he selected the guns and ammo. In the end, they purchased ten grand worth of guns and ammo. A small investment for a lick worth millions.

Both brothers spent the night boo loving on the phone with their boos. In the morning, they set up surveillance on the trailer park. The activity on the outside proved the riches inside.

"I wonder if that's cash," Sun said aloud as they watched a man pull up and hop out with a heavy bag.

"It ain't his laundry!" Rico cheered. "We need to run up in that joint now!"

"I feel you," he agreed.

In the few hours they'd been watching, several men dropped of big bags and left with smaller ones. It was dough for dope all day. A silence fell over the car as they contemplated breaking their plan and moving now.

"Fuck it, let's roll," Rico suggested. Nothing good has ever been proceeded by the words *fuck it*. No one ever said *fuck it* and did anything good. It wouldn't happen today, either.

"Yeah, fuck it," Sun agreed. Both men rolled their ski-masks down and cocked their weapons. As soon as the man left with his smaller bag, they rushed in with theirs.

"Call it now!" the agent yelled as he watched the robbery unfold. His partner scrambled to get his radio to his mouth to call it in. In seconds, local and federal agents were en route.

"Hands up!" Rico shouted as he charged through the flimsy trailer door. The addicts smoking meth barely raised their heads at the intrusion before going back to smoking.

"What in the hell is going on out here?" a hillbilly demanded as he came up the back hallway with a shotgun in his hands. Sun didn't have time to explain so he let him have it from his own shotgun.

"Anybody else got any questions?" he asked as the man tumbled backwards down the hall. Rico was snatching bags of cash while Sun eased down the hall.

"I got one!" another redneck shouted and came out shooting.

"Ugh!" Sun grunted as the shotgun blast lifted him off his feet. He fired back while sailing backwards in the air. He caught the man in the neck, nearly knocking his fat head off.

Two more men rushed out of the back rooms, firing wildly. Sun was on the floor so Rico let loose with his chopper. The threat ended when their lives did. Sun popped up and felt his chest to see if the slug had gone through his vest.

"Whew!" he exclaimed, seeing that the vest had held. His chest still felt like it had been hit by Thor's hammer.

"Yo, let's get this dough and bounce!" Rico shouted. The junkies on the sofa still hadn't budged.

Sun ran into one of the rooms while Rico hit the other. They met back in the hallway loaded with cash. They flashed a smile at one another and rushed back up front. The smiles vanished when they opened the front door.

"Shit!" Sun shouted when he saw a sea of police. He backpedaled inside the trailer. Rico raised his gun and sprayed the cars.

The police opened fire back as he ducked back inside.

"What are we going to do?" Sun shouted over the gunfire.

Two addicts tilted over dead from strays while another kept right on smoking. Bullet holes opened above their heads as the police kept shooting. As much as they like shooting unarmed men, they were even more excited to fire at armed ones.

"Fight or go to jail," big brother advised. Both men knew it was a battle that they couldn't win. To fight meant to die.

"We fight then," Sun said since jail was not an option. They gave each other a pound and a hug and came up firing.

Chapter 21

"Dear Diary, Yay, it's Sun and Shyne's first day of school. Their father is in town for the special occasion, although, really I think he here for some booty. Those kids lucky we got them up on time cuz we fucked all night!"

"Freak!" Shyne shouted, giggling, and got back to reading.

"As soon as I made sure they got inside the school, we came straight back home and got to it again. Killa had just found his stroke when the phone began to ring. I pushed him off of me when I heard the principal calling. We rushed up to see what was wrong and this bitch started flirting with my man!

"It's bad enough I have to compete with ugly ass Sincerity. Okay, she ain't ugly, but still. I'm tired of being a side chick. Speaking of side chicks, I think my son might be one. His punk ass ran and left his sister to fight alone. I'm worried about that girl. Sometimes I look in her eyes and see me. I don't want her to be me..."

"Dear Diary, so, Killa takes us to his projects yesterday. He wants them to learn Karate so who better to teach them than Karate Joe? At first glance, I thought he was ca-crazy, but he knows his shit!

"The old man let it slip that he has a daughter named Sincerity. He knows the twins are Killa's kids, too, but hasn't said anything about it. I'm gonna use him to get to her so I can kill her..."

"Dear Diary, I told that bitch to leave my man alone! I warned her and I threatened her, but what she do? She sent my man pictures of her pussy..."

"Oh shit!" Shyne exclaimed after reading about Yolo feeding their principal to the pigs. She decided to share this with the only person she could and grabbed her phone. Before she could dial Sun's number, Bryonna called. "Sup, yo?"

"Sun got shot! Both him and Rico. They both got shot!"

****

Shyne didn't hear a single word Bryonna spoke as they drove to the airport. She was far too worried about her brothers to answer any of her questions. Since she didn't know anything about their mission, she couldn't answer anyway.

"How did you know? Who told you?" Shyne finally asked once they landed in Nashville.

"The police called! They said...how did they know who he was? He leaves both his ID and his phone at home!" she said, catching on to what Shyne was saying.

Neither knew that Sun and Rico had been under federal surveillance for months or that the Feds executed a search warrant at Sun's house as soon as Bryonna left with their daughter.

"I'll take the kids to the hotel while you go check on my brothers," Shyne suggested as she led the march to the rental car agency and got a car.

"Two subjects shot it out with police today at a Northside trailer park. Police say they received a call about an armed robbery in progress..."

"It's not them!" Shyne shouted and cut the radio off. As much as they both wanted to believe it, the heavy police presence at the hospital said otherwise.

Sun and Rico managed to shoot several police officers before falling under a barrage of bullets. Two cops died at the scene while two more fought for their lives along with Sun and Rico.

"Stay with Auntie Shyne," Bryonna told her daughter as Shyne came to a stop a block after passing the hospital. The spoiled child could sense the urgency and didn't protest.

"Aunt Shyne gonna get us some ice-cream," Shyne said as they pulled away.

"One of those punks passed!" a cop announced as Bryonna drew near. The other police cheered as she walked in hoping that it wasn't her husband he was referring to.

"Sun Forrest, I'm um...his wife," she said to the lady at the front desk.

The woman smiled as she typed the name in. Whatever came up on the screen wiped the smile away instantly. "He died in surgery," she replied stoically.

Bryonna promptly passed out.

****

"Answer your phone, girl!" Shyne fussed as she tried Bryonna's phone once more. The deal was that she called back in an hour but three had passed and she still hadn't heard from her.

"Hello?" a strange voice asked unsurely. Shyne almost hung up but didn't. "Are you trying to reach Mrs. Forrest?"

"Um...Yes, Mrs. Forrest. Why do you have her phone? Who are you?"

"I'm Nurse Rodriguez. If you are a family member, can you please come down to the University Hospital?" she pleaded. Shyne looked at her sleeping niece and debated on leaving her sleep.

"Yeah, I'm on my way," she decided then decided to wake Little Yolo. The baby in her own belly kicked as they went out to the car. All eyes were on Shyne as she walked into the hospital.

"Isn't that the sister?" an agent asked when he recognized her from Baltimore. "We should arrest her, too!"

"Nah, she's got enough problems," the other replied since he knew what news was awaiting her inside.

"I'm looking for my friend. She came to check on her husband a few hours ago," Shyne stated at the front desk. She tried to sound casual despite the high profile situation.

"Bryonna Forrest?" the nurse replied since she was the only one who fit the description. Shyne confirmed with a nod and held her breath. "She went into labor."

"Labor? She's not even due yet! She isn't even as far along as me!" Shyne frowned.

"I believe it was from the shock of hearing that her husband passed in surgery. She..." Shyne passed out, too, upon hearing the grim news. When she awoke hours later, she was in a delivery room about to give birth to her third child.

"Wha-...um?" Shyne stammered as she awoke in a roomful of activity. Nurses were bustling around while a doctor sat between her legs.

"Glad you could join us! Just in time, too," the friendly doctor said, looking up at her.

Shyne opened her mouth to ask a series of questions until she felt the familiar feeling of a child leaving her body.

"A boy!" a nurse cheered happily. She had six girls of her own so was happy to see anyone have boys.

"Sun Forrest," Shyne said immediately. Her world needed a Sun so she named her child after him. "What did my sister have?"

Shyne noticed the grim faces in response to her question. One nurse turned away and another left the room. The other busied herself with the newborn.

"I'm so sorry. Mrs. Forrest miscarried," the doctor said genuinely sad. He loved bringing new lives into the world so the stillborn baby broke his heart.

It took Shyne several attempts at speech before she was actually able to get the words out. "How is she? My sister," she croaked as she choked on the sorrow.

"I'm very sorry."

"Thank you," she said appreciatively. She really appreciated when her husband barged in.

"Are you okay?" Asad demanded as he came over. He glanced over to his son but was focused on his wife.

"Sun is gone," she said and finally got to cry. She knew tears were a sign of weakness, but it's okay to cry in front of your husband.

"Gone where?" Asad asked painfully. Sun was his first and only real friend beside her.

"He..." Shyne got stuck on the words and couldn't go any further. "Bryonna lost her baby. Can you go check on her? Please..."

"Sure. What about..." he asked, nodding toward their newborn. The nurse had wrapped up her duties and brought him over.

"This... is your son, Sun. Say hello to your father," Shyne sang. They both realized just how much their child looked like Sun. Neither could stop the tears that flowed.

No one thought it could get any worse but it could and it would. It was about to get much worse.

Chapter 22

"Dear Diary, so Killa has an engagement ring in his pocket. Yes, I go through his pockets, wallet, phone and anything else I can find. Not that I don't trust him cuz 1. I know he has another woman and 2. He always keeps it real.

"I have no idea if it's for me or her. I mean, I could see him marrying me. We're two of a kind. Ying and Yang. Only thing is... I took that shot. Man, I wish I could take that back.

"He could marry me, though! Especially after the way I sexed him. I rode that dick sideways, backwards and forwards. He tried to put it on me but it backfired. Anyway, so after we finished, he hit me with the news that he was going out of the country to see his people in a couple of days.

"I insisted that he take the twins. It's not fair that his other kids get to know his grandmother and not mine. I saved that old bat's life. That's gotta count for something! He said that he was going to. He said when he gets back that things would change. He said that if it wasn't for Sincerity that things would be different. I can read between the lines. He wants me to kill her while he's gone."

"Girl, how you get that out of that?!" Shyne demanded and shook her head. She noticed she was still in the hospital and that Asad was sound asleep in a chair. She was relieved that she didn't wake him and went back to reading.

"Dear Diary, I'm going to have to kill Karate Joe. I know, I know. It's fucked up, but what else can I do? How else can I get to her? Killa knows I be in his phone so he don't have shit in there about her except some pictures of her pussy which I deleted and replaced with ones of my own."

"WAKE UP, SHYNE!" Shyne heard in her mother's voice. It was so vivid that she opened her eyes and saw Bryonna standing there.

"Hey," Bryonna greeted softly and reached for her hand. "Congrats on your new baby."

"I'm so sorry," Shyne moaned. She wanted to comfort her friend, but was in need of comforting herself when she broke down into deep heavy sobs.

Bryonna couldn't do anything but hold her tightly and let her cry. She could feel the warm tears on her back as she got it all out. Poor Asad sat helplessly across the room rocking their newborn.

"I'm so sorry about your brothers. I would bring them back if I could. I would gladly trade places with Sun," Bryonna said, finally getting a chance to cry herself.

"I know you would," Shyne said as the roles reversed. She tried to comfort her. It took a while for her grieving brain to catch up. "Wait... Why you say brothers? What happened to Rico?"

"Oh my God! No one told you? He also died in surgery! I'm so sorry. He's gone, too. And my son, my baby!" she replied and broke down once more.

Asad couldn't take the grief and walked out. Not only was it too much for him, he also didn't want the baby to absorb the grief. He took a seat in the waiting room and gently recited Qur'an in his son's ear.

****

Shyne was too distraught to handle making the funeral arrangements for her brothers. However, she did make the call to inform Shonda of the bad news only to find out that she was pregnant with her brother's first child and that they'd recently gotten engaged. Now, instead of a wedding, they were having a funeral.

Bryonna and Little Yolo joined Shyne and family for the long ride to New York. The fourteen-hour trip seemed to take an eternity to make since the mission was to put her brothers into the ground.

The only thing that made it worse was having to face her mother.

Yolo had made her a promise to take care of her brother and she'd failed. Now he was being buried right next to her. Rico wouldn't be far away since he was being buried next to his own mother.

The grief-stricken family hadn't said two words since they'd left. Each was utterly consumed with grief. The kind of grief that tore families apart.

"We have to go now," Asad said gently as he came up behind Shyne at her mother's grave. Bryonna stood staring at Sun's headstone in disbelief. The service had ended hours ago and it was now starting to get dark.

"Huh?" Shyne asked when she registered her husband's presence.

"The kids are getting restless and hungry. We have to leave," he repeated.

"Yo, B, we gotta go," she called over to Bryonna at the adjacent grave. The spot next to it was reserved for her.

"Go ahead. I'm gonna stay with my husband," Bryonna decided in her grief. "Go with your Aunt Shyne."

"No, Mommy! I want my daddy!" her daughter protested.

It took several minutes to get them both back into the vehicle. Shonda said her final goodbye to Rico and then joined them. She had flown up, but would ride back down with them to visit Killa.

****

"I can't do this anymore," Asad said as he drove south. He was talking to himself, but had said it loud enough for Shyne to hear from the passenger's seat.

"Can't do what?" Shyne wondered. They'd known each other since they were in the first grade and she'd never heard the word *can't* come out of his mouth.

"This. All the death and grief. Pretending I don't know what you guys do. How many times have you come home smelling like gas? I'm not slow, you know!"

"Of course, I know, baby!" Shyne reeled. She reached for his free hand only to have him pull it away. "You're just upset. We all are. We'll talk about this when we get home."

"No! There's nothing else to talk about... I want a divorce."

Shyne gasped loudly and reeled backwards as if she'd been slapped. The words stung harder than any slap and to make matters worse, she knew that he was right. She was dangerous and a danger to her family.

"I understand," she croaked painfully. She rode with her face to the window so that he wouldn't see her tears.

She wasn't the only one crying in the vehicle. In fact, there wasn't a dry eye in the whole truck.

****

What was left of the once happy Forrest Clan entered the hospital in silence. All faces were balled up tight from grief and anger. Shonda led the way up to ICU then stepped aside so the immediate family could go in first. That meant Shyne, who stepped into the room alone. She stood there and listened to the steady beep of the machine that monitored her dad's heartrate.

"Hey, Daddy," Shyne greeted, twisting her lips like *ain't this some bullshit*. She noticed a slight uptick in the beep when she spoke, like he got excited from hearing her voice.

Shyne took his hand and the beeping slowed as he relaxed from her touch. She watched the screen go up and down with the beeps. It took several minutes before she was able to muster enough strength to deliver the bad news.

"Sun died," she forced out. With that out the way, the rest of the news came freely. "Rico, too. They died together. Yo, they took them cops to war! You know they took a few of them with them!"

Killa's heartrate increased along with the beeps of the machine. The line on the screen bounced form the top to the bottom, like a vintage Ping-Pong video game as she spoke. Alarms began to sound and that brought medical staff running.

"I'm so sorry, Daddy! I let you and mommy down," she pleaded as the room filled with doctors and nurses.

"Code blue!" a doctor yelled as he tended to the patient.

"Ma'am, we need you to step outside!" a nurse demanded.

"That's my father! I'm not going anywhere!" Shyne shot back. She had to shout to be heard over all the noise in the room. It was total chaos until it went silent.

"Flat line!" the doctor shouted when the beeping stopped. A flat line on the screen increased the urgency. A nurse wheeled over the paddles and applied some gel. The machine let out a wail once it was fully charged.

"Clear!" the doctor shouted and applied the defibrillator to his chest. The room went silent as he attempted to shock Killa's heart back into action. Killa's whole body rose off the bed when he hit the button.

"Come on, Daddy!" Shyne pleaded. The electric shock got a beep and a pulse on the machine but remained flat.

"Clear!" he repeated and shocked him again. He shocked him twice more before calling it. "Time?"

"Eleven-forty-two," she said, giving the exact time that the legend, the myth, the Killa had died.

Chapter 23

"N-o-o-o-o!!" Shyne screamed loud enough to re-start his heart and the machine. Neither happened, though, and her beloved father was covered with a white sheet. She broke down and let out a heart wrenching howl. "N-o-o-o-o! Daddy, don't die!"

"Wake up, Shyne!" Shyne heard again in her mother's voice. This time, it was so clear and close that she could feel the heat from her mouth. Shyne felt hands on her shoulders that lifted her completely off her feet. "Girl, wake up!"

"What's wrong with her?" her father's voice asked from a distance.

Shyne stopped struggling and cautiously opened one eye. She quickly closed it to avoid the apparition. Next, she opened the other eye and it confirmed the vision, so she shut it. Finally, she opened them both and saw her mother holding her up and her father standing behind her.

"Mommy!" she squealed and wrapped Yolo in an anaconda like hug. "You're alive! You and daddy are alive!"

Yolo looked back at Killa who shrugged his shoulders.

Their daughter's screams had interrupted an intense lovemaking session that marked his departure out of the country. Their moody daughter had been locked away in her room all day.

"Of course we're alive! Girl, you must have had a nightmare," Yolo comforted. She instinctively checked her child for injury and fever.

"No, it was real! Where's Asad?" Shyne demanded, turning to look in her bed.

"And why would Asad be in your bed, little girl?" her mother wanted to know. Her father scrunched his face up wanting to know the same thing.

"Chile please, that's my husband. We got three kids. Where else he gonna be?" she huffed, searching under the covers. "Asad? Baby?"

"What's going on?" a sleepy eyed Sun asked as he wondered in.

Shyne's eyes lit up when she saw her twin and she rushed over to greet him. "You're alive, too!" she cheered and knocked them both down from the impact. He frowned and wiggled as she planted kisses all over his face.

"Get her off me!" Sun pleaded to his parents. Neither helped him, of course, since they thought it was cute.

Yolo took the opportunity to look under the bed.

"He under there?" Killa asked. Asad's little ass was in trouble and didn't even know it.

"No, but this is!" Yolo announced, coming up with her diary. "Girl, what are you doing with this?"

"Huh?" Shyne asked, dumbfounded.

Yolo didn't buy it and twisted her lips dubiously like prove it. "Don't huh me, girl! Did you read my diary?" Yolo whined at the intrusion. All of her inner thoughts, fears, hopes and dreams were contained in the pages. Her very soul had been laid bare in the book.

"Yes, Mommy," she lowered her head and admitted. She thought the show of contrition might save her ass but it didn't.

"Why I oughta..." Yolo growled and tried to get to her. Luckily, Killa stepped in between them and stopped her. "Nosey little ass!"

"I'm sorry, Mommy," Shyne said and broke down in tears. Real ones this time and they did the trick.

"Come here, baby," the mother sang and hugged her daughter.

Both Killa and Sun thought it was a trap and braced themselves to jump in and rescue her. After all, it wouldn't have been the first time.

"Let's leave them," Killa suggested when Yolo began to cry, too. He escorted his son out of the room and took him down to the den. He kept him occupied with a video game while Yolo spoke with Shyne.

"I really wish that you hadn't read my diary. You really, really...
Invaded my privacy," the mother stated plainly.

"I'm sorry. I wish that I hadn't read it, too. It gave me nightmares.
I dreamt that you and daddy's other baby mama had a fight and fell
off the roof. You both died and me and Sun had to go to foster care
and the boys were picking on Sun, so I set them on fire. Then we went
to school and I burned the school down! And then we went to college and I burned a girl up cuz she was burning and wanted to give
Sun some. And then..."

Yolo pressed her lips together really hard to prevent from laughing. Her poor daughter was completely traumatized by her diary. She
only hoped she hadn't read all the sexual passages.

"And then me and Asad got married. It was just in time to cuz I
was getting horny. Then we had Malik and Amina. And then big Sun
and my other brother Rico died and we had little Sun. Then..."

"How you know about Rico?" Yolo interjected. She felt silly
when she remembered it was in the diary along with everything else.
"Oh, okay."

"So, Sun and Bryonna was married. It's crazy cuz me and her
were best friends and we don't even talk in real life. We going to,
though, cuz she cool! All them girls at school were hoes, 'cept us! We
were good girls!"

Again, Yolo struggled not to smile at her daughter's ramblings.
Just like the diary, it gave a glimpse of who she was, how she saw herself and her future. The mother was pleased that her daughter intended to be a wife and mother above all else. Those are the most honor-
able and most important jobs in creation.

"Well, baby, it's late. Your dad is leaving in the morning so he
needs his sleep."

"Y'all wasn't sleeping," Shyne spat, twisting her face. "I know
what you guys be doing in there."

"Well, Miss Thing, we 'bout to do it some more, so take your nosey little butt to sleep," she shot back.

"Mommy, please don't kill Karate Joe! He's our friend. He taught us how to defend ourselves and each other," Shyne pleaded.

"Kill Karate Joe?" Yolo reeled, fanning herself like a southern belle, "Where in the world did you get a- You read my damn diary!"

"Yes, and you gonna fight Sincerity. She's going to kill you, Mommy, and you're going to kill her. You're going to die! I seen it!"

Yolo eyes went wide as her daughter recounted her plan to lure Sincerity up to the rooftop. That part wasn't in the diary, but it was exactly as she planned. The child had a true dream that shook Yolo to her core.

"I promise I won't kill Karate Joe. And, I won't fight Sincerity on the roof," she vowed. She still planned to kill Sincerity, it just wouldn't be on the rooftop. Maybe a sniper's shot from a rooftop, but there would be no rooftop battle. "Now, give me some sugar."

"N-o-o-o-o! I do know where your mouth has been!" Shyne shrieked in disgust. She raised her little had as a consolation. "Fist bump."

"Can't stand you!" Yolo laughed and left her hanging. She walked back down the hall to her bedroom.

Killa was on the bed. He was laid on his side, propped up on an elbow, posing. His dick hung down like it was posing, too. "Is she okay?" he asked, like the concerned parent he was.

"Huh?" she asked, still looking at his dick as if it had spoken. If it had, she wanted it to repeat itself.

"I said," he interjected, bringing her attention to his handsome face. "Is Shyne okay?"

"Far from it! That little girl needs help, bad!" Yolo said, shaking her head.

"Poor baby."

"Me or her?" Yolo asked, pushing him onto his back. She took him in her hand then her mouth while rubbing his muscular legs.

"Huh?" he asked as he watched himself grow thick and hard between her lips.

That's exactly what she wanted and got up to mount it. "We can't...ssss...keep living l-l-like thi-s-s," Yolo hissed as she worked her way down his dick. Once she reached the hilt, she squeezed and rocked.

"I kn-kn-know," he agreed and gripped her ass.

Yolo snatched his hands off her and pinned them on the bed. This was her show and she wanted total control. "You have to decide...me... or her," she insisted between squeezes and rocks.

"I know," Killa agreed again. In fact, he had already come to that conclusion and made his choice. This visit to his grandma was to give her the news before breaking the news to one of his baby mamas and breaking her heart.

Things with Sincerity had grown cold and distant when he returned from New York. He could no longer give them both want they needed

"That's right, papi! Give it to me!" Yolo moaned as Killa went stiff and exploded inside of her. She squeezed and rocked some more to milk him dry.

"Like I said, things will be different when I get back," he said just before he began to snore.

"Well, why don't I murder Sincerity while you're gone to make it easier for you?" she whispered as he slept. "Shake your head *no* if you don't want me to... Okay, great. I will!"

Chapter 24

"Can we go with you? Please, Daddy!" Shyne whined as the family rode to the airport to see Killa off. It was a good performance just like Yolo instructed.

"Not this time, baby girl, but guess what? Your great-grandma is coming back with me and she wants to meet you guys!" he replied. He started to warn them about her deadly grandma hugs but shook his head at the thought. No one had warned him, so they would have to find out the hard way, just like he had.

"Yay! Grandma!" both kids cheered since neither had met any grandparent before.

Yolo slipped into a funk at the thought of it. Nurse Marquita had told her about her birth, about her mom's death as she gave her life to give life to Yolo. The PG version that she was given was that she was young and pretty and died quietly. The truth was she was a dirty addict with a minus T-cell count from having full blown AIDS. And that Yolo was a medical miracle, having survived and being HIV free. The white John who'd impregnated her mother had donated his high IQ to her cause. He'd also taken the virus home to his wife and they'd both died, too.

"What's wrong?" Killa asked, seeing that she had drifted off somewhere.

"Nothing, I'm good. We're good either way," she said, twisting her mouth. She had news for him, too, but chose to wait until he came back. By then, Sincerity should be dead, or she would be.

"Mommy, please don't kill Karate Joe!" Shyne moaned with her slick ass. She hadn't bought her mother's response last night so she had decided to put her on blast in front of her daddy.

"Huh?" Yolo said like she didn't know what she was talking about.

Killa twisted his lips and cocked his head at her dubiously.

"In your diary. You said..."

"I know what I said! And I know what I told you!" she snapped and turned to Killa. "I was just writing stuff. I promise not to hurt a hair on that man's head. He helped our kids!"

"Yolo," Killa said, which said a lot.

"Babe, you know that girl is crazy!" Yolo said, trying to keep a straight face.

"She is, Daddy!" Sun co-signed, nodding his cute face up and down.

"Whatever!" Shyne huffed and whipped her head as if her afro puffs would move.

` The festive mood grew suddenly somber as Killa exited the expressway to enter the airport's parking lot. He usually left at night or while the twins were in school to avoid the goodbyes. He had to deal with it when he left Sincerity and their sons down in Atlanta.

"Cheer up, guys, I'll be home in a couple of weeks. And, I'm bringing Grandma," Killa comforted.

"Okay, Daddy," the twins said stoically. Yolo was quietly pleased at their father's discomfort. It was good to see he felt it as well. They all chitchatted their way to the long ass security lines and said their goodbyes.

"Love you guys!" Killa said and hugged the twins off their feet.

"We love you, too!" they giggled as their feet kicked in the air. When he finally put them down Yolo was waiting on her turn.

"Love me, too?" she asked hopefully as they embraced. The twins were almost ten and he still hadn't told her those words. He acted like he did, and treated her as if he did, he'd just never said it.

"Mmhmm," he nodded.

It was close enough and Yolo squeezed him even harder. "I love you, too," she gushed. Tears of joy streamed down her face. Sun twisted his lips like it was corny while a romantic Shyne shed a tear of her own.

The family waved, smiled and blew kisses as their daddy made his way through the security area. Four hours later he was clear and they turned to leave.

"Can we go to the gun range?" Shyne asked once they reached the car. They had become accustomed to being treated anytime Killa left.

"You guys don't want to go to Chuck E. Cheese? Or Six Flags?" she offered.

"No! We want to go to the range!" Sun cheered.

These were definitely Killa's kids.

****

Meanwhile, down in Atlanta, Sincerity dealt with Killa's departure in her own way. She had grown tired of being juggled along with another woman; especially that damn Yolo. She still wanted to kill her if she ever got the chance. She knew full well that's where Killa was when he wasn't with her.

When a woman's fed up, there ain't nothing you can do about it. Sincerity was definitely fed up, so she fed her vagina to a gangster name Sweet. Unlike Yolo's bald vagina, she kept a thin strip of hair pointing to her pot of gold. It looked like a Hitler mustache on Sweet when he pressed his face against it.

"You tryna make me cum again, ain't you?" Sincerity challenged as he literally sucked another orgasm out of her. All he could do was nod his head up and down since he had a mouthful of pussy. That extra movement was all it took to send her over the edge.

Sincerity had met Sweet in an upscale club while Killa was out of town. He sent bottles of champagne to her before approaching. She insisted she had a man, and he insisted he just wanted to eat her pussy. It took a couple of months before she gave in. Now every time Killa went to visit her, she went to visit him.

"Guess it's time for me to get a nut," Sweet said with a wet face. She wouldn't let him fuck her but instead would watch him as he masturbated. He kneeled between her legs and began to stroke himself. Tonight, he added a twist and ran one of his thick fingers in and out of her juice box.

"Fuck me!" she decided. She grabbed his dick and pulled him on top of her before she changed her mind. Once he hit that cervix, there was no way she would change her mind.

She asked to be fucked and that's exactly what she got. Had she asked him to make love to her, he would have gripped her ass and worked it real slow and easy while planting soft kisses on her neck and face. However, she asked to be fucked, so he lifted her thick legs on his muscular shoulders and got after it. He pounded her pussy like it was his. When she came again, she wasn't sure that it wasn't his. It could be his since Killa didn't seem to want it.

"Grrr!" Sweet growled and snatched himself out of her a millisecond before he came. They both watched as he stroked himself and came all over her stomach.

"I gotta go!" Sincerity blurted and bolted. She grabbed her clothes and dressed on the way out to her car.

"You'll be back!" Sweet laughed as he watched her tear out of his driveway. "Damn, that bitch got some good pussy! Fuck her man!"

"Fuck Killa!" Sincerity told her reflection. "That bitch can have him! No, she can't! Fuck that! Don't let her win, Sin!"

Sincerity went back and forth in her pain and confusion. She hated being taken advantage of but didn't want Yolo to win. If Killa was going to keep fucking her, then she would keep fucking Sweet. She almost turned the car around to go back and get some more of Sweet's dick.

"I had him first. Fuck Yolo!" she decided. "I'm going to kill that bitch myself!"

Chapter 25

Cameisha had gotten in some trouble down in Brazil and fucked it up for everyone. The family was forced to move up to Belize and set up shop. Grandma Deidra missed New York and her other great-grands so she insisted on moving back to The Bronx. Killa was taking her back when he returned. In the meanwhile, he planned a nice little vacation. Sincerity and Yolo took a lot out of him. That's why he decided to finally pick one.

"Yolo!" Grandma shouted in disbelief when Killa told him his decision. "She killed your child! Tried to kill me!"

"She saved your life instead. Doc would have killed you," he reminded.

Deidra rubbed her neck where the deadly device had once rested. It was true, she had saved her life. "But still... What about Sincerity?"

"I'on know," he admitted. He knew about her friend but didn't know just how far things had gone. "Knowing those two, one of them will be dead by the time I get back home. I put my money on Yolo."

"Bet, a thousand," Grandma said, extending a pinkie to confirm the bet.

"A grand!" he agreed as they twisted pinkies.

This is one twisted family.

****

"Now look!" Yolo demanded as she briefed her children. "You guys stay together. Don't touch anything, don't set anything on fire, don't talk to strangers..."

"Cuz anything we say can be used against us in a court of law!" Sun warned his sister. Yolo pressed her lips together to keep from laughing.

"Mommy, this just like my dream. You left us to go kill Karate Joe! And then, you die!"

"I'm not going to kill Karate Joe!" Yolo shouted, causing people to stare. She lowered her voice and went on. "I promised I wouldn't touch him and I won't. I have to see a lady and I'll be right back. Promise!"

"Okay, Mommy! I believe you," Sun said eagerly. He was eager for her to leave so he could run around the museum. The bows and arrows in the Native American display had his name written all over them.

"Okay, Mommy," Shyne relented. She did want to check out the smoke signals in that same display.

"Okay then. See you guys in an hour," Yolo said. She kissed Sun and got a fist bump from Shyne before heading up to The Bronx.

Yolo found out that Sincerity had an aunt up on Trinity Ave and went to find her. She wasn't hard to find posted up in the park reading a book. Yolo made a few passes to make sure the coast was clear before approaching her. When it was, she came up behind her.

"What the fu-... Chill, B," Rashida said when she felt the metal ring go over her head. The gun pressed to her temple killed her protest. "Yo, I got money and a blunt in my purse. Go on, take it. Just don't shoot!"

"I don't want your money or your purse," Yolo growled, pressing the barrel deeper into her temple. A tug on the trigger would have fed the pigeons brain matter for lunch.

"Did I fuck your man?" Rashida wondered. It wouldn't be the first time a woman stuck a gun in her face about fucking their man.

"I doubt it! Anyway, get your niece on the line. On video chat," Yolo said from behind where she could be seen on screen.

"Which one?" she asked since she had several. She even breathed a sigh of relief since it was one of them who in trouble and not her.

The sigh was premature since she was the one with the DC 2000 around her neck.

"Sincerity! She's been fucking my man. Now get her on the screen!"

Rashida quickly complied and made the video call. Sincerity cocked her head curiously when she saw the call. The two didn't really kick it like that so she wondered why she was calling. She couldn't figure it out so she took the call.

"Sup, Auntie?" Sincerity asked almost curtly. It took a second for her to see Yolo standing behind her. "The fuck?"

"Hey, Sin. You know we gotta settle this shit, right?" she asked.

"Hell yeah! I'm sick of you stealing my time with my man!"

"I could say the same thing, but I won't. Truth be told, it won't be over until death does us. One of us," Yolo explained.

"Just tell me when and where! I'm there, you can believe that," Sincerity dared.

"How 'bout at Rashida's funeral?" she asked.

"My funeral!" Rashida exclaimed. "I ain't dead!"

"Yeah, you are," Yolo said and hit the switch. The woman's hand still held the phone up as her head sat down next to her.

"I'm gonna make you pay for that. bitch! It's on and poppin'!"

"'Til death does us. Okay, bye!" Yolo laughed. Once the drama was done she grabbed her journal and made an entry.

"Dear Diary, Guess what?" Yolo wrote, *then paused to look at the test strip once more. It still said what it said the same thing so she wrote, "I'm pregnant!"*

Chapter 26

"So, let me get this straight..." Sun began then paused dramatically. His sister let out a deep sigh like *here we go again* and shook her head. "All that was in your dream?"

"Yes," Shyne said exasperated. "The whole thing, all of it was just a dream."

"So, we ain't young killers going through growing pains, school daze or part of the family business?" he mocked. "Oh and I'm glad I ain't married to Bryonna. Her hair nappy!"

"No it's not! It's natural, just like mine!" Shyne protested on behalf of all the perm free girls. Well, at least herself and Bryonna, since most little girl's parents had their hair fried, dyed and laid to the side by first grade.

"Anyway, I'm glad it was just a dream." Sun said wistfully. He loved his parents dearly and didn't know what he would do without them.

"I guess," Shyne said twisting her lips. She'd enjoyed being married to her best-friend, Asad. They were engaged in real life so... maybe her dream would come true. Hopefully her mother would survive this time.

*****

"I'm gone kill this bitch! That's my word! I'ma murder that bitch!" Sincerity vowed after watching her aunt get beheaded.

"Who?" Sweets asked. He was slightly amused by the tough talk and a little aroused as well.

Once they'd open the door to them having sex he and Sincerity went at it every chance they got. Why not since she was certain that Killa was sexing Yolo on his frequent visits to New York.

"My man's girlfriend is who!" she fumed. She was mad at Killa too but once Yolo was out of the picture she would have him all to herself. In the meanwhile, she decided to be spiteful.

"What you doing?" Sweets asked hopefully as Sincerity kissed her way down his chest and stomach.

She didn't make it to his belly button because his swollen dick head was blocking the way. Sweets moaned as she began to lick around the rim. Licking led to kisses which led to him getting his dick sucked.

"Oh," he answered since her mouth was full. Not as full as it was about to be when the tingling began to creep up from his toes.

Sincerity decided letting him cum in her mouth was going a little too far and spit his dick out just before it began to spit. She was generous enough to tug on his thick shaft and milk him dry. She kept right on tugging to ensure it stayed hard. It did so she tossed a leg over him and mounted him.

"That's why I quit you," Killa mumbled as he watched the couple copulate in the bed he slept in when he was home. He closed the lap top when Sincerity began whining about an impending orgasm. He had seen enough so he didn't need to see that.

****

"I'm so glad to be going home! Belize is beautiful and all, but... there's no place like the Bronx," Grandma Diedra admitted as their plane lifted off the runway.

"True that," Killa agreed and then slipped back into his own mind. Tried to anyway, but his grandma had other plans.

"So, when can I meet my great grandbabies? Let me see their pictures again," she insisted.

Killa quickly handed over his cell phone in hopes that the photo gallery would keep her busy enough to let him think. It was funny how as much pussy he got while with Sincerity he was in his feelings about her sharing hers with another. Bugs Bunny was correct, it ain't no fun when the rabbit got the gun.

"Oh my," Diedra blushed when her nosey ass ventured into the videos on his phone and saw Yolo riding him backwards.

"That's what you get," Killa fussed and gently snatched his phone away. He then swiped to the twins and handed it back.

"Beautiful. Just beautiful," she gushed at a young Sun and Shyne. He looks so much your dad at that age."

"I think he looks like me," he insisted.

"And who you think you look like? Act like too. Your granddad was a beast back in his day. The stories I could tell you!" Grandma sighed with a love struck gaze.

"Someone needs to write a book about you guys one day."

"I'm sure someone will, one day," she agreed. She was right too because it's one hell of a story.

****

"What?" Yolo snapped when she caught her daughter staring at her.

"You tell me," Shyne snapped back. She sometimes forgot it was all a dream and she wasn't grown. The stern look that spread on her mother's face reminded her real quick. "You look... scared."

She would never admit it but that was the foreign feeling eating at her insides. Butterflies fluttered in her tummy and she felt anxious. She wanted to write it off as being excited to see her boo when the plane landed but that was just a part of it.

Another part was how would Killa's grandmother accept seeing her? Would she forgive her like he had, after all, she did save her life. Part was killing Sincerity's aunt and starting a beef that could only end in death. Another part was telling her that Killa was about to be a father once more.

"Scared! Scared of who? Scared of what? Shit fear is scared of me!" Yolo huffed and puffed to prove that she wasn't scared. Shyne didn't buy it and so twisted her lips.

"A-yo, Ma, they plane just landed!" Sun said saving his sister from getting popped in public. He pointed up at the arrival board that displayed the flight information from Belize.

"Listen guys. Grandmothers hug real hard, so take a deep breath and brace yourself," she warned as they made their way to the gate.

"Like an anaconda?" Sun asked wide-eyed with excitement.

"Worse!" Yolo assured him. She stifled a laugh at her daughter's turned up face.

No sooner than they arrived at the gate Killa and Grandma departed their plane. Killa instinctively scanned the area for danger. He looked over his family to take in his surroundings. Once he deemed it clear his eyes doubled back and a smile spread on his handsome face.

"There they are," he told his grandmother pointing to his kids. Diedra squealed and took off towards the twins.

"Brace yourselves!" Yolo warned a millisecond before she scooped them up and hugged them into the air.

Killa prayed a silent prayer as the air was squeezed out of his kids. He and Yolo shared a quick glance that gave hint to wild sex as soon as possible. Grandma released her death grip a moment before Sun passed out.

"How are you guys? You are so pretty! And you're just the most handsome little boy! I'm so happy to finally meet you..."

"Hello, Miss Forrest," Yolo greeted gingerly, hiding behind a weak hand wave. She had never felt so insecure in her life.

"Yolo," Diedra greeted with a nod of her head. Killa let out a sigh of relief since his grandmother didn't flip out. Yolo too smiled at the non-violent reception. Lukewarm was better than red hot.

The family followed Killa out of the terminal. Sun and Shyne flanked their grandmother and engaged in lively banter. They kept up the conversation on the ride over to the Bronx. Yolo visibly tensed up when they reached the projects.

"What did you do?" Killa wondered when he peeped her reaction.

"Who? Me" Huh? Um..." Yolo stammered and stuttered. Karate Joe gave them a bow as they pulled into the parking lot to everyone's relief. "See! He's fine!"

"Karate Joe!" Sun and Shyne cheered and jumped out of the car before it came to a complete stop. They ran over to hug their sensei.

"How cute," Diedra gushed. "Y'all come on upstairs so I can feed you! You too..."

"Thanks," Yolo said accepting what she was given. She followed Diedra inside while Killa waited on the kids.

"Killa-son," Karate Joe greeted with a bow. "Your timing is bad. Sin is here."

"Where? Here?" Killa asked near panic. He knew his baby mamas would one day clash. He just hoped today was not that day.

****

"Okay. Um... grandma, we can't stay. Gotta get out to the Island to um..." Killa offered. He looked to Yolo for help but got none since she had no idea what he was talking about.

"Not before they eat some of my macaroni and cheese, fried chicken, candied yams sweet potato pie..." Grandma insisted. She named several more of his favorites even though she had him at macaroni and cheese.

"Oh, okay," he groaned. Lively play could be heard from the courtyard so the twins looked out the window to investigate.

"Can we go play?" Sun asked since he was the spokesman of the twins.

"No-yes!" Killa and his grandmother both replied. Yolo saw a chance to earn a brownie point and so sided with Diedra.

"Sure, just don't get dirty and watch out for each other," she needlessly insisted. They were definitely going to get dirty and they would certainly look out for each other.

The twins took off like they had been shot out of a cannon. The only obstacle in their path was the multiple dead bolts, chains and locks that adorned the heavy, steel project door. The adults watched in amusement as they struggled to get free. Five minutes later they made it out to the hallway and ran towards the elevator. Killa and Yolo hit the window to watch their kids.

"Let's hit the stairs!" Sun suggested when the elevator passed them on the way up. No way could he stand to wait the ten minutes it would take to return. He didn't wait for a reply before rushing into the stairwell.

"Eww!" Shyne reeled and crinkled her cute face as the stench of stale urine, weed, shit and sex invaded her personal space and hit her nostrils.

"Hold your breath!" Sun shouted behind him as he took the stairs two at a time. Shyne was dainty but just as athletic and hopped down on his heels.

Sun saw a kid around his age showing out on the monkey bars and made a bee-line over so he could show him how it was really done. A group of girls turned their noses up at Shyne so she followed her brother to the monkey bars.

"This will be interesting," Killa mused when he recognized the child doing flips and dips.

"Sure will," Yolo agreed when she peeped Sincerity on a bench. She eased back and made her way out of the apartment.

"Not bad," Sun said when the kid dismounted with a back flip with a twist. He personally never added the twist but would today. If that could do it, then so could he. Meanwhile, Shyne cocked her head curiously as she looked at the boy.

"Let's see what you got then," the kid dared. Others came near to see the battle.

Sun sauntered over to the bars and looked up. He spit into his palms and rubbed them together. It had no significance and was just plain nasty but looked cool. Sun hopped up to the bar and went in. He did every move the other kid had done, including the twist and flip dismount.

"Not bad yourself," the kid said when Sun landed. He ignored the fact that he'd spit in his hand and stretched his out to greet him. May as well since he'd spit in his as well. "I'm Rico. What's your name?"

"Sun," he replied and shook his brother's hand.

Chapter 27

"How sweet," Yolo sang as she came up on Sincerity. Killa lost his breath when he saw the two come face to face.

"Mmhmm. Now my son can comfort yours when I murder you," Sincerity growled through clenched teeth. Both knew now was not the time nor the place for their showdown. No, not in front of their kids.

"Oh shit!" Killa moaned when Yolo took a seat on the bench. Grandma heard fear in his voice and came over to investigate.

"Mmhmm... Baby mama drama," Diedra laughed and then went back to cooking her ten course meal. "Guess I better make a little more."

"I just don't see how this is funny to you," he said to his chuckling grandmother.

"Yeah... No... Actually it'll be me who murders you," Yolo said nonchalantly as Rico and Sun introduced Xavier and Shyne.

"When? Where?" Sincerity asked eager to get to it. She knew that the lovely little lunatic had a part of Killa's heart and that she would never have him all to herself until she was dead.

"Oh whenever... wherever," Yolo sighed. "Hands, guns, knives, whatever."

"Machetes... cuz I'm going to cut your head off just like you did my aunt," she warned.

"Speaking of head... I guess I'll give my man some when we go home," Yolo teased.

"Have fun cuz I'ma keep your head in a jar once you're dead. I'ma put it on the mantle at our home," Sin shot back. She'd had enough so stood to leave. Yolo looked her up and down and could clearly see what Killa saw in her. The other woman was dead fine and she would be fine with her being dead.

****

"Come eat!" Grandma shouted from the window. Sun, Shyne, Rico and X all took off running towards the building.

Sun and Shyne, and Rico and Xavier silently all wondered why the others had responded to their grandmother's call. Into the building they all went, and then up the pissy stairs and down the hall. Reaching the door Xavier opened the door and led the way inside.

"Hey, Pops!" he cheered and rushed over to embrace his father. Killa wasn't his biological father, but he was the only father he ever knew so it was the same thing. Besides being a father is what happens after you bust a nut.

"Sup, guys," he greeted and hugged both him and Rico. "I see you've beet your brother and sister."

"Who?" all four kids demanded. It was now clear to Shyne how much Rico looked like their father. Xavier favored like him too so he looked like family as well.

"No wonder you so dope on the bars!" Rico said, accepting his brother instantly

"You too!" Sun said cheesing widely from the compliment. The moment was broken up by a knock on the door.

"That must be Sincerity. I invited her for dinner as well," Diedra announced as she went to open the door.

Yolo wondered if she was being catty but figured she was being fair. It wouldn't matter anymore once she and Sincerity fought it out. Then the old lady could deliver her plates to the cemetery.

"Hello, everyone," Sincerity sang as she breezed into the apartment. "And what are your names?"

"I'm Shyne and he's Sun, with a *u*," Shyne greeted as sweetly as Sincerity had asked.

Yolo realized that the woman had an advantage over her with Killa's grandmother. She also peeped her trying to publicly take the high road in front of her and decided to do the same. The whole time over dinner the two women tried to *out polite* the other.

"Let me help," Yolo offered when Diedra stood to clear the table.

"No! Let me!" Sincerity hopped up and announced. Both women scrambled to collect as many dishes as they could carry at one time.

"Why don't you two, do the dishes together," Grandma replied with a mischievous smirk.

"No! I'll do them," Kill interjected. The last thing he needed at the moment was for those two to be in a kitchen full of knives, pots, pans and spatulas.

The kids settled in front of the TV and played video games while their grandmother watched. Meanwhile, Yolo and Sincerity sat across from each other and glared. They were still staring when Killa returned with dishpan hands.

"They really need to install dishwashers in this place," he grumbled.

"Bruh, this the projects," Grandma reminded him. The kids all snickered at both their pops getting checked and their grandma's use of slang.

"You should move to... with us," Sincerity offered, catching herself just before she disclosed the location of her home to her enemy.

"Or Long Island... Wyandanch," Yolo said, extending the invite to Sincerity.

"Guess, I better get these guys home," Killa said and stood.

"Can we spend the night?" Shyne pleaded and pouted. Killa formed his mouth to say no, but his grandmother beat him to answering.

"You sure can!" she said looking at Killa daring him to say something. "All my grandbabies are spending the night!"

The last remark was directed at Sincerity who lowered her head in agreement. She had given up her unit long ago but could spend the night with any one of her childhood friends or her dad.

"Well, I guess you can take me home then," Yolo purred seductively.

"Let's bounce," he replied. After kissing his grandmother and kids he hit the door. A head nod served as goodbye to Sincerity. Yolo stuck her tongue out at her as she followed him out.

"I'm out too," Sincerity announced and stood. The kids were so engrossed in playing with each other that they didn't even see her leave. She rushed from the apartment before the first tear could drop.

Even Sincerity had to admit that Killa and Yolo made a killer couple. She would never possess him the way she wanted until she was in a box six feet under the earth. A lady had just exited a taxi as Sincerity stepped out into the night. On a whim she rushed over and jumped in the backseat.

"Where to?" the cab driver asked his new passenger. Dispatch didn't know about this fare so it was going straight into his pocket.

"Um... JFK," she decided. If Yolo was getting some dick tonight then she was too. She pulled her phone out and called Sweets down in Atlanta. "I'm on my way. I'll call you when I land."

****

"You can thank Sincerity for this," Yolo said breaking the silence as Killa drove back out to the Island.

"For what?" he replied as she unbuckled her seatbelt and leaned over. It became clear when she fumbled to free his penis from the prison of his pants. "Oh!"

Yolo pulled on his dick until it grew long and hard in her hand. She then teased it with licks and half kisses until it throbbed in anticipation. Killa leaned his seat back to give her head room to give head.

"Mmm," he groaned when she finally granted him access to her hot mouth. He slowed the car down to thirty-five miles an hour as he fought to maintain his lane.

Yolo didn't even pause when Killa pulled up to the tollbooth. The female attendant started to flirt with the handsome driver until she noticed the head bobbing up and down in his lap. Instead she twisted her lips and made change for a twenty.

"Okay, that's enough," Yolo said when she felt the telltale signs of an orgasm. She sat up straight and put her seat belt back on.

"Y-y-yo... w-w-what... y-y-you doing?" he asked frantically at the abrupt ending.

"Making you wait," she giggled. She knew that he'd be so horny by the time they reached home that he'd really beat it up.

Killa mashed the gas in an effort to get home quicker. Beating it up was exactly what he had in mind. Now, with the kids away for the first time he planned to fuck her all over the house. Both had a surprise in store for the other and both decided to wait until after they made love to give them.

When they pulled into the driveway both hopped out and ran for the door. Yolo scrambled to get the key in the lock because she was super horny too.

"Step aside!" Killa demanded so he could kick it open like the police. Luckily for them both she found the key and got it open. They stepped in just enough too close the door and then went at it.

After wrestling tongues, groping and pulling each other's clothes off they were both hot and naked. He was hard as a rock and she was wet as a bubbling country creek.

Yolo turned and bent over the arm of the sofa. Killa leaned in and playfully bit one of her caramel ass cheeks. He then kissed the other before spreading them to lick her labia from the behind. He started to stop when she was on the brink of orgasm like she had, but didn't.

"Oh... bae... bae!" she proclaimed as she bust a nut on his tongue.

"Mmhmm," he agreed with his handiwork and then stood. He then aimed his dick at the puddle he'd left and plunged deep inside.

Yolo gripped the pillows and took the pounding. The sound of skin slapping skin rang out in the empty house. Her vagina sang a squishy symphony as he stroked her to another orgasm. She almost made it to a third one but came up short when Killa came inside of her.

"Whew!" he exclaimed and slumped over her back. He almost fell asleep in her pussy until she flexed it around him and called his name.

"Killa, let's go upstairs. We gotta talk," she announced sheepishly. Killa pulled out and stood on wobbly legs and followed her to the stairs.

"Shit!" Killa remembered his bag and rushed out butt naked to get it.

"Really?" Yolo asked shaking her head when he returned. The good thing was that they were both wide awake and alert.

"So, what you got to tell me? About Rashida?" he asked, proving not much gets by him. He kept tabs on his family whether he was near or far.

Sincerity's change in demeanor had prompted hm to install cameras to keep an eye on her. Her affair had helped him make his decision on who to be with. Now it was time to let his choice in on it as well.

"Okay see, that was an accident. Her head just fell off while we were talking and um..." Yolo began but saw that he wasn't buying it. She did have an ace up her sleeve so decided to use it. "It's hard to remember stuff when you're pregnant and stuff."

"I guess. So, what you wanted to tell me?" he asked.

"I just told you. I'm pregnant," she repeated and studied his face for a reaction. She was more concerned with his expression than what would come out of his mouth.

"Oh," he answered with a blank face. His lips twisted like they did when he was in deep thought giving her nothing to go on. He let out a sigh and dug into his bag.

Yolo tensed wondering what could be in the bag that pertained to what she'd just said. She was slightly offended that all he'd had to say was *oh*. *Oh* what?

"Oh! Oh my!" she reeled when he produced a ring box and flipped it open. The shiny three karat solitaire spoke for itself, but she still wanted... no needed to hear the words from him. "What is that?"

"A ring," he frowned at the silly question.

"I know it's a ring, but what kind of ring? What does it mean?" she asked coyly.

"Cuz we need to get married. We're good for each other and bad for bad people," he replied.

"Well, what about Sincerity?" she asked as he slid the ice on her finger, not that she really cared since she still intended to murder her.

"She cool," he shot back coolly. He understood that she was fed up but her actions still stung none the less. "I want you to leave her alone."

"Huh?" Yolo asked with a goofy grin. Killa gave her his *don't play* face and she said, "Okaaay."

"You didn't say yes though," he reminded, lifted his brow.

"Hell yes! Fuck yeah! Na'am! Si," she rattled off yes in every language she knew.

Chapter 28

Yolo and Killa awoke the next morning twisted together like a pretzel. He managed to get his morning erection inside of her and they had sex twisted together and just like that a new position was born and they dubbed it... the pretzel.

"I see why they call you Killa!" Yolo exclaimed winded from an orgasm.

"Cuz I be killin' shit!" he proudly proclaimed as he rolled out of the bed. "'Bout to hop in the shower. You coming?"

"I can't walk!" she giggled. "I'm 'bout to get up."

"Mmhmm," he replied dubiously when she reached for the remote. Yolo hadn't had a break from motherhood since becoming a mother so he left her alone.

"Anybody need dead?" Yolo sang as she turned to the news. She scanned both the local and the national new stories searching for some really foul person in need of a really brutal death. They could make a honeymoon out of it.

Killa washed contently under the stream of hot water. His grandmother's treatment of Yolo showed that she respected his decision even if she didn't agree with it. She was family and would be treated as family. Diedra had certainly made mistakes of her own in life, but that's another book.

"Oh... my... God! Killa! Help! Come quick!" Yolo screeched in terror. It terrified Killa to hear stark fear in her voice. What the fuck could scare her?

"What? What's wrong?" he asked as he rushed into the room. Yolo was balled up against the headboard covering her face. All she could do was point.

"Look!" she said pointing at the TV without looking up.

"The fuck!" Killa growled hotly. He was instantly furious when he saw what was on the screen. It was one of those beauty contest with little girls dressed like grown woman—faces full of make-up wearing ball gowns and bikinis. He couldn't find the remote so he simply snatched the TV off the wall and throw it.

"Is it gone?" she pleaded and trembled. Who could blame her since that's some sick shit!

"Yeah, babe," he said and crawled on the bed to comfort her. She was still shaking when he took her in his arms.

"JonBenet Ramsey ass shit! We need to kill all those sick fucks!" she whined.

"We are… going to kill all those sick fucks!" he corrected.

"Xavier, take your brothers and sister over to the A&P and get me some butter and eggs," Grandma said so she could fix breakfast. Of course, she also had an ulterior motive in mind.

"On Ogden? Why we can't go to the bodega?" X asked since he'd just got jumped by some teens over at the A&P. Rico had gone back over there with him to straighten it but the three teens had been a little too much for the two of them.

"Because I said so! Besides that damn bodega charge twice as much for everything. Like I said, take Sun and Shyne with you."

"We'll go, Grandma!" Shyne announced. She and Sun had never had a grandmother before so had fell instantly in love with the woman. Between the two of them they'd used the word *Grandma* a few hundred times since last night.

"Let's bounce then," Xavier agreed. He had no problem fighting them again. Win, lose or draw but there'd be no surrender, no retreat.

Grandma watched her grandbabies traipse through the courtyard. Once they had a decent head's start she slipped on her sneakers and headed for the door, but stopped short.

"Almost forgot my phone," she remembered. Not that she was expecting a call, she just wanted to record the fight. "World Star!"

****

"A-yo, I got beef with Lil-C on Ogden," X advised. The twins had no idea what that meant but nodded in agreement like they did. "You guys just cross the street if they out there."

"They gon' try to jump us again," Rico sighed. He didn't mind fighting either, but preferred a one on one—a fair fight.

"Can we stop and get a newspaper?" Shyne asked. She answered her own question by heading over to the corner store. She returned a moment later rolling a section of the paper into a club just like Karate Joe had taught them. In fact, he'd taught them to make a weapon out of just about anything. Her three brothers all smiled at the clever idea.

"I got the sports!" Sun called and grabbed that section. Rico twisted up the business section to give the bullies the business while Xavier took the world news.

"Yo, Lil-C, there go X," Corey called out when he saw X and Rico coming their way. They didn't notice Sun and Shyne on the opposite side of the street.

"Yo, I'ma pretend like I want a one with him. As soon as we start, you two jump in!" Lil-C advised. He and Xavier had fought a one on one once and he'd gotten his ass whipped. Now he had the upper hand since his boys were with him.

"Ready?" X asked Rico as he shot a glance over at the twins. They rushed ahead, crossed back over and were now coming up behind Lil-C and company.

"Ready," Rico replied gripping his makeshift Billy club. Grandma was read too and pressed record.

"Yo, I thought I tol—," Lil-C popped off and got popped in his mouth. The rest of the statement along with a tooth got knocked back down his throat.

Rico and the twins pounced on his friends while X pounded Lil-C into a fetal position.

"Don't... no... body... pick... on... my brothers!" Shyne fussed as she swung and kicked as she defended her brothers—it was a far cry from her dream of beefing with her brothers.

X landed one last kick to the seat of Lil-C's pants as he scurried off. His friends ran off with him leaving Killa's kids to celebrate. Grandma too as she ended her recording and headed back to the projects.

****

"Uh oh," Killa groaned when he checked his phone as he and Yolo ate a late breakfast.

"What?" Yolo asked matching his worried tone. "The kids oaky?"

"I guess. Grandma sent me a video," he replied. Knowing his grandmother it could be anything. She'd once sent him one meant for one of her gentlemen friends by mistake. Killa couldn't un-see what he'd seen no matter how hard he tried.

"Prob'ly some cute stuff with the kids. Let me see!" she insisted rushing around to his side of the table.

Killa pressed play and looked away. He could not stand to another twerk video in his life. Yolo smiled brightly as she watched her kids beat the older boys into submission. Sun and Shyne moved as one just like X and Rico. They'd all been trained by the same master and they were all just as dangerous.

"Told you it was some cute stuff with the kids!" Yolo cheered. She hit play again and watched it again and then once more.

"Okay, that's enough!" Killa insisted so he could use his phone. Grandma answered on the first ring. "Sup, Grandma, what you doing?"

"Tryna upload a video," she replied sounding frustrated by the process. "'Bout to cook something for my babies. You coming to the city?"

"Yeah, in a few hours. Sup with Sincerity?" he asked and looked at Yolo to see her reaction. Yolo had a ring on her finger and another bun in the oven so the name didn't even register. She'd won and once she put Sincerity in a box she'd be free of her forever.

"Your guess would be better than mine. I hears she got into a taxi last night, but don't know where she went or if she back or..."

"Aight, aight! Let me hit her up and see what's up," he cut in. They said their goodbyes and he dialed Sincerity.

"Mmph!" Sin fussed as the head of Killa's dick popped up on her screen as Biggie's *Big Poppa* ringtone sounded off.

"What?" Sweets asked. "You look like you just bit a lemon!"

"No, but I did just get a bad taste in my mouth," she fussed. She was mad at Killa, but blamed Yolo for all her problems.

"Speaking of a taste in yo' mouth..." he suggested and pulled the sheets back to reveal his dick.

Killa turned on the camera app just as Sincerity went down on him. He watched for a second while Sweets reached around to play in her pussy.

"Oh my! Is that..." Yolo exclaimed as she peered over his shoulder. Killa quickly turned it off and put the phone down.

"Yeah, I guess she got herself a boyfriend," he shrugged. The nonchalant gesture didn't match the sting of pride that came out in his tone.

"Is that... your place? You got cameras in your house? You got cameras here too?" she fussed looking around the room.

"Yup. Everywhere!" he lied. Yolo was a lot of things and loyal was at the top of the list. She wasn't just crazy, she was also crazy about him. He'd been her goal since she was a teen. He didn't have to worry about her at all.

"Well, since she giving head on camera..." Yolo purred. Killa didn't have much left in him after a night of sex but didn't protest when she pulled out his penis. Besides, who says no to head?

Chapter 29

"Welp, I'm going to pick up the twins," Killa sighed. Not that he minded their presence but being able to spend time alone with Yolo was rare. People may wonder how he chose her but the truth of the matter is they were just alike. Two peas in a pod, on the same accord. No one else on the planet could understand them as they did.

"I'm gonna see if Christi can come and watch them so we can pay a visit to those Little Miss America people," Yolo replied. She used the word visit as if they were going for tea and crumpets instead of murder and mayhem.

"They could stay in the city. Being in The Bronx will do them some good," he replied. He knew his kids were sheltered and wanted to expose them to the grimy realities of life. No place can do that better than The Bronx.

"As long as they don't end up on *World Star* again!" Yolo fussed. She was kidding though because she'd watched the video at least twenty times already.

"I'll talk to her about that," Killa said lying. He'd posted the video to his social media accounts.

Killa got up and walked out without looking back. He knew if he did he would get turned on and they would end up in bed once more. That's was it three in the afternoon and he was just leaving the house. Mobb Deep rapped to him the whole way to the bridge. It was only fitting that KRS One escorted him through The Bronx.

He spotted his children playing in the courtyard when he arrived. He paused to watch his offspring as they did the exact things in the exact same places as he'd once done. Footsteps behind him snatched him back into the present. He snatched his gun and spun.

"Whoa!" Little Villain said raising his hands in surrender. "I don't want no problem. Definitely don't wanna get hit with that! What the hell is that?"

"Desert Eagle, .50 cal," he replied and handed it to his young friend.

"Damn, Unc!" he exclaimed feeling the weight of the heavy artillery. "Who you gon' shoot with this? Elephants? Tigers? Bears?"

"Pedophiles," he replied accepting it back and tucking it away in order to exchange a pound and a hug.

"No wonder you walk with a limp," Villain laughed as they embraced. "Yo, your seeds are wild! They beat up Lil-C 'ndem this morning. The video has gone viral! But I still went 'round there and shoved my gun in his mouth to make sure it's over. It is."

"I bet," Killa laughed loudly. The sound was like a dog whistle to his kids since they all popped up from playing when they heard it.

"Daddy!" Shyne screeched and took off. The little girls she'd been jumping rope with watched on curiously. Being a daddy wasn't cool where they came from, so none of them had one. God willing, music and media will one day promote fatherhood as much as they promote the bullshit. But until they do these kids are on their own.

The boys were too cool to scream Daddy and take off running. Instead they said, "Sup, Pops," and walked real quickly to their dad. Shyne jumped into his arms so they had to settle for handshakes.

"What you guys been up to?" Killa asked. The four kids shared conspiratol glances before Xavier spoke up.

"Oh nothing. Kid stuff," he shrugged.

"Aight. Y'all finish playing while I holla at grandma," he said. He planted a smooch on Shyne's cheek that made her giggle then put her down. She ran off back to her project friends and was met with a million questions. They all wanted to know what it was like to have a daddy. Rico and Sun raced back over to the monkey bars while X hit the basketball court.

"Smells like home," Killa laughed as he entered the pissy stairway. The smell helped him take the stairs three at a time until he reached his floor.

"I told you guys not to keep running in and out this apartment! Pee on the stairs like everyone else! Except you, Shyne. Girls don't pee outside," Diedra fussed from the kitchen. She was frontin' though because she was absolutely delighted to have her grandkids underfoot.

"It's me," Killa greeted as he entered the kitchen. Grandma tilted her face up to accept the kiss she knew was coming. Killa planted it on her cheek and then hit the fridge.

"I see where them boys get it from," she said as he inspected the refrigerator.

"Don't let Shyne fool you, that little girl eats like a horse!" he laughed.

"Well, she's my little pony! What a sweet girl," Diedra cooed. "I don't know where she gets if from."

"Speaking of her mama," Killa answered her question. "I gave her the ring. Asked her to marry me..."

"Did she say yes? She better had! I don't know who she think she is! What, she waiting on Prince Charming or something?"

"She said yes, Grandma. Can you help her with the wedding, please?" he asked. It was one of those rhetorical questions since he knew she'd say hell yes.

"Hell yes!" she shouted. There weren't many weddings in the projects so this was a treat. She went on rambling about flowers, dresses and carriage rides. Killa waited for a chance to jump in the conversation, like it was double-dutch.

"Oh, we gotta go out of town for a few days. You want to watch the twins or I can..."

"You can nothing! Them babies staying right here until you two get back! I'll tell Sincerity... Where is she, anyway?"

Killa twisted his lips trying to find an answer. Last time he'd seen her she was giving head but he couldn't say that. His silence turned his grandmother's head in his direction. She read the distress on his face and did what she does best.

"You made your choice and I support you. I love Sin, but I love you more," she said and made it all better. They parted with a hug as he set out to kill some pedophiles.

****

"Hey, babe!" Yolo greeted when Killa returned. "Want something to eat? Drink? Want some pussy?"

"I'm good. What you doing?" he wondered as she flipped through Shyne's preschool pictures on the computer.

"I been going back and forth with the Little Miss America people. Told 'em I had a daughter and they asked for pictures," she explained which explained half the story.

"So, why they old pictures?" he asked of the five year old pictures.

"They said nine is too old. They like to get them at age four, five tops," she replied through clenched teeth. Killa was just as disgusted, but it was about to get worse...much worse as a matter of fact. A moment later they got a reply. A sick, disgusting reply from a person who was nearing the end of their life.

"She's very pretty. Do you have any of her in a swimsuit? A bikini if possible. A video would be even better. Can she twerk?"

"Twerk! Bitch, I'll..." Yolo growled and typed. Luckily Killa was there to stop her before she blew her cover.

"Chill," he advised as he pulled her hands away from the keyboard. She was so mad that she was literally shaking as he lifted her out of the chair. He took her place and type a reply.

"No. We were hoping you could help us with that. Would it be possible to leave her with you guys for a while, so you can mold her for competition?

"Argh!" Mr. Trump grunted as he came in his pants.

"What's wrong dear?" his wife asked with her dense Honduran accent. She rushed to her husband's side and saw the wet spot growing in his slacks. The woman was so grateful that he'd plucked her from the Tegucigalpa slums that she turned a blind eye to his perversions; that's why she was going to die right along with him.

"Th-th-they as-as-asked if we could k-k-k-keep her a w-wh-while!" he stammered with excitement.

"Yes!" she shouted and typed the reply in for him. She gave included their names and address as she set the date.

"This Trump is about as dumb as the other one," Killa said shaking his head.

"You mean Mr. Grab 'em by the Pussy?" Yolo laughed at the dumb ass. People can say whatever they want about the billionaire, but he is one funny mother fucker.

"Book a flight. Let's go see about his ass," Killa ordered rubbing his hands together greedily.

They weren't the only killer couple plotting a murder.

Chapter 30

"Mm...mm...mph," Murda grimaced as he looked down and watched himself slide in and out of his girlfriend. The colorful display of their sex was amazing. She had a dark brown complexion, black vagina lips that surrounded pink insides that exuded a thick white cream on his light brown dick.

"I know right," Malice said with a giggle and a squeeze of her already super tight, black box.

That extra pressure was more than the man could take. He snatched out and skeeted on her back. She reached back and fondled her clit so she could cum too while Murda sat back and watched the show. And what a show it was as she thrashed around from a strong nut.

"Let's get a shower and go handle this business," Murda said as he stood to his impressive 6'1" height.

"Mmm... 'kay," Malice purred and rolled her pretty ass out of the bed. Her face was even prettier than her ass and heavy tits, despite her being cross-eyed in one eye. The short bob the short girl rocked framed her face like a pretty brown picture frame.

Malice and Murda hailed from the man streets of Bedford Stuyvesant, better known as Bed-Stuy, Brooklyn and also known as Do or Die Bed-Stuy. Its murderous stick-up kids put the die in *do or die.* The majority of their capers ended in murder. A few with a strong tolerance for bullets survived. A fat dope boy from the projects had survived and made back what he'd lost and plenty more. And that's why Malice and Murda were going to pay him another visit.

"Need some help with that?" Malice asked as Murda washed his genitals.

"We gone be here all night if yo do," he laughed. Most of their time was spent smoking weed and fucking. Not to mention shopping with all the free money donated to their cause. Quite a few dope boys just put them on payroll to keep from being robbed. It was some real bitch shit, but it beat getting robbed.

"I get a raincheck?" she asked, staring down at his dangling dick. It was the only one the 20-year-old had ever. She'd spent her childhood in foster homes trying to keep different dicks out of her.

Murda came into her left when she was fifteen. The foster parents she was living with at the time sold a little dope on the side to supplement their income as foster parents and one day the hungry young robber came along and kicked the door in.

The couple had refused to come off the money so he shot the wife. The husband hadn't minded since it left him alone with his money and the girl. A frustrated Murda had almost given up on the lick until the cute teen spoke up.

"Kill him and I'll show you where he keep his money and dope!" she blurted as he turned to leave.

"Alice!" the foster father shouted in disbelief. "Don't tell him shit! I'll take you shopping!"

"Where?" Murda wanted to know. They could handle their Family Drama on their own time.

"Kill him and I'll tell you!" she insisted then added, "You gotta take me with you too.

Murda shrugged and murdered the man. "Now, where?"

"You gotta take me with you," she insisted and crossed her arms over her chest.

"WHERE?" he shouted and placed the hot gun barrel on her forehead.

"WHATEVER!" she dared. Being dead would be better than the next foster home.

"Oh, okay, little girl!" Murda relented. He wasn't that old himself at eighteen, but she had a baby face.

"Say word!" she demanded. It meant something to her since her word was her bond.

"Okay. Word," he sighed and was bound to it as well. He didn't have much so his word was sacred.

Alice showed him the stash of money and dope after she packed her meager belongings. He took her to his rented room and gave her the bed. He never touched her until she turned eighteen. That's how she got the name Malice. Her pussy was that good.

Neither of them had made it far enough in school to graduate so they lived off the land. They shoplifted and boosted before moving up to armed robberies. On their first lick as a team Malice caught her first body, a man. Then her second, third as well as her first woman. Dead people can't testify.

"What?" Murda asked of the sideways smile and faraway look on her face.

"Just reminiscing," she said, snapping out of her daze. "Quit playing so we can go!"

"Me? I... Okay," Murda said shaking his head. They stepped from the shower, dried off and got dressed to kill.

****

"Remember last time we was in Birmingham?" Yolo asked as they boarded their flight. "And you wouldn't give me none!"

"Well, I'm sure you won't have that problem this time," Killa assured her. His voice was thick with lust causing her to squirm in her seat.

"Shoot we might not even make it to Birmingham," she dared.

"Probably won't," he agreed. Both waited impatiently until the plane reached cruising altitude and a tone beeped signaling that passengers could remove their seatbelts. As the tone sounded they both popped up out their seats and rushed to the bathroom.

Yolo attacked as soon as they got inside and closed the door. She slammed her mouth against his so hard that their teeth clicked. Killa reached down to lift her short skirt and got a pleasant surprise.

"Mmm...no panties, huh?" he said gripping her full ass cheeks.

"You keep me too wet for panties," she giggled. Her girlish giggle was followed closely by sultry moan when he slipped a finger inside of her.

Yolo scrambled to free his erection while he finger fucked her. It felt good but his wood would feel even better. Once his quivering dick was free from its confines she spun around and bent over the sink.

"Here...we...go," Killa said as he worked his way inside of her wetness. His knees buckled slightly when he felt her hot box surround him. He now knew what a pizza felt like inside a brick oven.

"Mmm," Yolo moaned and clamped her vagina down tight. She did it for him but it caused her to cum that much quicker. "I'm...cumming!"

"Me...too! Argh!!!" Killa grunted and let go. The text book quickie only took a couple of minutes. Then they were using the tiny sink and paper towels to clean up as best they could before exiting. They received a warm round of applause as they stepped out.

Another couple rushed in right behind them for their own quickie.

"What is this, The Mile High Club Convention?" Yolo asked as they returned to their seats.

"I guess. And you 'bout to leave a puddle on these people's plane," Killa laughed. He was sleep a minute later and would be until the landed.

Chapter 31

"How we look?" Murda asked as Malice returned from her surveillance of Fat-Boy's Brownstone. They already knew the layout of the place since it was the scene of their first robbery. Murda was sure that the dope boy now had security measures in place and he was right.

"Got cameras on the front, a bodyguard smoking a blunt on the front stoop and I saw two more in the window," she relayed. "Dude out front tried to holla when I passed by. He's our ticket in."

"Get in and let me in. Dude prob'ly in his room with that jump of he brought home," he said. They'd seen Fat-Boy come in from the club with a mixed girl. She was part black, part Spanish as well as part flesh and part plastic. Only a doctor would have put tits and ass that big on a woman her size.

"Aight, Daddy. Watch me work," Malice bragged as she flipped and twisted a butterfly knife. She then stuck it in the garter belt on her left leg under her little skirt. Her right thigh housed its twin making her legs a deadly combination.

Murda admired her shapely ass as she walked towards the Brownstone. She put a little extra in her already nasty walk since she knew he was watching. She turned and blew a kiss just before she reached dude on the stoop.

"A-yo, sup Ma? What yo' name? Damn you cute. You got a man? Come smoke one," he rambled. He threw all of his best lines out hoping to catch. Pretty much the way a fisherman casts multiple lines into the water.

"Um...nothing. Malice. Thank you. Yes. Okay," she replied in answer to all of his questions leaving him confused. Luckily she sat next to him and plucked the blunt from his fingers. She filled her cheeks with smoke then blew it out without inhaling. "You stay here?"

"Umm... Yes. No. I be... Work... My man, Fat-Boy, stay here. I'm security," he said proudly. He name dropped hoping to impress her and it seemed to work.

"You want some head?" Malice offered causing him to choke on his next toke.

"Hell yeah!" he cheered. No man has ever turned a pretty girl for head and he would not be the first.

"Well, let's go inside," she purred and reached into his lap. His instant erection jumped at her touch. "Dang! You hard already!"

"Hol' up one minute!" the flunky pleaded as he jumped to his feet. He then quickly rushed inside and was met by the other two bodyguards.

"Sup?" the larger of the two men demanded as he reached for his gun. He gripped it, but didn't pull it from behind his back.

"Yo, where Fats?' he whispered, looking around.

"Knee deep in that bitch he brought home, I assume." The other replied. "Why? What you got goin' on?"

"Bagged a dime outside. She wanna suck a nigga off. I'ma bring her in the bathroom?" he suggested hopefully.

"Bruh, you can't be brining no crack heads up in bruh shit!" the first one barked. The second one went to the window and took a peek at Malice out on the steps.

"A-yo, that ain't no crack head! Shorty bad!" he announced.

"She gon' have' to suck all of us off," the first one insisted.

"Bet!" he replied and rushed to go get her. Malice turned and smiled up at him when he came back out.

"Come on!" he demanded as he snatched her in by her hand.

"Hey now," the large guard greeted as he looked her up and down. He was so focused on her tits that it took a minute for him to look at her face. "Cockeyed too!"

"They suck the best cock!" the other one laughed. Malice cracked her pretty smile despite being hurt as well as outraged by the insult. All her life she'd been teased about her wandering eye.

"I do. Now who's first or y'all all wanna go together?" The nasty niggas contemplated the idea for a second since it was kinda gay.

"Okay. Sure. Bet." They all agreed since they were all kinda gay themselves.

"Bring 'em out, bring 'em out," she rapped and squatted. The men surrounded her and whipped out their dicks. She along with the three men all looked at the three dicks surrounding her as she went for the dual butterfly knives.

Suddenly the room exploded in extreme violence. Malice hit the two inside guards on the insides of their thighs. She ruptured their femoral arteries which would cause death in mere minutes. Only they didn't have a minute, because after slicing their arteries she popped up and twirled around slicing both of their throats to their spines.

"What the fu—," the one who had invited death into their lives began to ask, but his words along with his jugular vein were cut with one swipe.

Malice quickly rammed the other knife into his Adams apple before he could scream. She then rushed over to the door and opened it to find Murda standing there with his bag of tricks.

"What took you so long?" he quipped as he walked inside. The bloody scene brought a crooked smile to his rugged face.

"Well, there was three of them," she said in her own defense. "Let's go see what Fat-Boy into."

"Let's," he agreed and handed her a nine millimeter with a long silencer attached to it. He carried one just like it as they crept up the stairs.

The sounds and smells of sex wafted down the hall as they reached the third floor. Fat-Boy left his door open most of the time since he had security, he figured no one would make it passed them to make it up there.

Fat-Boy had earned his nickname by eating himself to over 400 lbs. Although he was severally overweight his riches afforded him plenty of pussy, but they had to ride him. And that's exactly what plastic girl was doing when they barged in. She was riding the big man so well that the two killers paused to watch.

"Si, Papi! Si, Papi!" the girl shouted as she bounced vigorously up and down on his dick. It was prelude that would conclude with her having an orgasm. Several seconds later the girl shook and shivered as she bust a good nut. People assumed she only fucked with Fat-Boy because he was caked up, yeah that much was true but he also had a long fat dick that got her off every time. Most of the caked up pretty boys she fucked couldn't fuck. However, fucking with Fat-Boy was the best of both worlds. Well, until tonight that is.

"Shit! I'm..." Fat-Boy grunted and groaned. She knew the rest and so scrambled to get him inside of her mouth. His cum tasted sweet from all the cakes, pies and cookies he ate all day. Plus swallowing it paid well. "Cumming!"

"Mmhmm," she giggled with her mouth full in between swallows.

"Bravo!" Murda clapped getting both of their attention.

"Fuck you niggas doin' in here?" Fat-Boy barked, assuming that it was his help. He leaned up and passed gas loudly when he saw Malice and Murda standing there instead pointing pistols at him. He was familiar with the sight being that it was the last thing he'd seen the last time they'd robbed him. He woke up a week later with tubes coming and going out of every hole in his body.

"I'ma bounce so y'all can handle your business," plastic girl politely offered and stood. Her fake boobs didn't even budge from the movement.

"Are those real?" Malice asked as she moved in closer. Murda kept his gun trained on Fat-Boy while she inspected them.

"Real expensive," the other woman quipped as Malice poked one with her finger. The Latino did a half turn to show off her butt implants as well. "They got a buy one get one free over on Jamaica Ave!"

"Do they have feeling?" the killer asked before firing a silent round into one of the girl's ass cheeks.

"Quit playing! Now I'ma be lopsided!" the woman protested as one cheek went flat.

"Yo, I got a buck in my closet. Take that shit and spare me! Matter of fact, I'll just start paying you every week like Santana do!" Fat-Boy pleaded.

"That sound good and all, but we got a rep to keep up," Murda replied.

"Yeah, we the new Killa and Yolo!" Malice bragged, like a groupie. The underworld revered the mythical couple that wiped out the entire Black Mob.

"Exactly! So, if we kill a nigga they gotta stay dead," he added almost making it sound reasonable. Truth be told he wouldn't mind adding another dope boy to his weekly tally. Would have too if plastic girl hadn't opened her mouth and fucked it up.

"Killa and Yolo? Please!" she laughed despite the silicone leaking down her leg. "The real Killa is seven feet tall and Yolo is a bad, green eyed bitch with an ass like Nicki and tits like Wendy Williams!"

Urban myths had made the killer couple larger than life. The new generation had no idea what they really even looked like. Either way Malice and Murda tried to pattern themselves according to what they'd heard. Everybody they dropped was a step closer to their goal to be the most notorious couple out of New York.

"I look like Yolo now?" Malice demanded after shooting the girl in her temple. She fell with a thud and didn't reply. "That's what I thought!"

"Stay dead this time," Murda demanded right before he shot Fat-Boy in his fat forehead. He and Malice then climbed onto the bed, aimed down at the dead dope boy and emptied their clips into his face and head to make sure that he compiled.

"You think we'll ever be as dope as Killa and Yolo?" Malice sighed as the lugged the money and valuables from their heist back to the car.

"We gone be doper! All we gotta do is find them, and kill 'em!"

Chapter 32

"Is everything ready? They'll be here shortly!" Mr. Trump fussed as his wife scrambled to get the house ready for their guest.

He still couldn't believe someone would give him their daughter to train. Then again those sick ass pageant parents who paraded their young daughters around in these sick ass were pretty fucked up too. Their local pageant was just a few months away but it was nothing like the national convention that was held in Vegas. Sick fucks from all over the country would converge there to exploit their kids.

"Si. Si..." she began and stopped when she realized she was speaking in Spanish—it happened whenever she got really excited. "Yes, I am ready!"

Her statement was still in the air when the doorbell began to chime. Mr. Trump gave the room one final last minute scan before he rushed to the door and pulled it open wide and smiled even wider.

"Good morning!" he greeted the lovely couple. His smile wore off when he noticed that there was no little girl next to Yolo in a tasteful dress and Killa, who looked dapper in a suit.

"Good morning. We're the Jones. Mike and Sally," Killa greeted in return as he stuck his hand out. He actually flinched at the feel of the man's cold, clammy hand. It felt like he was dead already, but not as dead as he was about to be.

"Where's the girl?" he asked looking over at the rental car they'd arrived in.

"At the hotel. I thought it would be best for us to check the place out first. You never can be too careful, you know," Yolo added.

"Si, come on in," Mrs. Trump offered. She had to nudge her husband out of the doorway so that their guest could enter. She then took Yolo be the hand to show her around while the men talked.

"So..." Killa began as they sat across from one another. Mr. Trump looked so disappointed that he had to stifle a laugh. He would've felt sorry for the man if he wasn't a sick pedophile about to be murdered. "Tell me about the program."

"Well," he began and didn't stop until he had given up all the goods on all the local organizers involved.

"Anyway, we should all do dinner. I would love to eat, eh... I mean, meet them," Killa said. "Tonight, if possible. And then we can drop our daughter off in the morning before our flight."

"Sure! Sure! I'll invite everyone over!" he agreed. He would agree to anything to get his hands on a young girl.

"Who?" Mrs. Trump asked, returning to catch the end of the statement. She put up a fuss about the last second meal as the Jones left.

"Yo! You should see the room they got set up for your daughter!" Yolo chuckled as they pulled away. "That bitch showed me little thongs and high heels! I can't wait to kill that bitch!"

"You don't have to. They invited us and all the others back to tonight for dinner!" Killa announced with glee. "They don't know it but they're gonna be the main course."

****

"I could get used to this," Sincerity heard herself say. She felt a tinge of guilt for admitting she kind of enjoyed her sons not being around. She'd had to care for herself as a child of crack head. Then she'd cared for her mother when she'd gotten sick. Then came Xavier and Rico. Sincerity had never gotten a chance to do her, and that's exactly what she was doing now laying in Sweets' arms.

"So, what's stopping you? Your man, who's with his other woman?" he dared.

His words actually caused her to flinch. Living it was one thing, but to hear it spoken out loud was even worse.

"See, I'd be wrong if I just left his as. Left him to take care of the boys while I drop in and out like he do," she said to see how it sounded. It sounded good, but could she do it. It could she really allow Yolo to win?

"So, what's stopping you?" Sweets asked as he gripped her ass. Her mouth opened to reply but he inserted his tongue. He moved down to her neck, breast and stomach. Her answer changed when he shoved her legs open and stuck his tongue inside of her hot box. He ran it in and out until she came all over it.

"Ain't nothing stopping me. Fuck Killa! Fuck Yolo! Now fuck me!" she demanded.

Sweets aimed to please so he aimed the head of his dick at her swollen lips and rammed himself deep inside. They wrapped up an hour later just as Killa and Yolo did the same.

****

"I...feel...like...like...I should give you an award. A trophy. A plaque. Something!" Yolo panted while trying to catch her breathe again. It had been stolen by a breath snatching orgasm courtesy of the spectacular back shots she'd received.

That's how you know that you beat the pussy up when a woman feels indebted to you. "How about some money? A car, maybe?"

"We straight," Killa proclaimed proudly. He knew he'd knocked it out of the park. After all, they didn't kill him Killa for nothing. "Speaking of killing shit, we gotta get ready for our dinner date."

They'd hit the hardware store earlier for party favors. They'd picked up a blow torch, hammers, plastic ties, rope hack saws and other assorted items. Now all they needed to do was shower and dress.

Yolo squeezed her vaginal muscles to keep him inside but he'd began to deflate so she ended up squeezing him out instead.

"Backfired," she laughed and rolled out of the bed. She followed Killa to the shower where they romantically washed each other. It was like they were saying *I love you* without saying a word.

"Grandma wants to help you with the wedding," Killa announced. He was getting married mainly for the benefit of Yolo, his grandmother and the kids, but he still looked forward to it.

"She does?" Yolo cheered and cheesed. It was pretty much the reaction he'd expected. It was the reason he'd set it up.

"Sure does. I think you should let her. It'll make you guys closer," he said, explaining his reason for doing it.

"I prob'ly should let her take the lead, huh?" Yolo reasoned herself. Everything except for the *I dos* were irrelevant anyway. "So, when you gon' tell Sinderella?"

"When I go to Atlanta," he informed. It was personal and therefore it had to be done in person.

Killa steeped from the shower signaling that the conversation was over. Yolo wasn't feeling him going to see his baby mama in Atlanta, but let it go—she wasn't a nag. She decided to trust in their bond and let him handle his business. After all, she was the one who was wearing his ring and carrying his next child.

The murderous duo got dressed to kill in farmer's coveralls and rain boots. Including the Trumps ten pieces of shit, child exploiters had agreed to join them for dinner. That meant five a piece. It was going to be a bloody night.

"I think I'll go with...this...this...oh and this..." Yolo sang as she selected her killing apparatus for the evening. A hardware store is always a great place to shop for weapons. Killa placed the garden shears, hatchet and chicken wire she'd chosen into a bag with the axe handle, his item of choice.

"Just like walking tall," he mused, taking practice swings with a club.

"You so sexy with some wood in yo' hand," Yolo said coyly, batting her eyes and lowering her head.

"Anyway... Let's bounce!'

****

"You guys are so lucky!" Mr. Harding gushed over the Trumps good fortune. Mr. Harding was the principal at the local elementary school, but he'd never had the opportunity to keep a child. He was left to jack off in his office while watching little girls on the security monitors.

"Not lucky," the arrogant host bragged.

"Soon our little pageant will be the best in the country! Everyone will have to come to us!"

"And I'll have to give each little girl a check-up!" Doctor Sharpe proclaimed. The perverted pediatrician had personally photographed every pubescent pelvis he'd come in contact with and peddled the pictures to other pedophiles.

"And I'll take a copy of each please and thank you!" the local Girl Scout troop leader announced. The middle age woman had a staggering collection of child porn.

"Yes! Our guests have arrived!" Mr. Trump sang as the doorbell chimed. He rushed over and snatched the door open to let death enter his home. His face wrinkled at their odd clothing. His mouth opened to ask about them, but Yolo hit him with a cattle prod that dropped him shivering and shaking.

"What's the meaning of this?" the juvenile judge in attendance boomed, like he was in his court room. He wasn't and to prove it Killa swung the ax handle to show him who was presiding over things. The crack to his kneecap sounded like a homerun hit at Yankee Stadium.

Mrs. Trump tried to make a run for it but Yolo tag her in the back with a Taser. Out came the plastic ties and soon they had a pile of pedophiles hog tied in the living room.

"I'll take her...him...this one...um..." Killa said picking out his five, like he would for a pick-up game in the park.

"Ooh! Ooh! I got a better idea!" Yolo declared, bouncing up and down with her hand raised. Killa shook his head and picked her. "Like Shyne said in her dream!"

"That was one, long, crazy ass dream!" Killa replied as she rushed from the room. He turned to the confused condemned to relay to them what was going on. "Our daughter had this dream where... Well, y'all nasty asses in trouble! Actually, y'all were already in trouble but now...yeah!"

Yolo proved him right when she returned with a gas can. A terrified hush fell over the victim's when they realized what was about to happen. They all started bitching and snitching as she began to dose them with the cold gas.

"W-w-wait! W-w-we're not the only ones!" Mr. Trump pleaded, catching Killa's attention along with a brief reprieve.

"I want all of you! Everyone associated with this little Miss America shit!" he growled.

"My computer. The password is unripen," he whimpered. Killa checked it before unplugging it and sitting it by the door.

"Okay, bye-bye," Yolo sang as she pulled a match from the matchbook. Killa stopped her just before she could strike it.

"Wait!" he intervened to their relief once again. It would be as short lived as their lives. "Why you get to light the match? We 'posed to split them.

"How we gone split 'em and burn 'em?" Yolo wondered. "Okay. Paper, rock, scissors!"

The future inhabitants of the fire watched as the duo came up with a tie after tie after tie. Killa and Yolo laughed and kept playing as if the winner would win a juice box instead of the privilege of setting them afire.

"Ah ha!" Killa cheered when his paper finally covered her rock. "I win! I win!"

"You win," Yolo pouted and hung her head. It always worked for Shyne so she tried her luck. Come to find out Killa was a sucker for a pouty mouth.

"Oh okay, you..." was all he could get out before Yolo struck the match and tossed it on the pile of shit.

Chapter 33

When Killa and Yolo arrived back in New York she took the car out to The Island while he took the train into the city. Every New Yorker who moved away has to ride the train to re-charge and reconnect when they came back home. Fond memories played in his head during the long ride from Queens to The Bronx.

He recalled first fights on the A train, a knife fight on the 4. A shoot out on the D train and getting some head the 5. His body was on autopilot as he absent mindedly made the transfers and connectors all the way uptown. He snapped out of it when he got off at Yankee Stadium. Back in the day he and his crew would hike up the hill but that was many murders ago. Today he stuck his hand up and hailed a gypsy cab.

"A Hunned and sixty-six and Ogden," he announced in reply to the driver's raised eyebrows asking him where to.

"Five bucks," he said putting the car in gear but not moving. Killa understood and slid a five and a one into the slot. He had jumped out of enough cabs in his youth to know what it took to get moving.

Killa got out on 166 and cut over to the projects. He made it a point to cut through the courtyard so he could catch up with Little Villain. As expected he was on his bench hugged up with a project cutie.

"A-yo, Ma. Give me a minute with my mans," he said when he peeped Killa coming. He was too far away to see his face but his swag was undeniable. "I'll be up in a minute."

"Psss," the girl sucked her teeth and got up. She put on a dazzling display as she walked away to ensure that he would indeed be up in a minute.

"Sup, Unc!" Villain greeted and stood for his mentor. This is the same dude who refused to stand for the judge in court—his refusal had cost him thirty days on Rikers Island, but so be it. Killa was far more important than any judge.

"Chillin', Nephew," he replied accepting the pound and hug. They both took a seat back on the bench as Killa asked, "What I miss?"

"Your kids wildin' out," he laughed. "Playin' and fightin', fightin' and playin'. Kid shit."

"'Round here it is," he sighed. It was good for his offspring to see this side of life. Now it was time to take them home to the other side. "I'll holla."

The men stood and exchanged another pound and hug before going in different direction towards different goals. Villain was headed towards for some good, down home project pussy while the family man was headed to see his family.

"Daddy!" came the shouts of his four kids when he walked through the door. The boys fell back and let the bully go first.

"Sup, baby?" he asked as Shyne jumped into his arms. He inspected her and her brothers for any damage. They all had their share of bumps and bruises from growing up, but ain't nothing wrong with that.

"Them kids!" Grandma Diedra announced, with her fronting ass. *Them kids* as she called them were her entire world. She had more fun than they did fussing cooking and running behind them. The daughter-less mother especially doted over Shyne.

"I already know," he said knowingly. "Time to go home you two. You two are going back to Atlanta tomorrow."

"Awe!!!" the four groaned as one. It was music to his ears to hear them getting along so famously.

"Have you spoken to S-i-n-c-e-r-i-t-y?" Grandma Diedra spelled out as if the kids couldn't spell. They all twisted their faces up as if she were crazy.

"N-o, but I will," he replied. It took a little doing to separate the twins from their grandmother and brother, but once the car service arrived he pushed the issue and pushed them out the door.

****

"Pssst!" Sincerity fussed as the ringtone of her ringing phone announced Killa's call. She rolled out the bed and stepped out into the hall to take the call. "What?"

"I'm on the way down. I got X and Rico with me. You do remember them don't you?" Killa said sarcastically. "So, you might want to clean up the house."

"I... Fuck you!" she hissed seeing he'd hung up. She had fallen out of love but was too proud to admit it. She now only wanted Killa so Yolo couldn't have him.

"Sup?" Sweets asked when she returned. He could tell by the look on her face that something was on her mind.

"You gotta bounce," she announced and tossed his pants on the bed.

"Your man, must be on the way," he chided as he climbed out of the bed. Her eyes shot down to his dick, making her wonder if there was time for a quick hayride. She shook her head no not knowing where he'd called from.

"Yeah, with my kids," Sincerity said feeling the need to explain. When a woman feels the need to explain she is your woman.

"Aight," he said and got dressed. He left without a goodbye or a goodbye kiss.

Sincerity grabbed the vinegar and water and ran a hot bath. She wanted to get right in case he wanted to get some. Her attitude may have been *fuck Killa,* but she would still fuck Killa.

Killa had called from New York so it was several hours before he made it home with their sons. The boys were in their feelings about having to leave Sun, Shyne, and their Grandma behind in the projects but perked up when they reached their own house. They were eager to see their mom again.

"Sup, Ma," Xavier greeted like a teenager does once they pass the mommy stage. Not Rico though, he rushed his mom and slammed into her.

"Awe, I missed you too," Sincerity sang with mixed emotions. She had missed him, them, but could live without it. She was pretty much a single mom considering that Killa only popped in and out of their home.

She chided herself for becoming a side chick to her own man. She couldn't quite place when the love was lost but knew that it was gone. She'd spent the last week smoking weed, drinking, fucking and sucking. Now it was back to...

"I'm hungry," Rico stated like he was starving to death.

"Me too. You gon' make dinner?" X asked like he was her man while the one who was supposed to be her man looked around the house.

"Lost something, yo?" she snapped since he still hadn't spoken.

"Actually, I did but..." he replied. He knew they'd lost what they'd had, but if it had been meant to be it would have been. "You guys go play until dinner."

"Y'all must gotta take," Rico nodded getting a dirty look from both his mom and dad. "Um... Okay. We'll go play until dinner."

"Good idea," Sincerity added. They watched their kids depart until they were out of sight. Then they engaged in an awkward silenced until she finally spoke up. "So..."

"Yep," Killa agreed and nodded. "I guess I better come right out and say it. Don't want you to have to hear it somewhere else..."

"Don't tell me...she...pregnant," Sincerity said twisting her lips and shaking her head.

"Well, yeah, but that's not it. We um... I um... We'regettingmarried," he blurted making it sound like one word.

Another awkward silence followed and again it was her who broke it. "I see," she said, like women do. It can be all sorts of shit running through their heads yet the only thing that comes out of their mouth is *I see*. That's some scary shit right there.

"Things have changed. We..." he began but was cut off by her hand.

"No need to explain," she said raising a hand to cut him off. "Like you said, things have changed."

"Yeah, It ain't *sweet* like it used to be," he quipped enjoying her flinch upon hearing her lover's name. She glared at him to see if he knew but couldn't tell. "Remember how *sweet* it used to be?"

"Un huh," she replied busying herself with cooking a meal.

"Well, I'll be in town for a few days, so I'll be back. Is that *sweet* with you?"

"Un huh," she repeated without looking up until she heard the door close behind him.

Chapter 34

"Sup yo. Good timing," Yolo greeted when she took Killa's call.

"Why?" he wondered and looked at his watch to jar his memory.

"Cuz, I was just about to play in my pussy," she moaned, signaling that she had already began.

"Then we need to make this a video call!" he insisted and hung up. He pulled up his app so he could get some face time with his pussy.

Yolo answered the video call and then propped her phone between her legs. Killa wanted to clap when she ran her wet finger in and out of her slippery box. A minute later it was squishing loudly as juice ran form it. Another minute and she came all over her fingers.

"Wish you were here," she moaned. "When you coming back?"

"Couple of days. I gotta see a man about a mule," he replied. "Talk to you tomorrow."

****

The man Killa had to see was Conrad Winston the Third. The mule was the toddler he'd left in his car to die. Police called it murder since he had been researching how long it took for a baby to die in a hot car. On top of that, several of his young girlfriends had reported how much he wanted to leave his wife and kid.

Prosecutors determined it would have been a lot cheaper to divorce his wife minus a child so, he minused his child. Left him in the back of his SUV at his office and went inside to work. The little boy's body had baked and his brains boiled in the intense heat.

Conrad came from a wealthy family and was able to hire the best lawyer in town. The slimy lawyer was so good he made it seem as if it was the child's fault that he was dead. His client was acquitted and Norman Deal had another feather to add to his cap. That's why he was going to get fucked up too, right after his client.

It took a couple of days of surveillance of his targets for Killa to lock in their routine. The client loved the happy endings provided by Miss Kim and her girls at the local massage parlor while the lawyer, on the other hand, had a penchant for black pussy so he frequented the various hoe strolls the city had to offer.

Killa now knew enough about their lives to end their lives.

The boys enjoyed their dad being in town even if their mom didn't. Sincerity loved and hated him at the same time and she hated it. What she hated most was his constant use of the word *sweet* whenever he came over. That and the fact the he wouldn't touch her. She would have let him but he never did.

****

"Sup, yo," Yolo giggled when Killa took her call. She was silly in general but even more so now in particular.

"What did you do?" Killa demanded. Knowing her, the mirth in her voice could mean anything.

"Oh nothing. Where are you?" she inquired. "Not in your room."

"No, actually I'm at the Happy Ending Massage Parlor in Gwinnett," he replied expecting some grief.

"Okay. Have fun. Call me when you get back to your room," she sang happily and clicked off.

Now, he really knew she was up to something, but now was not the time to ponder about it. No, now was the time to give ol' Conrad his happy ending. He wouldn't be too happy about it but Killa sure would.

"Qisas," Killa recited the Arabic word for just recompense. The unique thing about the word is that it could be good or it could be bad. Either way it was exactly what one had earned. In Conrad's case it would be bad, very bad. Killa leaned back as Conrad pulled into the parking lot. He had that *I'm gonna get some head* smirk on his pudgy face. He made a whole other face when Killa shoved a gun in his face when he got out.

"Don't shoot! Take the car! Take my wal—yeah my wallet!" he agreed when he remembered that his credit card was on file inside the massage parlor. He may be about to get car jacked but he was still getting his dick sucked. After all, the show must go on.

"Get back in your car and do exactly what I say. Do you understand?" Killa asked in a slow and deliberate tone to make sure that he did. Conrad nodded his fat face up and down.

He got back behind the wheel and Killa slid in behind him. He followed his turn by turn directions like Killa was a human GPS. Eventually they pulled into an auto body repair shop on the south side of town. Conrad let out a sigh at the thought of his vehicle being chopped up inside the shop. He loved his vehicle, which is why he'd kept it even after using it to kill his child.

"In there," Killa said pointing to the paint booth with his pistol. Conrad compiled and pulled in. "Shut it off."

"What kind of car thief are you?" Conrad fussed. He was losing his reserved space in Yung Ho Fat's mouth. Space was limited already now it would take extra to squeeze in.

"Not a very good one since you get to keep your car," Killa replied as he cuffed the man's hands to his steering wheel. He took his keys and walked over to the control booth.

Auto Paint booths are essentially large ovens. The extreme temperatures actually baked the paint onto the cars. Or in this case baked a deadbeat dad to death just like he'd done his child. Qisas.

"Wait! Where are you going? What about me? It's getting hot in here!"

"So take off all your clothes..." Killa sang and laughed. Of course Conrad couldn't since he was strapped in the hot car just like his son had been. Now he would die a miserable painful death just like his son had. Qisas indeed.

****

"Welcome back, Mister Jackson!" the desk clerk cheered when Killa returned to his hotel. She blushed and fawned like he was a rock star. He kinda was so he was used to it.

"Sup," along with a head nod was all the cute girl got out of him. Not too long ago she woulda got the dick, the whole dick and nothing but the dick but now he was engaged to be married. Engaged to a lovely little lunatic who was at home with their children, or so he thought.

"Daddy!" Shyne cheered as she rushed her father when he entered his room.

"Sup, Pops," Sun greeted since he was now too cool to jump into his father arms like he had just two weeks ago. Killa laughed and gave him a pound and a hug. Yolo sat back in a chair with a devious smile upon her face.

"Knew you was up to something," he told her.

"Mommy said you have her medicine and she can't live without it!" Shyne explained urgently. "She gotta take a shot?"

"Oh, she gon' get her medicine, alright. Tonight," he assured them. "Back shots."

"Plus, since their birthday is next week, I figured it would be nice to have a family vacation. The kids would love to go to the Aquarium. Right kids?" Yolo prodded.

"No, you said...," Sun began but got cut off by a stern look from his mother. "I mean, Yes. The Aquarium."

"Okay, but we're going to need..."

"A bigger room," Yolo finished. "I rented a suit upstairs. Let's feed the kids so I can get my medicine."

Chapter 35

Killa gave Yolo her medicine all night long. Not just back shots, but side shots and orally as well. Obviously it worked well because she was still slobbering and snoring when awoke the next morning. She was sleeping so well that he hated to wake her, so he took the twins to breakfast, leaving her behind.

"Mommy not feel well?" Shyne asked as they drove away from the hotel.

"Mommy is feeling great!" he replied triumphantly.

"I heard her praying last night," Sun added. "She kept shouting *Oh God* over and over and over!"

"Well, yeah," Killa laughed. "Anyway, you guys want some waffles?"

"Okay, but no bacon. I'm Muslim and I don't eat pork," Shyne huffed indignantly. Father and son looked at her and twisted their lips.

"So, why didn't Asad come down with you guys?" Killa asked. Both he and Yolo were amused by her dream of them being married with eight kids. That part he wouldn't mind at all coming true, but they would not grow up to be killers. No, he and Yolo could and would handle the family's business.

"Cuz mommy's a hater," Shyne spat, crossing her arms over the little nubs on her chest. No one could disagree so the car moved on in silence.

****

"Why didn't you wake me up?" Yolo pouted when her family returned. Waking up and finding the suit empty had cast her back to her lonely childhood, where she'd had no siblings or friends. Actually, she'd a friend, but fucked that up when she killed her.

"You looked like you needs some rest," Killa replied handing her, her take out plate. She couldn't protest any further once her mouth was full of food. "I have some business to handle later. I'll um..."

"Boy, stop. You know I'm coming with," Yolo cut in. Killa fixed his face to pretend like he didn't know what she was talking about but she shut that down. "Uh oh, better get Maaco!"

"Aight yo. I'll hit my homie Ra and see if he and Dre can babysit while we take out some trash."

****

And trash was exactly what Attorney Norman Deal was. After getting Conrad off for killing his kid he then helped a rapist beat a rape charge. He used pictures from the victim's social media accounts to portray her as a slut. Have him tell it sluts can't be raped since they give it away for free. The client got off but now he was about to get offed.

"So, our little friend loves putting his little pink meat into sweet black pussy," Yolo nodded as she reviewed Killa's notes on the lawyer. Despite having a wife and family at home he still frequented the hood in search of hoods. "This cat is about to get caught in a rat trap!"

Norman was a creature of habit and his main habit was an after work blow job before going home. Getting his dick sucked relaxed him and allowed him to overlook whatever stress awaited him at home. Makes sense, but also made it easier for the killers to kill him.

"Where are all my hoes at?" Norman said in a mock pimp's voice. Actually, he sounded like pasty white man trying to sound like a pimp. Let's count that as strike number one for the night. Mind you, you only get three.

There were no hoes out on any of the hoe strolls or hotels that littered the street because Killa had chased them off. Posing as a cop wouldn't work since they sucked more cop cock than the law allowed, so instead he'd said he was from the health department and the hoes had scattered like hoes do when someone from the health department comes around. Think roaches when the light comes on.

Yolo looked super sexy in a halter top with a pair of teeny tiny shorts. Her stomach had a slight roundness to it due to the child taking form inside of it, but it still looked better than the tore up whores who slung pussy and tonsils around here.

"Damn shame," Yolo mused to herself when three cars collided trying to get over to her. She turned down five more *dates* as both the tricks and treats call them, before Norman pulled in. "Date?"

"Hell yes! Hop in!" he insisted. Once he saw how cleaned and pretty she was he decided to take a trip around the world. Yolo had the same thing on her mind.

"I got a room. I...," she suggested causing him to roll up the windows, park the car, get out and lock it before she could finish her statement.

"Let's go!" he cheered and lagged behind to see her behind. Yolo switched for him as a going away gift.

"You ever had some rat-trap head?" Yolo asked, making it sound sexy and exotic instead of excruciating and painful.

"I... Um... No, I can't say that I have. How much extra is it?"

"For you...it's free. You deserve it," she said swiping her key card. How this man didn't take off running after hearing that is a mystery. He'd never done anything good to deserve anything good and definitely not for fee, so he should have known that it was bad. Real bad.

Once they were inside she pointed to the bed and demanded, "Strip!"

"Clark...Kent...has...nothing...on me!" he bragged as he came out of his clothes. From the way he stood proudly displaying it he obviously thought tiny pink dicks were the shit.

"Lay on your back and give me your hands," she ordered so she could secure them with plastic ties to the bed. He opened his mouth to protest until she reminded, "Rat-trap head."

"Oh yeah. Okay," he agreed and compiled. The next time his mouth opened she stuffed one of his expensive socks inside.

SA'ID SALAAM

"To muffle the screams," she answered the question on his face. It asked another when Killa came out of the bathroom.

"Don't mind me. I'm just here to observe," Killa said raising his hands in surrender. Both men turned to Yolo as she pulled the heavy rat trap arm back. The tiny erection shrunk into a baby shrimp.

"NO MEANS NO, Mr. Deal, and SPOILED KIDS DON'T DESERVE A SLOW DEATH IN A HOT CAR," Yolo laid out as she inched the trap towards his inch of dick. He tried to plead his case but the sock in his mouth saved Yolo from hearing his feeble excuses. It also saved her from hearing the opera high note he hit when the trap clamped shout on his balls and dick.

"Ouch," Killa winced in sympathy for his genitals, not him, as Norman thrashed, bucked and moaned in pain. He was calling them all kinds of Niggers from beneath his gag. They paid him no mind as they dug in their bag of tricks.

"Uh-oh," he surmised when they made their selections. He'd accepted that his life was over, but the heavy duty sling shots were just pain disrespectful.

"Couldn't find any stones, so we're going to use marbles. I hope that's okay?" Yolo leaned in and asked. She couldn't make out his muffled reply so she took it as a yes. "Okay. Bye-bye."

"So long!" Killa added before they took turns stoning the adulterer to death with marbles.

****

"I'm going to pick up X and Rico," Killa stated in a tone that Yolo knew not to protest.

"Want me to ride with you?" she offered sweetly, but Killa saw right through it. She wanted to find out where Sincerity lived so she could kill her.

"No, but you can go to the airport and pick up Asad. His flight lands in an hour," he replied. "He's family too."

"I know. I know. I'm just not ready to see my babies growing up. That dream Shyne had was crazy! All them damn babies!" Yolo said, shaking her head. "It wish Christi could have made it."

"She did. She'll be here in a few," Killa said proudly. The look of love in her eyes was as good as a coochie coupon. He gave her a nod and walked out of their suite.

"You sir, have earned a double coochie coupon," she told his back as he departed.

"What's that?" a nosey Shyne asked, scrunching her face up. She went to public school so she knew what a coochie was, but what did it have to do with a coupon is what she wondered.

"None ya," Yolo quipped. The child needed no explanation for that or deez. Both she'd learned the hard way from her mom. "Sun, can you behave long enough for me and your sister to run an errand?"

"Yes," he said a little too quickly for her taste. It really was a complex question which should have required more though on his part.

"By behave I mean, no damage, no fire, no EMS, PD, FBI, DEA, ATF, um..."

"Oh," he replied and twisted his lips in thought just like his dear old dad does. "I should be able to behave, for a couple of hours."

"Where are we going?" Shyne fussed with a hand where her hip would one day be.

"Does it matter? No! So come on," Yolo fussed back. Sometimes Sassy Shyne forgets who she got her sass form. You can't out sass the master.

****

"Y'all father here," Sincerity hissed when she saw a car pulling up in the driveway. Her heart grew colder towards him by the second. Now she just wished he would go home so she could spend time with Sweets.

"We know," Xavier said since Killa had texted him to come outside.

"Yessss!" Rico cheered and pumped his fist. He wasn't sure what to be excited most about. Seeing his dad, his siblings or the aquarium. It was all good either way.

As much as Sin didn't want to see him it irked her that he didn't come inside. Not to be so easily dismissed she tugged her shorts up into her crotch and stormed out to his car.

"Oh my!" Killa mumbled to himself when he saw the print of her pussy in the polka dot shorts. It grew larger and larger as she got closer and closer until it was right in his face.

"Up here!" she demanded, stealing his attention form the marvelous mound between her legs.

"Sup yo?" he replied. Her face was just as pretty as the plump print which is why he'd stayed outside.

"How long you gonna keep them? I got shit to do!" she fussed folding her arms over her heavy breast.

"I'ma keep them overnight. Have a sweet time," he said sarcastically. Luckily the boys piled in the car preventing a shouting match. Sincerity made sure to sling her ass from side to side as she marched back into the house. Killa watched it like a hypnotist's swaying watch.

"Dad? Earth to Dad," Xavier laughed.

Sincerity called Sweets and told him to come over the moment she got back inside.

Chapter 36

"I bet it's Christi!" Shyne insisted as she and her mother ventured into the airport. It was a good bet since she knew there was no way in the heaven above or on the earth that their big sister would miss their birthday. Turning ten is a big deal when you're nine.

"How much?" Yolo dared, extending a pinky to make it official.

"Then again," Shyne conceded. Her mom was a little too cocky for comfort. She would just have to wait and see.

The mother and daughter reached the gate just as the flight began to unload. Minors flying alone are first to board and fist to get off. Yolo watched her daughter closely to see her reaction. She was not pleased to see her go from sassy to groupie mode in a blink of an eye.

"ASAD!" Shyne screamed, like he was one of the Beatles and took off. She only made it three steps before skidding to a stop. She did a 360 and ran to hug her mother. "Thank you, Mommy!"

"Um... You're welcome," Yolo said instead of saying *don't thank me, thank your father!* Now it wasn't as bad when her daughter hugged the boy.

Asad was delighted to see his fiancé/bestfriend. He cheesed widely during their brief hug. He was still shy and reserved so he broke the hug off soon after it started.

"As salaamu alaykum," he greeted through his smile, like ventriloquist.

"Wa... Alaykum... As Salaam," Shyne greeted happily. Even yolo had to admit how cute they were. She had to respect that he didn't want Shyne to be his girlfriend, side chick or baby mama. He wanted her to be his wife.

As Salaamu...," Asad said to Yolo, but was cut off.

"Yeah, yeah. Come on," she fussed. She still had to give him a hard time.

****

"Well, hello there, Miss Shyne," Christi called when they returned to the suite. Once again Shyne lost it when she saw her big sister.

"Christi!" she cheered and tackled her. "I knew you were coming!"

"You know I wouldn't miss you guys birthday for nothing in the world!" she replied.

The twin's birthday was the following day but the family celebrated being a family. They headed over to the Dave and Busters for dinner and games.

Sincerity and Sweets were doing pretty much the same thing at her house. Isn't that what 69 is after all? Dinner and games.

Sweets twirled his tongue around Sincerity's swollen clit while she swallowed as much of his dick as she could. She took a quick pause to cum then went back to work until he did. They both swallowed and then changed positions. Sweets beat it up from the back until she came once more before flipping her on her side and doing it all over again. Then he put her back on her back, legs on his shoulders until he got the same result again.

"Okay! Okay! Let me ride it," she panted, not sure if she could survive another orgasm.

"All aboard!" Sweets said taking position on his back. He gripped his dick and held it straight up, offering her a seat. She took it and rode off into the sunset. Sunrise actually since she rode all night.

****

"What the..." Christi wanted to know when she saw a white man palm a little girl's booty under the guise of helping her on one of the games, but he had clearly copped a feel.

"My daughter," he chuckled as if that explained it.

"Un huh," she replied and stormed off to find Yolo. She found her and Killa engaged in a competitive match of hoops.

"Take that! Take that!" Killa gloated as he pulled ahead. Suddenly with ten seconds left Yolo launched her come back.

"Ungh! Ungh! Ungh! Yes!" she cheered and bounced as she claimed victory.

"Rematch!" Killa insisted and swiped the card. He got no reaction and swiped it again. "Now I know we didn't run through a hundred dollars already?"

"We need more money!" his four kids demanded since they too had ran through the hundred dollars he'd put on each of their cards.

"Oh, come on!" he fussed and took them to reload their cards.

"Yolo, this man just felt this little girl's booty! He claimed he's her father, that makes it worse if you ask me," Christi spat and frowned from the nasty taste of what she'd witnessed. "I should call the police!"

"Nah. Just show him to me," Yolo said and took off. She was heading in the wrong direction until Christi pulled her towards the right one.

"There he is! And... It was her, with the blonde hair," she said pointing them out. Yolo glared at the man, watching his every move. Child molestation was a capital offense punishable by death in her book. After being a victim she'd vowed to kill everyone she could.

David Morton's eyes played pinball bouncing off all the children's booties as they played. He didn't seem to discriminate between boys or girls, black or white. He was already in trouble, but when Yolo followed his eyes to her daughter's backside he earned a closed casket. She was about to save his family fifteen percent on cremation.

"Distract him for a minute so I can talk to the girl," Yolo demanded. Christi stared back skeptically but complied. As soon as she had his attention Yolo made her move.

"Excuse me sweetheart," Yolo sang. The little girl flashed a bright smile and blinked her big, blue eyes. "You just won a hundred dollar game card. Just write your name and address on this paper."

"Gee, thanks!" she swooned and jotted it down. She quickly traded it for the game card and rushed off to use it.

"Kids give up the info so easy," she laughed to herself just as Rico rushed by. She shrugged her shoulders and tried her luck. "Rico, write your address under hers."

Rico scrunched his face up at what he thought was an odd request. He assumed she already knew it so quickly jotted it down so he could back to playing. He took off just as Killa came over.

"What are you up to?" he asked, seeing the mischievous smile spread across her face.

"A child molester," she sang happily. Feeling his own daughter up in public. "Look at him now!"

"GRRR!!!" Killa growled when she pointed him out. His hand was shoved deep in his pocket so he could pull on his pecker while watching the children at play. "I'm going to follow him home and burn it down!"

"I saw him first! He's mine!" she protested. "Once we put the kids to bed I'm going to murder Mr. Morton."

"Aight, but I do believe I have a coupon," he whined.

"And you can cash it in as soon as we get back! Then, I'll go see about our friend there.

****

"Okay, boys in one room, girls in the next. Me and Mommy will just get another room," Kill announced when they all returned to the hotel. He'd already gotten a room so it wasn't a problem.

"Just like my dream!" Shyne recalled of the separate condos they had in Atlanta. "Except for you, Mommy, you were dead."

"Tell me more about his dream," Christi requested and got an earful. The girl talked her all the way through the lobby, up the elevator, down the hall and into bed.

Meanwhile, in the other room it was, "Fuck me, Killa! Fuck me, Killa!"

"Whew! No we...," Killa exclaimed and paused to yawn. "Need to go see..."

"I know, Bae. Sleep tight," Yolo chuckled as he began to snore. She started to jump in the shower to wash the sex away but changed her mind. Murder always made her horny so she planned to wake him up when she got in.

Yolo quietly crept around the room and got dressed. She had Sincerity's address so she lifted Killa's keys to let herself in. "Thank you, Baby," she whispered and slipped out of the room.

A coin toss decided who she'd murder first. As bad as she wanted it to be Sincerity the toss came up tails for the booty grabber. It would have to be business before pleasure so she input his address into the GPS. She followed the turn by turn directions until she turned into the driveway.

"I ain't got time to play with you Mr. Morton," she said as she screwed the silencer on the pistol. She marched up to the door and prepared to pick the lock. The number one rule in lock picking was to check to see if it was actually locked first. It wasn't and so she slipped inside.

Yolo lifted her gun eye prepared to murder anything moving. A cat moved and got murdered on the spot. She then paused to listen for anyone or anything else. The silence gave her the green light so she crept forward. She assumed from the design of the ranch style home that the last room was the master. The door was ajar so she peeped in for a peep.

"GRRR!!!" she growled seeing the little girl in the bed. Not only was she in her father's bed, but she was wearing a custom made nightgown.

Mrs. Morton had died a year ago and Mr. Morton had forced her duties upon the child. Not only did the girl have to cook and cleans she had to perform her deceased mother's wifely duties as well.

"Son of a bitch," Yolo muttered as she crept over and picked the girl up. The poor child was so tired that she didn't even stir when she carried her into her own room. "Now, it's time to catch a predator."

"Hey," Mr. Morton fussed when he felt water splash on his face. He popped up and got popped with a pistol. "Owww!! Who are you?"

"Miss Jackson, soon to be Mrs. Forrest. I'm form the Child Protection Agency. Well, not really, I just made that up, but I'm still here to protect a child," she rambled.

"Where's my wi— daughter?" he fussed searching his bed and then the room. "Is she safe?"

"She is now!" Yolo replied and sent a slug into his open mouth. His brains looked like watermelon as they flew out the back of his head. Ther3e were thirteen rounds left so she tugged on the trigger until it clicked empty. It'd be a closed casket, just like he deserved.

"Next!"

Yolo stopped back in the girl's room and took one of her tiny thong outfits. She smiled at the name and number on the label. It was good for business but bad for the tailor. Her last act was to call 9-1-1. She couldn't allow the child to wake up and find the body on her own.

"9-1-1, what's your emergency?" a clerk asked as dryly as possible so that the caller would know she didn't give a fuck.

"Some man came into my house and shot my daddy," Yolo said in her Shyne voice. She didn't have time for the twenty questions to come so hung up. They had the address from the system so she took off.

****

"Eh," Yolo said of Sincerity's house as she pulled to a silent stop in front of it. It was actually a pretty nice house, but she would never admit it. She grabbed her gun to kill and phone to take pictures since she was pretty sue Killa wouldn't let her hang Sincerity's head on the wall like a deer. Pictures would be the next best thing.

She took the house key off the rest of the key chain and eased out. Security cameras captured her approach but no one was watching. The couple inside were in a deep cum coma from hours of sexing. Sweets was ass naked stretched out on Killa's bed. Sincerity was slobbering on his chest while snoring softly.

"Oh my!" Yolo gasped softly when she snuck into the bedroom. She raised the gun to finish her but realized she was already finished. Instead she raised the phone and shot her, him and then them. Then she videotaped the couple in bed together. She smiled broadly at Sincerity and whispered, "Thank you."

Yolo returned to the hotel and slipped back inside of the room. She slipped her SD card into Killa's phone then slipped inside the bed. Now all she had to was wait.

Chapter 37

Murda had an extra pep in his step as he ditty bopped through Prospect Park. It was a beautiful Brooklyn day and he had a bad bitch by his side.

Malice was killing shit in her high heels and short skirt with the high hem that threatened to show off that pretty, black ass of hers at any moment. She'd topped it with a crispy white wife beater that allowed her braless nipples to poke through like a pair of jet black eyes. And all eyes were on her as her heels click clacked across the pavement.

"Yo, Murda! Sup, Malice," Men, women and teens greeted as they traipsed through. Their popularity grew right along with their murderous rep.

"Sup. Peace. What's happening?" Murda replied proudly. He was impressed with himself but the person he wanted most to impress sat ahead engaged in a game of chess. "Wait here, baby."

"Okay, Daddy," Malice said and took a seat. She smiled back at all the smiles pointed at her as she watched her man walk over to the chess game.

The older man had been toying with his opponent until he saw Murda making his way towards them. He slid a night, pushed a pawn and slid his queen. "Check mate. Let me talk to this youngin' for a minute," he told his friend.

"Got damn it!" he exclaimed at the sudden check mate. He'd thought he had him this time, after twenty years of losing.

"Marvin," the man said by way of greeting when Murda sat down and began setting the board back up.

"Murda," he corrected, but with an air of respect. "You must not watch the news, old man."

"Something told me that was you. I guess you had your ol' cock-eyed girlfriend with you," he replied of the quadruple homicide over on Flatbush. (A dope dealing daddy lost his two children trying to hold out on his stash. They usually try to hold on to it, but they also usually give it up when you threaten their children. Not Papi though. He held out even after Malice had shoved a pistol down his toddler's throat. He held out even after she'd pulled the trigger painting the wall brain matter pink. Didn't give it up after she murdered his infant and wife either. Murda finally got tired of playing with him and murdered him. The duo then searched the house and found ten kilos and a hundred grand. The murders made the news alright but you never know who watches the news.)

"Of course. She's the Yolo to my Killa," he nodded and pushed a pawn. The man knew that opening move and quickly countered it.

"Yolo, Killa," he chuckled. "I don't know much about her, but him! He's the second most dangerous man that ever came out of Highbridge. His uncle was the first. You couldn't shine they shoes!"

"Highbridge in The Bronx?" was all Murda heard. He was getting tired of getting dissed every time he invoked Killa's name. There were five kids on the court proclaiming to be the next LeBron, and no one was shooting any of them down. "Check."

"Nice move," he replied without answering the question, but answering the check. Murda knew the man well enough to take it as a yes.

"Check," he repeated and moved his horse. "One day the city gon' know my name. Kids gon' pretend to be me."

"Or not," the man replied and moved out of check. He saw it was futile and tripped his king over before Murda could check mate him.

"Here," Murda said and sat a brown paper sack on the board. The man waited for him to leave before scooping it up and putting it in his pocket.

"Thanks, son," he whispered to his back as he walked away. His own dad had never showed him any love so he didn't know how to show any to his.

"Is he ready to meet me?" Malice asked excitedly. Her smile lit up the park when she did.

"Not yet. He said you pretty though," he said leading her in the opposite direction.

****

"Why didn't you wake me?" Killa protested when he joined his family in the suite.

"You was sleeping so hard!" Yolo replied. "You must have had a long, hard night."

"Um... I'm not ten," Christi announced point at herself. The kids may not have caught the sexually charged wordplay they volleyed back and forth but she did.

"I'm ten either. You know what I'm saying?" Xavier flirted again. He had been at it since he first saw the cutie. He was relieved to find out he wasn't related to her by blood and pushed up.

"Boy, stop!" Christi dismissed once more. She actually thought it was cute but he was way too young. She still wasn't fucking and didn't have many dates— and zero second dates for not fucking and the first.

"Anyway, y'all get dressed so we can go to the aquarium now that daddy's up," Yolo announced. She and Killa retreated to their room to do the same.

"Have fun last night?" Killa asked once they reached their room.

"A ball! I wonder if it's on the news?" she said and hit the remote. She watched Killa strip to shower and though about joining him. She'd bathed already and getting in now would defeat the purpose.

"In Breaking News out of Brooklyn, New York. The bodies of the Ortiz family were found murdered in their home. Two children were brutally murdered along with their parents. Police have tentatively linked this case to several others involving children..."

"You hear this shit, yo?" Yolo fumed. Once a baby killer herself it now burned her up when the victims were children. It took having some of her own for her to see the light. She was still a lunatic though.

"Yeah, I do! We need to look into that once we get home! Well, me. It's time for you to chill so you can have a healthy baby."

"Healthy, smealthy. You go, I go," she shot back. Quietly though, so he couldn't hear her.

"I heard you," he replied, proving it wasn't quietly enough. He traipsed out naked, swinging and bouncing.

"Now see... Christi gone have to take them kids by herself if you don't get dressed," she dared.

"Round two!" he cheered and chased her around the room. She tripped on the bed like a damsel in a B movie.

The couple giggled, kissed and fondled one another until a rock hard erection grew between them. They both stared down at it like they were trying to decide what to do with it. Unfortunately, Killa's phone rang and interrupted the day. The MC Lyte ringtone told them who it was.

"Yes, Miss Shyne?" Killa answered and braced himself. His daughter was born without a filter and anything could and would fly out of her fly little mouth.

"We ready!" she huffed. Killa chuckled as he pictured her little hand on her imagery hip and her face twisted up.

"Five minutes, if that's okay with you?" he asked hopefully.

"I'll give you three now put Mommy on the phone," she insisted and quickly adjusted her attitude. See, Shyne was sassy, not crazy.

"Yes?" Yolo demanded. "Un huh. Okay. Yeas, dear," she said and hung up. "Your daughter wants a flame thrower for her birthday. I told her yes."

"Shit, she better use a can of Lysol and a lighter like we did when we were kids," he laughed. Yolo had been waiting on the chance to show him the video and this was about as good as it was going to get.

"Babe... Um...," she began, stopped, stammered and then continued. "I was by Sincerity's house last night and..."

"And what? Didn't I tell you to leave her alone? She is my kid's mom! You can't kill her..." he fussed while she pulled up the video. His mouth dropped open when he saw the naked man in his bed. "Did you?"

"No. The only thing I shot was a video and some pictures. I left them both alive. Why do I get the feeling you already knew?"

"Cuz, I did. I know everything you do, no matter where I am," he advised.

"I know and I don't mind. I ain't got shit to hide. You are the only man I've ever wanted since I was sixteen," she vowed.

"Aight, Aight with all the mushy stuff. We gon' mess around and make Shyne kick the door down!"

"Oh, speaking of kicking doors down," Yolo cheered as she dug out the seamstress' tag from the little lingerie. "A present!"

****

"Look!" Yolo said, pointing at Asad and Shyne. The rest of the boys had separated, leaving them on their own. Her parents watched as he escorted her around and protected her.

"Kids mimic what they see," Killa proclaimed. He would be honored for Asad to be his son-in-law. "Think they'll really get married?"

"Nope. I'm sure of it!" Yolo replied.

It took until nightfall for the family to take in all that the aquarium had to offer. They ended up back at David and Buster's for dinner and more games. Xavier and Rico got to spend another night with their extended family before having to return to their miserable mother.

"Why can't we just stay with you guys?" Rico wondered aloud as their father drove them home. The car was cast into silence as Killa searched for an answer.

"I'on know," he shrugged when he couldn't come up with one. "I'll talk to your mom, see what she thinks."

"Me too?" X asked sheepishly. He was old enough to know he had a different father, but Killa was the only dad he'd ever known. Being a dad trumps being a father any day. Anyone can bust a nut, what happens afterwards is what really matters.

"Why wouldn't you?" Killa dared. He'd never treated Xavier like anything other than his son. "I'll talk to your mother."

Sincerity twisted her lips when she saw Killa pull up in the driveway. To make matters worse he got out and was headed towards the house. She blew her breath on her hand to see if it smelled like semen. It did so she rushed to brush her teeth since the boys had a key. Killa did too and used it to let them all in.

"A-yo, Sin. We back!" he called up the stairs. "We had a sweet time!"

"You not funny! If you got something to say just say it!" she fussed upon her return. She didn't offer her sons a hug and they didn't mind. Sincerity had become distant and moody as of late and they were the ones who had to deal with it.

"No, nothing," he said with a sarcastic smirk that just pissed her off. "Anyway, the boys want to ask you something. Go on."

"Can we go stay with our father?" Xavier blurted out.

"First of all, your father is number twelve on the Knicks, the one you said sucks!" she spat with venom dripping from her mouth.

X slinked off in defeat and went upstairs. He was hurt more by her tone than her words. Plus number twelve did suck. Meanwhile, Rico stared up at her since she couldn't run the same thing on him.

"What? You wanna go stay with you father? Shit go 'head! I don't care!" she spat and stormed off. The confused kid looked up at his father for an explanation.

"I'on know," Killa shrugged and went up behind her. He paid too much for the house to knock down doors so he let himself in the room. His eyes shot to the unmade bed forcing a scowl onto his face.

"What?" Sincerity dared. "I know you know so why don't you just come out and say it!"

"If you know I know then why ask? It is what it is. We fell out of love," he reasoned. "I can't be mad at you for wanting more than I had to offer."

"But why her? She killed your son, or did you forget?!"

"No, I didn't, but I did forgive," he replied. Shyne wasn't the only one who'd read Yolo's diary. The details of her childhood in her own words broke his heart.

"Well, whatever! The boys want to stay with you they can! For the first time in my life I'ma do me!"

Chapter 38

"Thots for tots!" a friendly voice changed when Killa called the number on the label of the tiny thong.

"What did you say?" Killa asked with an incongruous smile on his face. He was thirty-eight hot behind what he thought he heard.

"Oh, that's my new tag line. I was going to go with tricks are for kids but settled on Thots for tots inside. Get it? Thots, tots!" he chuckled like he wasn't speaking to the most dangerous man on the planet. Any planet for that matter. Pick one, any one.

"Where are you?" he asked through clenched teeth to prevent cursed and threats from spewing from out.

"1325 Peachtree. Bring your child with you so I can measure them personally," the pedophile pleaded.

"How many people work there?" Killa needed to know. Had he said many he would have got a bomb to blow it up.

"Just me. One man show," he replied proudly.

"I'm on my way," Killa said and clicked off. Yolo was right there waiting on him when he hung up.

"Please, please, let me come! You should see the look on your face right now. Actually, it's turning me on," she admitted.

"You can come, but just as an observer," he agreed and got dressed.

"Aren't you forgetting something?" Yolo asked when he didn't go into their bag of tricks.

"I have what I need," he growled and marched out. Yolo had to practically jog to keep up with him.

She had to remind him of his speed the whole way over. Their flight left in a few hours so they had to make it quick. He found the address and skidded to a stop out front. Again Yolo had to jog to keep up as he stormed inside.

"Thots for..." were the last words the man would speak in this life. He opened the door and caught a right jab right on his chin.

"Dang!" Yolo cheered as the man's broken jaw hung to one side. The nasty uppercut that followed lifted him off his feet and deposited him on his ass.

The man raised his arms to block the blows but the blows broke them as well. The sounds of a though ass whipping reverberated around the room. Killa added a few kicks and stomps to the fray while Yolo looked around.

"Jackpot!" she cheered when she found his list of clients. They had to get it too. It was only fair. "Hurry up!"

"O...kay!" he replied while issuing two final stomps. The first one broke his neck and ended his life. The second one was just for kicks. The two made their way back to the hotel so that they could head over to the airport.

Christi was headed back to Cali while the rest of the family was headed back up north. And across town Sweets was headed south down to Sincerity's vagina since he now had it all to himself.

****

"What are we doing here?" Malice asked as they rode up the hill to the Highbridge section of The Bronx. Even coming from Bed-Stuy it was a scary place.

"On a mission," was all she got. He circled a few blocks before deciding to post up in Nelson Park. He parked and grabbed the equipment he needed for his mission. A gun, of course because this was Highbridge after all, and a bag of loose crack to feed the crackheads like pigeons, after all they were a lot alike.

Malice wore a pair of jeans so tight that the crotch clearly outlined her bald vagina while the back shaped her ass into a perfect heart. They also held her pistol behind her back like a holster.

"A-yo," Murda called out to a passing junkie. He held out a crumb of crack as she ambled over.

"Dang, you tryna get head with a bad bitch sitting next to you? Girl, you better start sucking that man dick!" she advised.

"Bitch, I take care of my man! The rock is for information!" Malice snapped.

"Information? Y'all ain't no police?" the addict added. She stuck out her hand to tell them whatever about whoever.

"You know Killa? Or Yolo? I heard they from around here," Murda prodded while pushing the product in her hand.

"Killa? Information? Nigga, I'd rather go to rehab than say shit 'bout Killa! So fuck you and you! Fuck both y'all!" she fussed and limped off.

The next few junkies had the same reaction at hearing Killa's name. This was his hood after all and so they were definitely Team Killa around here. No one had heard of Yolo so they made shit up for fee hits of crack. None of it matched so the couple were no further than they had been when they arrived.

"Yo, you know Killa?" Murda asked one last time. This time he held up the whole bag of loose rocks.

"You mean, Xavier Forrest, 1137 University Projects. Grandmother name Deidra, baby momma named Sincerity. I don't see them 'round much but her dad is Karate Joe. He up on the roof now," the junkie said pointing over towards the projects. Had she known more she would have told it too.

"Good looking," Murda said and handed over the dope. He then turned to Malice and demanded, "Let's go!"

All eyes were on the newcomers when they entered the projects. Meanwhile, there eyes were fixed on the man running around the ledge of the roof. Murda turned to cop a bag of weed while Malice went into the building. Bronx pee smells just like Brooklyn pee so she didn't flinch when she entered the pissy elevator.

"Yo, let me cop some of that loud," Murda asked a young dealer called Hot slinging on a park bench.

"Got that fruity shit," the salesman bragged. He was twelve going on thirty and had his own little operation going.

"Six for a hunned?" he asked of the twenty dollar sacks of colorful, fluffy weed.

"Nah, this shit so good I ain't gotta give no play," Hot declined. He was a street vet, but still green enough to not realize he was being stalled until Malice returned.

Karate Joe stopped on a dime when he heard the roof door open. Without lifting his blindfold he quickly ascertained the race, gender and age of the newcomer. He lifted it to get a look at the young lady.

"You must be Karate Joe," Malice stated seductively. She battled her eyes coyly, but it lost a little of its effect with one crossed.

"I am. And you are?" he flirted back and smiled. "You come for lessons?"

"My name is Alice. I'm a friend of Sincerity. Is she around?"

"She's at home," he replied skeptically. Any friend of hers would know that she now lived in Atlanta.

"Okay, well tell her I came by," she shrugged and turned to leave. "Oh, can you give her my new number?"

"Sure," he replied and drew near as she dug into her purse. When he was close enough she snatched out her pistol and fired a round into his forehead. Both Hot and Murda paused at the sound of the gunshot. This was the projects after all and gunfire was as common as the ice cream truck.

A moment later Malice came out and headed toward them.

"Ready," she smiled as he finally wrapped up the drug deal. He collected his weed and fell in step with Malice. Hot shook his head as he watched her fat ass fade from view.

"Well?" Murda wanted to know. "What he say?"

"Nothing. So, I killed him. Now, when Sincerity, who I bet is Yolo, comes to bury him we'll bury her and Killa," she explained.

"See, I knew there was more to you than your good looks," he cheered at her plan. It made perfect sense since no one around here knew anything about Yolo. If Marvin was Murda and Alice was Malice then Sincerity must be Yolo.

"Of course, I got some good as pussy too," she giggled. It was clear that she was the brains to his brawn, but she was smart enough to play dumb. A smart woman knows how to lead from the back, and let her man think he is.

Chapter 39

"I know your bitch had something to do with it! I'm gonna murder her as soon as I get up there!" Sincerity shouted when Killa took her call.

"Who, did what?" he asked calmly. Yolo was out with the kids like she was most days. She took to being a stepmom as easily as she had to being a mom.

"Killed my father! I know she's behind it!" she insisted. She had just got the news and none of the details so she filled in the blanks herself.

"I don't know what's going on, but I assure you Yolo had nothing to do with it. Matter of fact, she just took Xavier and Rico school shopping," he said. "I'll go into the city and see what..."

"No! You stay the fuck away from my father! I'm on my way up to New York right now!" she fussed.

"Aight, yo," he sighed just before she hung up. He slid his throwback shell toes on and headed out to his car. Not before calling Yolo to fill her in.

"If Shyne pick-up one more mini skirt I'm gonna choke her little ass out!" Yolo vowed when she took his call. "Gon' tell me that's what all the girls at school are wearing! Do I look like all the girls at school mother? No, I don't!"

"Yo, somebody killed Karate Joe. I don't know, so don't ask. I'm on my way into the city now to see what's poppin," he sighed heavily from grief.

"Wait for me!" she said, ready to cut the shopping trip short. Karate Joe didn't just teach her kids to defend themselves he'd taught them self-esteem and patience. There is no greater gift than patience.

****

Killa knew the flight to New York took two hours plus another four hours to get through security but he still found himself speeding to the city. He was so deep in though that his vibrating phone didn't register until he'd missed the call. Seeing that it was his grandmother he quickly called her back to hear what she'd heard.

"Oh Lord! They killed Joseph!" she spat. The anger and frustration was evident in her tone. She had known the man for fifty years and he would truly be missed. "Broad daylight. Shot down like a dog!"

"What are they saying?" he asked meaning the mean streets. Gossip about who fucked whom and who killed them floated freely in the projects, but never with the police.

"Nothing yet, but I got, I got my ear to the streets. I want you to handle this! You heard me?" she said ordering a hit. It wouldn't be the first one and he'd heard her loud and clear.

"Copy that," Killa agreed and hung up. He bust a few lefts and rights until he turned right up into the projects.

A somber mood hung over the projects when he entered the courtyard. He saw Villain giving young Hot the business and went to investigate. He liked the kid and hoped he wouldn't have to gun him down in public. He would too, right on the spot if he had something to do with the murder.

"Sup yo?" Killa asked when he pulled up on the two talking. A crowd formed so notes could be compared.

"Tell him what you told me!" Villain demanded impatiently. "Tell him!"

"Yo, Unc, some nigga came through with this broad. Bad bitch with a fat ass. That shit looked like the Hope Diamond, B. Like an apple! Like..."

"Stick to the story!" Villain urged with an open handed pop to the back of his head.

"Oh yeah!" the kid smiled like kids do. "So, dude wanted to cop some weed while the chick went into the building. Son kept talking about the weed and we heard a shot! Then the bitch came back and they bounced."

"What they look like? What was their names?" Killa asked looking around the crowd for anyone to answer.

"Dude said his name was Murda. He 'bout yo' height and color," Hot replied. "Oh! And the bitch was pretty but she had one of them eyes like Biggie."

"A lazy eye? Like she cross-eyed?" Killa asked to clarify.

"Yo, a cock-eyed bitch and some nigga was in Nelson Park asking about you!" a junkie added. "I told them to fuck themselves!"

"Me too!" the addict who'd given up the info lied. "I ain't told them shit! Un uh. No sir. Ain't say shit 'bout you and Sincerity or Karate Joe!"

Killa and Villain squinted at her and both clearly saw through her bullshit. NO, is a simple answer, all the extra proved she was lying. They looked at each other and gave a discreet nod. As soon as the session ended Villain stopped her from leaving.

"Yo, Val, you still got the two for one blow job special?" he asked quietly.

"Only on Tuesdays. That's a slow day," she explained. "I can do buy one, get one half price though."

"Sounds good," he agreed since fifteen bucks is a good deal on two blow jobs.

"Let's go over to Nelson," he suggested. There had already been enough murder in the projects for one night. Killa made small talk with the locals like a rock star after a concert. He let Villain and Val get a good lead before he followed.

When Villain suggested Nelson Ave Killa automatically knew he meant the condemn building that overlooked the park. It may have been condemned but it was still home to many families. Power was borrowed from the street lights and water carried up from the fire hydrant. The mailman even fucked with the program and picked up and delivered mail.

"Come on with it!" Val insisted from on her knees in front of Villain as Killa arrived.

"I'm good," he declined. He would rather stick his dick in the dirty water flowing in the gutter than in her mouth. The gutter was cleaner.

"What did you tell them?" Killa demanded. The junkie knew him well enough to know not to lie so came clean. "You got Joe killed?"

"Can I take one for the road?" she requested and lifted her head accepting her fate. Death would be the best sleep she'd had in years.

"Go 'head," Killa agreed. He and Villain watched as she pulled out what was left of the crack she'd received as payment. It was her forty pieced of silver. She loaded a large rock on the tip of her well used shooter.

"Give these to my comrades," she bequeathed and lit her lighter. A large orange flame danced on the top causing the crack to sizzle as she inhaled. It took almost a full minute for her to take a pull. Once her lungs were filled she gave the nod.

"Death before dishonor," Villain said as he and Killa snatched her up by her pants. They ran over to the edge of the roof and tossed her over it. It was raining crackheads in The Bronx.

"Or shortly after," Killa added as he turned away. Villain watched until she touched with a splat.

****

"Well? You get him?" Grandma wanted to know as soon as Killa walked into the apartment.

"No," he replied and went mute. Whatever happened to Karate Joe had something to do with him and he wasn't ready to reveal that part yet. No, not until whoever had done it was in the past tense.

"Why in the world would anyone kill Karate Joe?" Deidra lamented. He had no answered and so stayed quiet. They sat in silence until the throwback wall phone with the long ass cord so it could be used throughout the apartment rang.

"Hey, Baby, I'm sorry about your loss."

Killa knew that she was talking to Sincerity so stood to leave. He wasn't in the mood for her and her attitude at the moment. The fact that she hadn't called him proved that she wasn't in the mood for him either. He kissed his grandmother's check and left.

"Thank you, Miss Deidra, we just landed at JFK. We 'bout to rent a car so we'll be there shortly," Sincerity said.

"Who is we?" Deidra asked since Sincerity made sure to keep repeating it.

"Me and Sweets, my new man. So tell Xavier we'll handle the arrangements. He don't even gotta worry about it," she huffed.

"Um...," Deidra said because what was to be said. Karate Joe belonged to the whole hood but ultimately she was his family. It would be whatever she said it was. "Well, just let me know, so I can pay my respects."

"We sure will," she replied and hung up.

"I hope I don't have to put hands on your baby father," Sweets nodded like a tough guy. He didn't quite understand the smile that spread on her face.

"I sure hope so too," she sighed. She would miss him if he did. 0.00 men walked the planet Earth that had their hands on Killa. The others were in it.

****

"Give it to me! Let it go!" Yolo hissed and clamped her vagina walls so he would have no choice.

"Okay," Killa grunted and let go. If she wasn't already pregnant she would have been now. "Shit! Fuck! Shit!"

"That's right, baby," she purred and stroked his back. "Now, tell me what happened it the city?"

"Someone killed Karate Joe," he huffed trying to catch his breath after that good nut.

"What?" She demanded, shoving him out the pussy and jumping to her feet. "Who? I didn't do it! Who?"

"I don't know and I know you didn't." The GPS said she was at the mall when it happened, but he would never tell her that he'd checked.

"Whoever did it was looking for me. They asked about you and Sincerity as well."

"Me? Why... I mean... What?" She frowned in confusion. A sudden epiphany caused her to snap her fingers. "Yo, they killed Karate Joe to lure us out. That's what I was... Eh. I mean would have done."

"Lure Sincerity? No me! They know I will be at his funeral. Be careful what you wish for cuz I'll be there too!"

Chapter 40

"I need to claim a body. My dad, he was killed on University yesterday," Sincerity sighed to the morgue clerk. Dealing with it was hard enough, but saying it out loud was something else. Anger turned into grief and pushed the first tear from her eye.

"That must be Yolo. She aight but her titties ain't like Wendy," Malice spat jealously. Even in grief, after a long flight and little sleep Sincerity was still a bad bitch.

"So that must be Killa," Murda guessed as Sweets wrapped an arm around her to comfort her. "He ain't no seven feet tall."

"You gone be seven feet tall once we knock them off," Malice mused. She was right too because however killed Killa would make history. His myth would grow larger than he ever was in life.

"Let's wait outside," Murda said eagerly to take his place in history.

"Ma'am? Excuse me, Ma'am," the clerk called out again. Sincerity had drifted deep in thought and tuned the world out.

Her father was the last tie to her old life. He was dead now and her sons were safe with their father. Even hatred wouldn't allow her to second guess Killa as a dad.

"Cremate him," she blurted as soon as it crossed her mind. "I'll come back and claim his ashes."

"Are you sure?" the clerk reeled. She had seen many knee jerk reactions by stunned love ones including this one.

"Yeah, do it!" she insisted and spun on her heels. Had she been asked again she would have changed her mind.

"Babe?" Sweets called as he chased behind her. He caught up to her just as she hit the front door. He walked her to the car trying to get her to talk.

"I'm fine!" she fussed and dug in her purse for the rental car keys.

Sweets noticed Malice rushing toward them. He first noticed her breast heaving up and down and then the shotgun. He turned his head to warn Sincerity and saw Murda marching with a Mac-10. The warning got caught in his throat just as the sound of gunfire shattered the silence.

Malice's first blast of the shotgun knocked Sweets legs off below the knees. He tip over and the second shot missed him but not Sin. She let out a grunt as the blast to the chest slammed her into the rental car. The shotgun was empty so it was Murda's turn. He to up close and personal by standing directly over the couple.

Sweets went out like a real G by covering Sincerity with his own body. The .45 caliber APC rounds didn't seem to mind. They sped through his torso and into hers. Both were dead by the time he fired his final rounds into their heads. He and Malice high-fived and got ghost.

****

"Why can't we come?" Rico demanded forcefully. None of the kids took the news of their beloved Karate Joe well. Especially X and Rico who'd lost their grandfather. Shyne side-eyed her other with a snarl.

"How about because I said so!" Killa snapped. He was in a murderous mood and short-tempered.

"We are having a private ceremony for his grandkids and family because he loved you most," Yolo said softly while mean mugging Killa.

"Sorry, you guys," he admitted. Sincerity wouldn't answer her phone to tell him about funeral plans and it frustrated him. So much so he almost ignored his grandmother's call. Almost, but he relented and took it.

"You got something on your mind, little girl?" Yolo dared Shyne who was still mugging her.

"What you said in your diary," she challenged and crossed her arms.

"And I was with you the whole day, so…" Yolo shot back and waited.

"Yeah, you was," Shyne admitted. "My bad, we cool."

Yolo left her fist bump hanging and focused on her man. His face was white when he plopped into a chair and dropped his phone. Yolo picked it up and saw his grandmother's face on the screen.

"Hello? Oh my! Okay. We're on the way," she moaned and turned to the kids. "Everyone get dressed. No questions and give me your phones."

Her tone compelled all the kids to comply without complaint. They handed over their phones and put on their shoes. Yolo wanted to make sure none of them found out about the murder before Killa could deliver the news. It was his job so Yolo kept quiet.

The ride out to the city was eerily quiet. The only sounds heard were those of cars passing by and the wind. Yolo remained quiet all through Long Island and Queens. When they reached The Bronx side of the bridge she finally spoke up.

"Bae," she said clenching his hand for support and comfort. She was suddenly relieved that she wasn't to blame for the grief to come. Killa looked over at her and sighed while nodding in agreement.

"X, Rico," he said to make sure he had their attention. He reached for the radio to turn it down and realized that it wasn't on. "There's been an accident."

"My mother?" Xavier asked and braced himself for the answer. He had an empty feeling the instant his mother's sold left her body. This would explain why.

"Yes, your mom. She's gone," he replied. Oddly enough it was Shyne who lost it.

"NO!!!" she wailed on behalf of her brothers. Not only did she share their pain but the thought of losing one of her parents, or both like her dream.

"It'll be okay," Rico said pulling her close. He discarded his own grief in order to comfort his sister. Killa realized at that moment that his kids were one.

****

"My poor babies," Grandma fussed as she planted kisses all over Xavier and Rico. She hit Sun and Shyne off to just so they wouldn't feel left out. To Yolo's surprise she got a hug too. "Where's my grandson?"

"In the courtyard," Yolo replied. He stopped to chat with Villain to see if the streets were talking and what they were saying.

"What the fuck?" Killa asked in astonishment. Karate Joe and now Sincerity. It proved that Yolo was right, except they didn't wait on the funeral.

"I know right. Who got beef with Sin? Maybe the nigga she was with?" Villain guessed.

"Not if they were asking about me and Yo. Black Mob? Mafia? Who?" He could have kept guessing because it could have been anyone of the victim's family or orphans he'd left behind over the years. He could never phantom it being a case of dick riding to the highest degree. That some clown wanted to be him so bad that he would kill to take his place.

"Well, it's whatever with me dawg. I'll ride or die with you wherever on whoever."

"I already know," Killa sighed. So would Yolo, so he stood to go to her. Villain and Killa hugged it out before he went upstairs. He was relieved to see his exhausted children stretched out in the living room.

"What the hell is going on?" Deidra fussed in a hush.

"I'm not sure. Pack a bag, you're coming to The Island with us," he insisted. His foot was down so she knew she had no choice. It didn't stop her from talking shit though.

"This is just like when she..." she said pointing her head at Yolo, "was trying to kill me! Done shot my neighbor, pushed them boys off the roof..."

Yolo was embarrassed by her tirade as she stomped off down the hall. A few minutes later she returned with her bag packed, still fussing. "Then the white man tried to cut my head off..."

"Boys, Shyne," Yolo called to wake them up. Once they were all assembled Killa pulled a gun and lead the way outside. Even he was shocked at the sight that awaited in the courtyard.

"Oh my!" he said in awe. It seemed like the whole projects was outside armed with whatever weapons they had.

The goons brought out their big guns while the chicks had .380s and revolvers. There were knives, bats and even a tennis racket. Proof that the hood fucked with Killa the long way.

Chapter 41

Marvin Sr. sighed when he looked out his peephole. The rain had kept him inside and he'd hoped it would keep unwanted guest from ringing his bell. A third ring signaled that his guest wasn't leaving so he sighed again and opened the door. "Marvin."

"Murda," he corrected and barged in. He knew by now that he would not be invited in so he invited himself.

His father looked behind him for the girl, but she wasn't with him. Murda went on to the living room and helped himself to a seat. The sofa still had the thick plastic on them they'd come with when he was a toddler.

"You heard? I know you heard!" he gloated when his father arrived.

"Heard what?" he shot back. New York was a violent city. They had so many murders most didn't even make the news. Meanwhile, reality stars and dumb ass billionaires made the front page.

"Killa is dead! I killed him," he said proudly. "Him and Yolo. Gunned they asses down at the morgue. Iconic ain't it?"

"Ironic too," the dad chuckled. "Son, I don't know who you just killed, but it wasn't Killa. The bat sign would be in the sky if you had. Flags at half mass, schools closed for the day!"

"Damn, Pops, let me find out you a dick rider! Give me my props. I hunted that nigga down, found his girl, killed her pops and when they showed up to claim the body I bodied them both. Me and my girl. Murda and Malice! Fuck a Killa! Fuck a Yolo!"

"Son, that man is gonna hunt you down and make you wish you'd never been born," Senior advised truthfully.

"Like you, Pops? Wish I was never born?" Murda growled as he rose to his feet. His father glanced left and he followed his eyes to a large rusty revolver on the table. "Go for it!"

Marvin Sr. was a street dude and knew crazy when he saw it. He knew that his only shot at living any longer was to Marvin Gaye his son. He launched himself over his chair and grabbed the gun on his way to the floor. It was a lightening quick in the old man's mind, but dreadfully slow in real time.

Murda whipped his pistol out in a flash and then waited for him to finish his move. Pops popped up and raised the gun a second too slow. A flash preceded the explosion that knocked a small hole in the front of the head and a bigger one in the back.

"Since you love Killa so much, tell him I sent you," he told his father's shell. He stepped over the body like a puddle and walked out.

****

"Guess what?" Malice cheered as Murda stormed through the door. She was too excited to wait and shouted. "I'm pregnant!"

"You what?" he snapped and frowned. "Yo, we got too much to do to be slowed up by a baby. Get rid of it!"

"But I... We, I thought you said...," she stammered in confusion. He came in her daily so how could he not expect it. She did, since he refused to wear condoms.

"This ain't the time, baby," he said softening his tone. "We the new kids on the block. The new Killa and Yolo. Once we put in a little more work we gone have people beating our door down to do hits for them!"

"Okay," Malice sighed. She came around a little more with each kiss he planted on her face. She noticed small red polka dots on his face and touched one. "Is this...blood?"

"Huh?" he asked to check for himself. He looked at his father's blood on his thumb and said, "Nah. Take your clothes off."

"Mmm...nasty," she giggled and began to strip. Murda unbuckled his belt and let his heavy jeans fall to the floor.

As soon as Malice was naked he turned her around and bent her over the sofa. She moaned again as he played with her fat lips. When she came in his hand he moved up and gave her the dick.

Knowing the pussy would be out of service shortly urged him to beat it up real good. It was real good to Malice too, who coated his dick with her own creamy cum.

"Argh!" Murda grunted and bust yet another nut in the young woman. Why not since she was already pregnant.

****

"She hates me," Yolo whispered in Killa's ear as Deidra cooked dinner.

"Did she tell you she hated you?" Killa asked since he knew full well that his grandmother would. "I didn't think so. She's just out of her element and grumpy."

"Well, the kids certainly enjoy having her. I don't mind it either," she admitted.

"Good because once I find these people I may not tell her. Just keep her with us. She's too old to be alone."

"Cool. Plus, she can stay home with the kids while we handle our business. We still have the client list from Little Miss America and the twisted tailor."

"I don't know about we..." Killa said placing a hand on her belly. The baby inside kicked in response.

"Yo, one more. Please," she pleaded. "You know doctors say that pregnant women shouldn't give up their hobbies. So, I'm still gonna ride that pony backwards and kill people."

"Is that right?" Killa laughed. He wasn't sure about the first one, but definitely not to the second one. "One more and that's it until you have the baby."

The word baby sent both inside their heads. Different heads yet the same thought. How did they get here? Arch rivals now about to marry, with kids.

"Come on, Miss Yolo, so we can look at some dresses," Deidra fussed.

"Go on, before you get in trouble," Killa laughed. "I got some homework to do."

****

Killa called his contacts in every borough and found the name Murda was grossly overused. Good for all of them because he was going
to murder everyone who used the moniker. Truth be told the couple
still wasn't even on the hood's radar.

Yolo wouldn't admit to being happy that Sincerity was dead, not
even to herself when she saw the grief and confusion in her son's eyes.
She was just as eager to hunt her killers down as Killa was. After all it
was supposed to be her and her boo who'd been swiss cheesed in that
parking lot.

Since they couldn't get a lead on Murda and his cock-eyed girl to
keep themselves busy they crossed off a few names from the tailor's
client list.

"How 'bout this one in Cali?" Yolo asked hopefully, although
she already knew the answer.

"How 'bout not," he quipped. School started back next week so
they couldn't fly across the country to kill someone. "How about this
one here, in New Jersey? We can take the kids and make a day of it."

"Sounds like a great plan," she agreed. It was too for the two vig-
ilante murderers, but for Mr. Michael David not so much.

The elementary school teacher in Camden, New Jersey allowed
his students to play dress up. He kept a supply of inappropriate
thongs and boy shorts for the little ghetto girls. They of course saw
nothing wrong with it since their mothers and grandmothers dressed
the same way.

****

"I'm glad there's not enough room for all of us. I don't want to go to no aquarium anyway! Fuck a fish! Only fish I wanna see is dipped in some corn meal and dunked in some hot grease!" Deidra groaned when she heard Killa complaining about too many people in his whip.

"You sure, Grandma, cuz we were taking two cars," Yolo asked sweetly. "You know Shyne's little fiancé is coming too so..."

"I been meaning to talk to you two about that. How are they *engaged*?" Grandma asked making quotation marks with her fingers. "At ten years old. I know he's Moozlum. This ain't one of those forced marriages is it?"

Yolo was forced to answer because Killa pressed his lips together to keep from laughing. It didn't work so he rushed from the room, leaving in a trail of giggles.

"No, Grandma. No one could force Shyne to do anything Shyne doesn't want to do. They are best-friends. Who better to marry than your best-friend?" she asked. The fact that she was marrying her childhood crush, mentor, role model and best-friend spread her cheeks into a big grin.

"True dat," Grandma giggled. She could definitely relate since she'd married her best-friend. She'd had plenty of suitors since her husband died, but none could measure up so she'd decided to ride it out on her own.

"True dat?" Yolo reeled in mock shock. "Are these ghetto children rubbing off on you?"

"Chile, please! I'm from Highbridge. We put the G in Ghetto!"

****

Killa did what Killa does and had all the info on their next target before they reached the city. Camden, New Jersey has a hefty murder rate already so they could stand one more.

As soon as Killa and Yolo got the family settled in at the aquarium they set off in search of Michael David. It wasn't hard since Killa had hacked into his car's GPS unit. That's the thing about technology, it can help you or harm you. Or in this case kill you.

"That's him?" Yolo asked scrunching up her face at the pretty boy. He was behind the wheel of a pretty new car with a pretty woman riding shotgun. Actually, let's just say that she was in the passenger's seat because Yolo actually had a shotgun.

"That's him," Killa confirmed by looking at printout of his driver's license. He fell in behind him in traffic waiting for the chance to strike.

"Hey now!" Yolo giggled when the girl dropped her head into his lap. "That's the way to spend your last minutes alive."

"Kinda sucks," Killa quipped. "Get it sucks?"

"Not as bad as your jokes do," she replied, shaking her head as they crossed into the hood.

The future dearly departed rolled his window down to cop a bag of weed, but he girl didn't stop bobbing below. The block was booming so he fell into the line of cars waiting to be served.

"Pull up," Yolo directed and racked the shotgun, putting one of the hollow point lead slugs in the chamber.

"Sounds so sexy!" Killa said of the shotgun. She shook her head again and hopped out.

"Uh, oh. It's about to be milkshake time," Michael warned and grabbed the woman's head so she couldn't escape.

"Hi," Yolo cheered just as he began skeeting on her tonsils. He turned his head in her direction just as she tugged on the trigger. "Bye-bye!"

"Damn!" Killa chuckled as the blast nearly knock his head off. A few tendons held it on his neck but tuned it around like the exorcist.

"Yeah, yeah. I bet," Yolo teased the screaming girl but let her live. She hopped back into the car and they headed back to the aquarium. Now that's gangster!

Chapter 42

"Awe, looks at my babies dressed alike!" Yolo cheered when Sun and Shyne came to breakfast in the same colors. She never could get them to dress alike like some twins sometimes do. Still couldn't because Shyne twisted her face like Sun stunk and marched back upstairs.

"Or not," Killa laughed. He looked his boys up and down inspecting them for the first day of school. They all had fresh haircuts and the latest sneakers. Xavier had the beginnings of a mustache and sideburns.

Shyne returned a few minutes later with a new outfit on. Her large afro puffs made her look like a mousekeeter. She joined her brothers for a multicourse breakfast. Yolo had just got in the habit of cooking some of everything since they all had such different taste.

Country boy Sun liked grits while Rico was an oatmeal man. Xavier was coo-coo for Coco-Puffs while Shyne ate waffles almost daily. Of course, she scrambled eggs, browned hash browns and fried beef bacon and sausage.

"Can I have a ride to school, Daddy?" Shyne pleaded in her baby girl voice. The tone that always made Killa say *sure baby girl* and give her whatever she'd asked for. It would have worked if her mom wasn't there to cock block.

"Hell no! Ride the bus," she insisted. Life was rough so she wanted her kids to experience it young and adapt to it. That's why she'd enrolled them in public school instead of a private one.

"Look at my great grandbabies!" Deidra chimed with double meaning. She may have been their dad's grandmother, but they were great in their own right.

"Morning, Grandma," they all cheered. They all lined up to hug and kiss her on the way out the door.

Sun, Shyne and Rico were all going to the same middle school while X was on his own in junior high. The younger siblings caught the same bus so he waited with them protectively. Shyne saw Bryonna and marched right over to her.

"Hey, girl! You look pretty. I love your hair!" she greeted and gave her best-friend a hug. Only they weren't best-friends yet like in her dream.

"Um..." Bryonna fussed as the strange girl hugged her. "Are you okay?"

"Yeah, right. Trust me," Shyne assured her. Bryonna twisted her lips, but let the strange girl have it.

****

"Who the new kid?" Forty asked looking Xavier up and down as they awaited their school bus. His cronies shrugged since none of them knew him.

Meanwhile, X squinted at him to see if he was the one. His dad had told him that one of the kids would try him since he was new. It would most likely be the bully who beat everyone else up so once he beat him he wouldn't be messed with.

"Yup, he's the one," X nodded as Forty came closer. He'd gotten the name Forty when he was three because he looked like he was forty. He had a full beard at nine and got carded to prove that he was under age.

"A-yo, who's you?" Forty demanded, looking X up and down. He locked in on the fresh Adidas and claimed them. "I want them sneakers!"

"Are you sure?" Xavier asked calmly. After all there's always a calm before any storm, darkness before dawn, a bark before a bite.

"Hell yeah! Let me get 'em," he demanded, sticking his chest out.

"Here it comes!" Grandma Deidra cheered from the passenger's seat and started recording.

"I told you!" Killa smiled from behind the wheel.

"You two are too petty," Yolo said from the backseat as she began to record as well. "*World Star!*"

Forty said he wanted Xavier's sneaker so he gave them to him. Unfortunately for Forty his feet were still in them. A vicious round-house kick sounded like a crack of thunder when it connected with his face.

Forty did a 360 spin only to find a front kick to his chest waiting on him. The bully went spiraling backwards before tripping and landing on his ass.

"Are you sure you want my sneakers?" Xavier asked again ready to stomp him out like a forest fire if he said yes.

"NO! They don't even look like my size! I hate Adidas!" the bully assured him with his hands up to deflect anymore kicks.

"Cool," X said and offered his hand. The confused bully looked at it trying to decide what it meant. He finally accepted it and was helped to his feet. "I'm Xavier, but everyone calls me X."

"For-For-Forty," Forty flinched wearily.

X had made his point. Word would spread of the fight and by day's end he had earned a rep and title—The Wrong Nigga to Fuck With.

****

By the end of the day Bryonna and Shyne were officially friends. She really didn't have a choice since Shyne kept stalking her. It was either that or a protection order.

Sun was content playing second fiddle to the popular Rico. When the school bus hissed to a stop Asad was waiting to walk Shyne home.

"Your mother let you have a boyfriend?" Bryonna gasped in shock.

"Of course not!" Shyne frowned. "He's my fiancé. We're getting married! And you and Sun gonna get married too."

"Oh no we ain't!" she fussed looking at Sun like he stunk. He was so wild and girls were the furthest thing from his mind.

"So, how was school?" Grandma Deidra asked as the children piled in.

"Fine. Great. Okay," they replied and sat down to a snack.

Killa was also upstairs enjoying a snack of his own.

"You go boy!" Yolo cheered as Killa licked her towards an afternoon orgasm. He threw it into overdrive when he heard the kids coming in from school.

"You're welcome," Killa laughed as he left Yolo shivering on the bed. He headed to the ensuite bathroom to wash the glaze form around his mouth.

"Mmm," she moaned in reply. "I definitely owe you one. Two if you let me come with you. Please! Please?"

"Yolo, we can't risk stressing you out. No more incubators," he replied sternly. Yolo couldn't argue that but still didn't give up. Her twisted mind twirled over a plan. The convention for the Little Miss American pageant was right around the corner and she wanted in on the carnage.

"You right, but how much stress... is it to hit a button?" she asked while pressing the remote control. She turned the TV on, off on and then off again to stress her point.

"Owe me two?" he double checked when he caught her drift. He could set the trap and let her hit the button that sprang it. As much as he wanted this group of pedophiles under his belt two blow jobs is two jobs.

"Make it three!" she said sealing the deal. He would have gotten one on the spot if one of their kids hadn't knocked.

"Pops?" Xavier called as he tapped on the door. He was given permission to enter so twisted the knob. "Pops, Miss Yolo...how...um... I mean..."

"What's her name?" Yolo asked. She knew girls would like the tall, handsome kid. It was only a matter of time until he liked them back.

"I'on know," he shrugged. "But, how do you know when a girl likes you?""Tell a corny joke," Killa advised. "If she laughs, she likes you."

"Oh boy!" Yolo gushed, shaking her head. She couldn't say yay or nay since she had no idea. She'd fell in love with a legend and had never liked any boys.

"All my jokes by funny though!" he insisted. "I was telling jokes today and err'one was laughing. Even my teacher!"

"Let me hear 'em, he dared, twisting his lips.

"Okay, okay, check it. What do you call a turtle with a hard on?" X asked with an enthusiastic grin. Both Killa and Yolo shrugged so he answered. "Slow poke! Get it? Slow...poke!"

Yolo and Killa looked at him cracking up and then to each other. Xavier was laughing so hard he laughed himself out of the room

"Yo, that was super corny!" Yolo insisted. "You know what that means?"

"Yup. All the girls like him, including his teacher!"

Chapter 43

"Yo, who that bad little black bitch right there?" Skull asked seeing Malice posted up at the bar. The sheer top she wore made her nipples look like an extra set of eyes scanning the bar.

"I ain't never seen her before," his second in command advised.

Murda nodded in approval when he saw their target nibble at the bait. Skull wanted more than a nibble so he went over to take a bite.

"Hey, little mama. I...whoa!" he reeled when she turned and one eye didn't. He shook off the shock and picked up his macking. "Yeah, you can't be from around here. I ain't never seen you in here."

"Me and my moms just moved out here. I really don't know nobody yet," she pouted sounding miserable and making his dick hard.

"Well, you know me now," Skull said, placing her hand on his dick.

"Grrr!!" Murda growled. He didn't like using his girl as bait for this reason. Malice felt her juices began to flow as the cock throbbed in her hand. She was loyal and faithful, but a dick in hand is a dick in hand.

"You want me to fix it?" she asked so seductively that it could only mean a blow job. His dick throbbed yes before his mouth said it.

"Yeah, fix it," he croaked hoarsely with desire. He pulled her off the bar stool and out of the bar. He popped the locks remotely as the neared a new Benz. "Get in."

"You first!" Murda demanded as he came up behind them. Skull cut his protest short when he felt the unmistakable cold of a steel barrel touch his temple.

"A-yo, B, chill. I got racks in the glove compartment. Take the whip and keep the money," he offered. It was far trade for his life.

"Yeah, and you got a lot more at home. We been watching you," Murda advised pushing him into the front seat. Malice pulled a gun of her own and got in behind him.

"You got a pretty wife and daughters," Malice sang making the threat sound like a compliment.

"Thank you," he replied since he didn't get it. "I got work at the stash spot. I don't keep no dope at my house."

"I know," Murda agreed still driving towards his house. "You keep your money there. Well, you did.

Skull shook his head at himself for putting himself in this predicament. Chasing some ass was about to cost him almost a quarter-of-a-million dollars.

"Still want me to fix it?" Malice laughed as if she could read his mind.

"Fix what?" Murda asked, missing the joke.

"He put my hand on his dick and told me to fix it," she lied. Murda had to force himself not to murder him on the spot.

"We'll see about getting it fixed when we get to your house," he growled. That came sooner than later as they pulled into his driveway minutes later. He hit the remote and raised the garage so they could pull in.

"Please be quiet, so we don't wake my family," the family man pleaded. "Take the money and bounce."

"Okay. Shhh," Malice whispered then began to shout. "Everybody up! This is a robbery!"

Malice ran through the house with her gun and rounded up his family. His wife and daughters were in a state of shock as they were gathered into the den.

"Daddy!" the girls cried and rushed to his side.

His wife knew why they were there so quickly recited, "8 left, 15 right, go pass 30 once and then stop on it!"

Murda looked to Skull who nodded in agreement to the combination she gave. He took off to clear it out leaving Malice behind to hold them at gunpoint.

"Do you suck his dick?" she asked as if there weren't children present. "He tried to get me to suck it at the bar, so I wondered..."

"My children are present!" Skull's wife protested. "Please get what you came for and leave!

"Oh, we are. Trust me on that. Now answer the question! Better yet, suck it now," she decided.

"I will not!" she huffed indignantly and snapped on her husband. "This is your fault! Just greedy and now look! You have these...these thugs in our home!"

"What I miss?" Murda asked with mirth when he returned—why wouldn't he be happy with all the cash, jewels and guns he'd found.

"Nothing. You just in time. She about to suck his dick," Malice snarled.

"Okay, bet!" he cheered and took a seat.

"I will not! Don't you see my two children sitting here?!"

"One child," Malice corrected and cracked the ten-year-old in the head with a fire poker. The room went into a shocked silence as the girl fell out with blood gushing from the gash. "One down, one..."

"Okay!" she pleaded to save her other child. She scrambled to get Skull's limp dick out of his pants and into her mouth. Their eight-year-old turned away and shut her eyes.

"Un uh, shorty. You gotta learn," Murda laughed at the girl.

"You got the money," Skull pleaded as his wife sucked his soft dick with tears streaming down her face.

"And now we want a show!" Malice shot back. "This kinda wack! Let the girl try!"

Skull may have fucked up and let this danger into their life, but he couldn't take anymore. He snatched away from his wife and made a move towards Malice. It was too little too late and Murda gunned him down.

"Sianora Senorita," Malice sang and shot the woman in her tear stained face. Then turned to the little girl. It ain't no fun in a foster house, trust me," she said softly and then shot her too. The girl fell dead next to her big sister, only her sister wasn't dead.

"All this blow job talk got a nigga horny," Murda said clutching his dick through his pants.

"Why, Mr. Murda, would you like me to fix it?" Malice purred.

"I sure would, Miss Malice," he said and then whipped it out. The girl cracked one eye and locked in on their faces as she sucked him off. They left the second he came and she called the police the second after.

****

"I'm calling about the reward," the cop said when Killa took the call.

"Sup, Phillipe, what you got for me?" he asked of his long time informant. Leave it to Killa to have cops informing him instead of the other way around. Even the police were vying for the ten-thousand dollar reward.

"Got a triple over in Queens. A mid-level dealer and his family, wife and a daughter. It was supposed to be a quadruple, but one of the daughters survived. She got a good look at both assailants. One black male and black female," he explained in cop talk. Killa waited patiently for him to get around to what he was looking for. He decided to cut pass the jargon and get to the point.

"Crossed eyed girl?" he cut in when his flight was announced.

"Yes. The victim said he called her Alice? She said Malice, but we assumed she meant Alice."

"Assume nothing!" Killa barked, like he was the chief of police. "Find out all you can about Malice and Murda."

"Okay. I..." the cop began and ended when he realized he was alone on the line. He shrugged his shoulders and got to work.

"What?" Yolo asked, seeing his temples jump from anxiety. Something was on his mind and she was right by his side to help.

"Malice and Murda. Murda and Malice," he sampled. "That's who killed Sin and Joe. They thought they killed you and me."

"Malice and Murda? That's wack!" she said twisting her face. "Who they think they are? Killa and Yolo!"

"You know what? I think that's exactly who they think they are!" he said as it all began to add up.

The bits and pieces he'd collected from all five boroughs all fell into place as one complex puzzle. A male, female stick up team had been knocking off dealers. This was the first time they'd left someone breathing. It was going to be a fatal mistake.

Chapter 44

"Wow!" Yolo proclaimed when they reached the St. Paul Minnesota airport. Hundreds of parents were there parading their little girls around in grown women attire for the upcoming pageant.

"Damn shame," Killa growled, looking at a six-year-old with a face full of make-up. "This is the kind of shit pedophiles love! These parents are fucked up!"

"And that's why they're about to get fucked up!" she shot back. "But, first I need an ice-cream sundae with a pickle and sprinkles!"

"Um, okay. Ooh! How 'bout a Fat-Fat burger?" he exclaimed, sounding more like Sun than himself, pointing at the concession trailer.

"All that pork!" Yolo fussed and frowned.

"Nah, it's all beef now. Come on! We can get your ice-cream too," he announced and led the way.

After stuffing their pretty faces at the gourmet hamburger stand the killer couple checked into their hotel. There was a time when they would have stripped and fucked the moment they reached the room, now they just crawled on the bed and took a nap like an old married couple.

"You up?" Yolo asked a few hours later when Killa began to stir next to her. She had awaken shortly before and used the ceiling to project her thoughts on like a movie screen.

The wedding, her kids, her life were all almost too good to be true. Never before had God's mercy hit home like at that moment.

"I am now," he said rolling over to hold her. His hand found its way to her belly, where their future child developed and grew, instead of between her legs to play in her plump vagina.

"What you thinking about right this second? Don't think, just answer," she pleaded. She heard the vulnerability in her tone and didn't try to hide it either.

"The wedding. My grandmother is going all out, huh? Well, at least she and the kids will enjoy it."

"Me too," Yolo admitted. "It's like a fairy tale. I know it's more than I deserve, but..."

"No buts," he comforted and wiped away her tears. "We can't change the past, but we can shape our future."

"We can make the world better, huh? Killing bad people is good!"

"Killing bad people is great! We're like super heroes! I'm Killa-man and you're Yolo-woman!"

"That is so wack!" she cracked up. All the movement from her laughing gave Killa a hard-on. Whenever she gave him a hard-on he gave it back.

Yolo shimmied out of her panties and lifted her. Killa slid in and slow stroked them both to orgasm. Then it was time for another nap. After all, they had work to do.

****

"Wow!" Yolo proclaimed once again when she and Killa entered the massive convention center in downtown St. Paul. "It's going to take a dam airstrike to blow this place up."

"I see," he agreed as he scanned the structure. Thousands of parents and spectators milled about exploring items available at the different booths.

"Look," Yolo giggled and pointed to a tribute to the late tailor who Killa had beat to death.

"Yeah. Look," he replied, pointing at all the others who'd took his place. The place was full of inappropriate shit for little girls. Both parents could feel their blood boil as they continued to walk around. The majority of the spectators were creepy, middle-aged men. Most lived with their moms and massive amounts of porn.

"Ooh, ooh! I know!" she bounced and cheered. "Your daughter told me how she burned down a funeral home in her dream!

"Why she my daughter when she crazy, but your daughter when she cute?" he wanted to know.

"Cuz," she answered, like it was an answer, and then filled him in on the plan.

"Damn, that just...might...work," Killa agreed as he looked up at the emergency sprinklers. "There's an adult only screening tonight so I gotta get busy!"

Killa was indeed busy as he rigged the building for destruction. He acquired a gas truck and filled the sprinkler system with high octane fuel—only the best for the worst. Next, he tapped into the security cameras, so they could watch the fireworks form their hotel room.

The final act was to put remote controlled grenades around the room. The cherry on top was an incendiary device that Yolo could light from bed.

"It's almost show time!" Killa announced into his headset. Night had fell and droves of pedophiles streamed into the venue. Killa could just imagine what sort of events they had planned for the evening.

Pin the tail on the toddler. Bobbing for babies. Skeet shooting masturbation contests. Whatever it was they were going to die while doing them. As soon as the lines emptied inside he went around and chained the doors. No one would be leaving.

"I'm ready!" Yolo sang happily. She sat Indian style on the bed watching through security monitors.

"Smoke," he ordered and she hit a button. On cue the smoke canisters popped filling the room with dense smoke. The sickos were having so much fun that they tried to play through it.

The smoke triggered the sprinkler system causing it to rain gas. That started a panic that started a stampede for the doors. The killer couple watched in delight as they trampled and fought to get out. Quite a few had died in the rush for the exits.

"Now!" Killa ordered before they could break free. Yolo hit the switch that would start the fire.

The gas soaked patrons let out a howl that shook even Killa to his core. The pedophiles got a head start on hell as they burned alive until they died. This fire would be nothing compared to the hellfire. Killa drove away in a state of satisfied contentment that came from killing people who really needed dead.

"Hey, Bae," Yolo sang when he took her call. "Can you stop and get me something to eat?"

"Sure. What?" He asked scanning both sides of the street for restaurants. He didn't even register the emergency vehicles speeding towards the orange inferno in his rearview mirror. They really could cut off the sirens and slow down since there would be no survivors.

****

"In breaking news out of St. Paul, Minnesota, a massive blaze decimated a convention center. Thousands died in an event proceeding the Little Miss America pageant that was scheduled for tomorrow..." a reporter reported happily. He obviously thought they were some sick fucks as well by the smile on his face and the glee in his voice.

Killa and Yolo," an old man nodded as they watched the report from the bar.

"Who?" Malice barked from his own stool. He and Malice were there stalking a big-time pimp with big-time money. Malice made perfect pimp bait dressed down. She was young anyway, but the school girl clothes made her look even younger.

AG, the pimp, liked them young. The younger the better. The perverted pimp kept a stable of teen girls renting pussy. He kept a house full of even younger ones for customers who like pre-pubescents. Once they turned 19 he sold them to other pimps.

"Killa! It's got his name written all over it," the knowing man replied. "That's what he do! Him and his girl Yolo, they kill bad people. And people who mess with kids are the worst!"

"But, they dead! I ki—heard they got killed in The Bronx!" Murda almost begged as he followed the man's eyes over to AG. He'd planned to rob and kill him anyway, but now he had a cause. After all, he didn't just want to be like Killa, he wanted to be Killa.

"Killa can't die. He got roots on him. A magic spell," the old man rambled as myth mixed with legend and lore.

Murda felt utterly defeated as he listened to the tales of the invincibility and immortality. He was so deep in his feelings that it didn't even register when Malice slid into the pimp's booth. He begin spitting some smooth pimpin' in her ear and the gullible girl began falling for his gift of gab.

AG slipped his hand under the table and beneath her skirt, passed her panties and found her pussy. The tender young box got wet in an instant from the contact combined with pimpin' he was whispering in her ear.

"Got damnit!" he exclaimed when she clamped her tight box and made it grab his finger. It was so tight that he almost couldn't pull his finger back out. When he did he gave it a sniff, a lick and then decided, "Come on in the back so I can suck that thang!"

"Okay," Malice said and stood. She expected Murda to follow so they could rob him, but he was too busy listening to the highly embellished stories about Killa.

"Step into my office," AG said, leading her into a store room. She looked over her shoulder for Murda but saw no signs of him.

AG picked her up and placed her on a crate of liquor so he could lick her. And lick her he did! He snatched her thick thighs wide open and pulled the fluffy fro over her pussy aside. She almost came instantly when he shoved his thick tongue inside of her.

"Oh wow!" she moaned in delight and disgust. Murda had cum in that very same pussy just hours earlier. Sure she'd showered but the way he was sucking he was sure to get some nut in his mouth.

"Mmhmm. Mmhmm," AG mumbled when he felt her young body began to quake. It shook shivered and then went stiff as she bust the best nut of her young life. The pimp swallowed as pussy juice along with semen flooded into his mouth.

Malice was so shaken up by the orgasm that she didn't realize that AG had pulled his dick out until it was in her. She looked behind him once again, this time hoping that Murda didn't show up. She pulled her legs wider so he could get to the bottom of her box.

"This...some...mmm...good...pussy!" he declared as he stroked it. "How...old are you?"

"18," Malice moaned. The dick was so good to her that she forgot to lie. Luckily for her, most girls lied about being older, so she quickly changed it to, "15...my...shit! My...birthday...mmm..."

"Mmhmm," AG agreed as he filled her box up with cum. She squeezed and released until she'd milked him dry. "I'm gonna take you home. You 'bout to be my bottom bitch!"

"Okay," she replied since she was confused by cum and pimpin'. She would've went too if she hadn't seen Murda when they emerged from the back.

"Oh, yeah," the young girl giggled when she remembered who she was and why she was there.

"Word?" Murda replied as the older man relayed Killa killing a dragon. The man was having a ball building the tall tales. Why wouldn't he since they were family.

"Word up!" Uncle Roscoe lied convincingly. He and Killa's grandfather were blood brothers and he was proud of his nephew. "Got a number? I'll introduce you."

"That's what's up," Murda said, scribbling his name and number down. He happily passed it over and then went to collect his girl.

"I gotta go. I'll be back," Malice vowed when she saw Murda stand. He shot her a quick glance and then headed towards the door. She rushed out behind him before AG could talk her into staying.

"Kill my nephew!" Uncle Roscoe grumbled as he staggered to the pay phone. He dropped in a couple of quarters and began to dial. "7-1-8...um...oh shit! I forget Deidra's number!"

Chapter 45

Murda wore a question mark on his face as he splashed inside of Malice. Niggas know how the left shit; especially their pussy and this was not how he'd left it. They'd had sex before going to the bar and were now having it again after returning. He had no idea that she'd got dicked down in the store room at the bar and she wasn't going to tell him.

"What's...wrong...da-daddy?" she asked as he stroked with a perplexed look on his face.

"Nothing," he fussed since his suspicion didn't make any sense. There was no way she could have been with someone else since they'd been together. He got distracted when she thrashed around in a fake orgasm. She further kept him from thinking by offering him some head.

"Let me suck it, daddy," she purred and pushed him off her. She scrambled to get him in her mouth before he could get back to his thoughts. It worked like a charm. After all, what's more charming than a blow job.

****

"How I look?" Malice asked and did a little spin so her little dress would lift as she twirled.

"Like jailbait," he said, seeing the cartoon characters on her panties. He was inspired to murder AG for pimpin kids just like Killa would do, but still planned to rob him as well.

"Good!" she giggled since that's what she was going for. Sneakers, pigtails and bubble gum lip gloss had her looking every bit of fifteen.

"So, what's the plan? What the nigga was talkin' 'bout?" Murda asked since he hadn't been paying attention at the bar.

"Well..." she began then paused to think about the thorough tongue lashing he'd given her. "He offered to take me home. You can follow and give me like...30 minutes to open the door."

"Then I'll swoop in like Killa and kill that low-life pimp!" he said.

Malice twisted her lips curiously at the statement. It was at that moment that she realized her man was a dick rider. She would live with it, like so many woman who have dick riding men do.

"Thirty minutes though," she insisted so she could get a nut first.

****

"Little mama from the bar?" AG asked and literally crossed his fingers hoping the caller was. He could still taste the unique flavor from her pussy on his tongue. A salted nutty flavor he couldn't put his finger on.

"That's me," she giggled girlishly getting a glare from Murda. She twisted her lips like *yeah right* for his benefit even though her pussy was throbbing from his voice. "Still want me to come over?"

"Hell the fuck yeah! Where you at? I'll come pick you up!"

"My big brother can drop me off. What's the address?" she asked and got it. She flirted a little more, a little too convincingly for Murda, and then hung up. "Let's get this money!"

"Aight, err'body out!" AG shouted once he got off the phone. He wanted to get the girl alone so he could turn her ass out properly. "Take y'all asses to the mall or a movie! Anywhere, but here! And don't come back 'til I call!"

The teenagers filed out of the house and headed over to the mall for a movie. It was rare that the kids got to be kids. They skipped and giggled happily, like young girls are supposed to.

Meanwhile, AG pointed a video camera at his bed to capture the action to come, and then lit a blunt to calm his nerves while he waited. He wouldn't have wait long.

"At least a half hour. Let me scope the place out, then I'll text you when we ready," Malice coached.

"Um...okay," he replied since he couldn't understand why he couldn't just rush in now since he had a gun and all.

Both Murda and AG watched as she rushed towards the front door. AG actually waved and thanked Murda for bringing her. Murda frowned as he waved back and told him he was welcome.

"Thank you!" AG cheered and snatched her inside. The fancy house was a blur of leather and glass as he rushed her to his bedroom. He started the recording with a remote control as he ordered, "Strip!"

"Everything/" Malice questioned, like a little girl as she lifted the t-shirt over her head. He was mesmerized by her flat stomach and heavy breast. Her firm tits didn't move an inch when she reached around and unhooked her bra.

"Damn, you fine!" he vowed when her cartoon panties came into view. A poof of pubic hair made her vagina look even fatter.

"Thank you," she giggled and got wet when he pulled out a thick dick full of veins. It was so hard that it quivered up and down like a diving board.

He extended his hand, like a gentleman, in invitation to his bed. She took it and was led to the center of the California king. The bed was large enough to host his frequent orgies with his stable.

Malice spread her legs so he could expertly eat her out again. That was his plan, but with a slight twist. He came around so he could 69 her from the top. He clamped his mouth on her hot box, and felt its juices began to flow, while lowering his dick into her mouth. She gagged slightly when he reached her larynx. That of course became his target.

The room filled with a sexual symphony of slurps, sucks moans and gagging. Malice came first which allowed AG to enjoy the blow job. He then took it a step further and fucked her face. It was so nasty and Malice loved it. She reached down and played in her pussy while he tapped on her tonsils.

"Shit!" AG grunted and pumped her mouth full of semen. She let it run out of the corners of her mouth instead of swallowing.

AG flipped Malice onto her side and lifted one of her legs high in the air. He then took aim and plunged deep inside. He slowly dragged his dick out to the hilt and then plunged back inside to the bottom. He did this over and over again causing her to cum over and over again. Eventually the good young pussy got the best of him and he came too, pushing against her cervix and skeeting on it like it was his.

"Wow!" Malice sighed, love struck form the good fucking. Her eyes fluttered as she tried to make sense of the numbers on the clock. Have them tell it she had been there for almost two hours. "Oh shit!"

"What's wrong?" AG asked as she jumped up and scrambled to get dressed. "That's just round one. I gots more pipe to lay."

"Okay, one second. I just gotta... don't move!" she insisted and slipped on her last shoe. She rushed to the door and snatched it open to look for Murda she didn't have to look far since he was standing at the front door.

"What took you so long?" You okay?" he asked seeing the flush look on her face.

"Yeah. I... Um... He in the room. Come on," she whispered and led the way. AG was stroking himself back erect when they arrived.

"Round t—... The fuck?" He shouted when he saw Murda and more importantly the gun in his hand. He rolled towards the nightstand where a nickel plated .357 resided. Didn't make it though.

"Oh, no you don't," Murda chuckled and put a slug in his back. Malice sprang into action and grabbed the gun.

"Man, what y'all want?" AG pleaded. "Who sent you, Pretty John? Gorgeous Greg? Sweet Dick Rick? Yung Pumpin'? Who?"

"Damn, pimpin' ain't easy, is it?" Murda laughed. "Ain't nobody sent me! I'm here for yo' dough and to free the underage girls you pimpin'!"

"Take the money, but not my hoes! Them little bitches was fucking anyway. For free at that! Leave me my hoes! She can stay too! I..."

Malice fired a round at the same mouth that had just made her cum. Her DNA was all in his mustache and goatee, but she had to shut him up before he said too much.

"Damn, Baby, you shoulda waited until we got the money!" Murda fussed.

"We'll find it!" she shot back and began to search. The nightstand gave up a few hundred and a whole lot of freaky shit. He had lubes and gels, flavored and unflavored. Glow in the dark butt plugs and cock rings.

"That's one nasty nigga!" Murda said, shaking his head at all the whips, chains, rubber and leather in the closet.

"Yeah, he is," she affirmed. And she would know since her box still throbbed from his recent pounding.

"Jackpot!" Murda announced when he came across a small cash box. The ten grand in small bills looked like big money. All in all it wasn't a bad lick. They left with guns, money and jewels.

Probably should've taken the video camera as well.

Chapter 46

"You smell that?" Yolo frowned and sniffed the air from bed.

"Smells like...smoke," Killa replied drowsy from a long day and good sex. Yolo was getting bigger by the day so side shots had become their favorite position.

"That damn Shyne!" she growled and rolled out of bed.

Killa thought about getting up but shook his head no instead. He enjoyed the view of her larger usual ass until she put on a robe.

"No, don't get up. I'll make sure your daughter hasn't burned the house down!"

"'Kay," Killa said and rolled back over. He was back asleep by the time she reached the steps.

"Shit!" Shyne fussed in a hush when she heard footsteps coming down the stairs. Her mind scrambled for a reasonable explanation, but had no luck.

"Really?" Yolo said, shaking her head. "Who makes a flame thrower in the family room?"

"Your sweet daughter?" Shyne cheered and cracked her famous smile. It always worked on her dad, but moms are different than dads.

"First of all... Actually, this isn't half bad," she said checking out the contraption until she caught herself. "Girl, go to bed!"

"Okay, Mommy," Shyne agreed. Grateful not to be getting her butt whipped she scurried off and darted up the steps.

"Let's see here..." Yolo mused as she further inspected and improved the device. After all, you never knew when you would have to set something or someone on fire.

****

"I have something you will want to see," Phillipe smiled and nodded over the phone as if in person. "Bring that reward money and meet me in the city."

"Aight," Killa sighed. Getting a lead on whoever killed Sincerity sure beat what he was doing now. "I'm on my way. Text me the address."

"Where you going? You have to try on your tux next!" Grandma Deidra fussed just as Yolo came out in her dress.

"I gotta..." he said and stopped dead in his tracks Seeing Yolo in a wedding dress brought reality crashing down. "Wow! You look great!"

"Thank you," Yolo blushed and gushed at the compliment. The baby in her belly kicked as if it shared in her excitement. Her hand went to her stomach to feel it. "Where are you going?"

"That's what I want to know!" his grandmother fussed as she adjusted her dress. It really didn't need the superficial tug here and pull there, but she wanted to seem useful.

"Cop called," he said since she would know the rest. Grandma Deidra didn't and looked back and forth between the two hoping for more info—with her nosey ass.

"Handle your business," Yolo said since it would be futile to try to go with him. She was so far along now that the rush was on to get married before she give birth.

Killa had driven his own car since he'd already had other plans so was able to leave the ladies behind. He entered the address he'd been given into his GPS and then followed the directions out to Brooklyn. Once he got there he parked in front of a refurbished Brownstone and called the cop back.

"Where are you?" Phillipe asked almost desperately. He had that ten grand reward already spent.

"Outside. I'm coming up now," he replied. He tucked a pistol in the small of his back and grabbed the envelope stuffed with cash. He could hear locks clicking as he approached and then saw the happy cop's smiling face.

"Come! Come! You won't believe what I have! Man, was I lucky to get it! He exclaimed leaving Killa no doubt that he was about to get his man...and woman.

Phillipe led Killa into a room with a large TV taking up most of the wall. He picked up a space age remote and triumphantly pressed play.

"You called me to Brooklyn to see a porno? Nice ass but..." he paused when Malice's cock-eye appeared. It straightened out for a second when AG's tongue touched her box. Then went sideways again when he shoved his dick into her mouth.

"Un huh! See!" the cop cheered. "But wait, it gets even better!"

It did too, when AG fucked her face. Killa wondered if Yolo would let him. Perhaps on their honeymoon. It got even better as the watched the pimp dick the girl down sideways. Everyone enjoys a good homemade fuck tape, and this was a good one.

"Heeeeerrrre comes Murda!" Phillipe announced as the killer entered the scene.

Killa's face twisted into a murderous snarl as they watched the robbery unfold. Neither flinched when Malice murdered the man who'd just fucked and sucked several orgasms out of her minutes prior.

"I like her," Killa announced. "I need an address for this... Malice and Murda."

"Cool names!" the cop gushed, like a groupie. "I'm tracking down a few leads as we speak. Give me a couple of weeks."

"I don't have a couple of weeks," he mused. "My wedding is a week away. You should come."

"Sure. When and where?" the cop asked.

****

"I need to call your Uncle Roscoe. We need to invite him," Grandma stated as she reviewed the sparse guest list.

"Wow, I haven't seen ol' Unc in a million years," Killa recalled. A smile turned up one side of his mouth as he thought about his colorful uncle. "Do you even know where he lives?"

"No, but I know where he drinks. Put your shoes on, let's go for a ride," she replied.

Killa let out an *I don't want to go for a ride* sigh but put his shoes on and complied. He twisted his lips the whole way out to Brooklyn. They pulled to a stop in front of the bar Roscoe was known to frequent.

"Grandma, it's...3 pm, you think Unc at the bar already?" Killa asked skeptically as the entered. The question was answered by Roscoe sitting at the bar sucking down suds.

"Deidra? Is that...my sister-in-law?" he cheered and stood, staggered, caught his balance and threw his arms open.

"It is," she replied and gave the dusty man a hug. He burped loudly when she put her grandma squeeze on him.

"Excuse me," he giggled and then got serious when he saw his nephew behind her. "Is that... Are you... Little X to the V?"

"I am," Killa smiled broadly at the nickname he hadn't heard in decades. Not since he became Killa.

"Ooh!" Deidra gasped as she was cast aside so that the men could embrace. Family is important to her so seeing them together touched her heart. "We came to invite you to the wedding."

"What! You getting married again? After all these years! I thought your mean ass would never..."

"Not me! Him!" Deidra fussed. She was mean, but that's not why she'd never remarried. Fact was that her deceased husband set the bar so high most men couldn't even see it let alone reach it.

"You? Son, many vaginas are better than one," he advised.

"Roscoe, when the last time your old ass seen a vagina? A real one, not in a magazine or on TV?" Deidra dared.

"I gets me some on the 1st of err' month. Buy me a shot when my check come. Use to anyway until someone killed ol' AG, matter of fact!" Roscoe recalled and patted his pockets.

"What you looking for, Unc?" Killa inquired. He knew the pimp murdered on tape name was AG so he had his full attention. I should mention that Killa kept the tape. He and Yolo watched it on the regular.

"This whippa-snapper was in here talkin' 'bout he was the new Killa, and he killed the old Killa and..." he rambled while searching himself. 'Must be in my other pants!"

"Other as in, you only have two?' she asked with a grimace.

"Only got two legs!" he shot back like it made sense. Meanwhile, an older gentleman approached real smooth like and asked...

"Can I buy you a drink? Car" Condo? Whatever," he inquired.

"Nigga, if you don't..." Killa cut in but got off.

"Sure," Deidra giggled. "White wine is fine."

"And so are you," the man replied and offered her his elbow. She took it and was escorted to his table.

"Um...?" Killa asked in confusion. Snapped out of it and said, "Let's find that number!"

Roscoe led the way out of the bar and a couple of blocks east. They entered a tenement building where he rented a flat. It took nine keys to unlock the joint before he opened the door. Killa braced himself for whatever and followed him in. It wasn't what he expected.

"This is...nice!" he exclaimed at the tidy little apartment. It was clean and nicely furnished with all the etceteras.

"Thanks," he replied over his shoulder as he entered his bedroom. "Oh shit!"

"What?" Killa called and rushed in behind him. He saw a defeated look on his uncle's face and a washed out paper in his hand.

"I washed it,' Roscoe moaned. He looked so miserable that Killa shared in his misery.

"Don't worry about it, Unc. It's cool," he sighed even though it wasn't. Malice and Murda were a threat. The sooner they were off the planet the better.

Killa led his dejected uncle back to the bar so he could collect his grandmother. A pretty girl on a corner smiled brightly when she saw Roscoe.

"Hey, Uncle Roscoe! We still on for Tuesday?" she asked eagerly.

"What's Tuesday?" he frowned and thought.

"The first!" she reminded and blushed.

"Oh yeah! But of course," he replied and perked up. The promise of pussy is something to perk up about.

Grandma was giggling and blushing too when they arrived back at the bar. Killa went over to the booth and took her by the hand.

"Call me," the man insisted as they departed. Uncle Roscoe took down the date and place with a promise to be at the wedding.

Chapter 47

The killer couple rented a wedding hall out in the Hamptons. They used assumed names, since technically Killa was a wanted man. The couple spared no expense on flowers, food or their cake. They prepared for hundreds although only a handful were actually invited.

Deidra was old fashioned and insisted on an old fashioned wedding complete with something old, something new, and something borrow—she wasn't worried about the something blue. She was the old, Yolo was the new and the stunning pair of diamond earrings she handed her were the something borrowed.

"Oh my!" Yolo exclaimed over both the earrings as well as the sharp kick from inside her belly.

"Are you okay?" Deidra fussed and came over.

"I'm fine," she replied, fighting back the urge to double over. "Is Shyne ready?"

"I'll check," Deidra said and went to do just that. Killa couldn't see his bride until the wedding so he, X, Rico and Sun and Asad had gone on ahead in his car. A limo would bring the bride along with Shyne and Grandma Deidra once they finally got ready.

"Yes!" Fussy Shyne fussed at the knock on her door. Her tone changed when her grandmother stuck her head in.

"Are you... Oh my! You're beautiful!" she gushed causing the flower girl to blush.

"Thank you," Shyne sang and posed in her white dress along with white flowers in her hair. Her little friend Bryonna wore the same dress with the same flowers in her natural hair.

"You guys come on. The limo is here," she advised before closing the door back behind her.

"I can't wait until you and Sun get married!" Shyne told her friend who promptly scrunched her cute little face into a ball.

"Your brother is disgusting! I would never marry him!" she vowed.

"Okay," Shyne sang in disbelief. Her dream had been so vivid that there was just no way it wouldn't come true.

****

"Don't be scared, Pops. You'll be okay," Sun said, patting his father on his head like a puppy. He'd come across him deep in thought and tried to cheer him up.

"Thanks, Sun," he replied, fighting back a smile. He wasn't scared, just reflecting on life. The life he'd lived and the life he'd yet to live. His crooked cop informant had texted him telling him that he knew where Murda and Malice were at, so he planned to murder them both with malice as soon as he and his family returned from their honeymoon.

The entire family, including Asad and Bryonna, were heading down to Belize for a week. Yolo was in her third trimester so this would be her last flight for a while.

"They're here!" Xavier called out when he saw the limo pull up to the side entrance. Yolo scurried inside dragging the long wedding dress in its plastic wrap.

"Show time!" Killa said with a nervous sigh. He heard it and tried again with more confidence. "Show time, fellas! Let's do this!"

"Where are all the people?" Shyne fussed as she entered the large empty hall. She scrunched her face up at the empty seats and the old man seated with the young girl in the front row.

"That's Uncle Roscoe," Sun explained to the question on her face. "And his girlfriend, but only on the first."

"Oh," Shyne replied since she didn't get it either. She and Bryonna took their places and waited for Yolo to emerge.

Deidra fussed over her future granddaughter as she dressed. Yolo did the best she could to keep a nagging tear from falling, but it was too heavy. She'd never had a real family, and therefore felt both overwhelmed and grateful. It's times like this that confirm that there was a God and she was grateful for Him.

"Stop all that before you mess up your make-up," Grandma said, even though Yolo wasn't wearing any. She did though and her own tears threatened to run her mascara. "And my friend Carlton is here."

Yolo got a good laugh after the good cry. Even she couldn't believe the pretty bride in the mirror was her. She smiled and the reflection smiled back. Only for a moment until another sharp pain hit.

"What? The baby?" Deidra asked urgently. She was old and wise enough to know that something was wrong.

"No, I'm fine," Yolo lied, bent over in half holding her belly. "Let's do this!"

"Girl, are you having contractions? You are, aren't' you?" she demanded.

"Please, I want to be married first. Tell them I'm ready!" Yolo begged and willed herself to stand up straight. She wiped the pain off her face and hit the door.

The Wedding March began to play and Shyne tossed flower petals in her path while Bryonna held her long flowing train as Yolo marched regally up the aisle. Her eyes were straight ahead on her prize; Killa.

Killa stuck his chest out proudly as he watched his bride coming towards him. He scanned the few faces in attendance and nodded. Uncle Roscoe gave a thumbs up while his rented girlfriend smiled. Deidra's friend Carlton smiled and nodded while Phillipe looked around nervously. Killa thought it was odd but his bride arrived and stole his full attention.

"Hey," Killa greeted with his killer smile. "You okay?"

"Nope, I'm in labor," she replied and barked at the preacher, "Let's go!"

"Um...okay...let's see here... Dearly beloved, we are gathered here..."

"Fast forward!" she demanded. "Get to the I dos!"

Sun was the ring man and giggled at someone else, besides him, getting in trouble. Villain was the closest thing to a friend still living in Killa's life so it was only natural that he was the best man. The crooked cop suddenly stood and made a beeline out of the hall just as the preacher sped through the truncated vows.

"Do you take her, do you take him..." he asked as Yolo doubled over in pain once more.

"We do!" they both shouted. No sooner had he pronounced them man and wife did a bullet slam into his forehead pronouncing him dead on arrival.

"Get down!" Killa shouted and tackled Yolo just as the place erupted in gunfire.

"Looking for me?" Murda laughed in between bursts of gunfire from a fully automatic pistol. Luckily for Yolo Malice's cock-eye caused her to miss her and hit the preacher.

Villain pulled a pistol form his back and returned fire. Murda sprayed the seats hoping to murder everyone in attendance. Rico and Asad huddled over Grandma Deidra risking their own lives to save hers.

"Ugh!" Both Villain and Murda grunted when their respective bullets found their mark. Both dropped from gunshot wounds.

"Murda!" Malice screamed. She fired wildly as she helped him to his feet and out the door.

"Everyone okay?" Killa asked frantically. Everyone answered yes, except for the preacher and Yolo.

"My water broke!"

****

Killa sent Deidra and the kids to the airport and on to Belize while he rode with Yolo in one ambulance and Villain was transported in a second one. His wound wasn't life threatening, but Yolo was months early once again. Killa paced the waiting room, like a lion in a cage. He planned to blow up the entire borough of Brooklyn just to get at two people. His phone had gone to voicemail before he even realized it had rang.

"This nigga!" he growled seeing that the missed call was from Phillipe. It wasn't hard to tell that the crooked cop had double-crossed him. He'd sold both killers out and had gotten paid twice. That's the thing about crooked cops, they're crooked.

"What the hell happened? I went to smoke a cigarette and heard shooting. I rushed back in, but they got away," he lied via voicemail.

"That's what's up," Killa nodded and smiled in agreement. Not because he believed him but because he still had his address.

"Excuse me, Mr. Johansen?" a doctor asked. Killa almost said no until he recalled that that was the name he'd used for the wedding.

"Yes. How is she? The baby?" he asked almost frantically.

"I operated on your friend, took a bullet out of his lung. He'll lost the lung, but will survive," he relied. It came as a relief, but he wanted to know about his wife and child.

"Mr. Mills?" another doctor asked as he approached Killa and his colleague.

"Yes," he replied causing the other doctor to frown in confusion.

"Would you like to come meet your daughter?" the second doctor asked with the proud tone of a job well done.

"Um, yeah!" Killa said. His knees wobbled on the first step, but he quickly got it together and followed him in. He walked in and found Yolo staring down at the bundle of joy in her arms.

"A girl, yo," she chuckled. She would have preferred another boy because Shyne was more work than her three sons combined multiplied by two.

"What's her name?" he asked getting a peek at the precious little newcomer.

"Deidra," Yolo announced happily. She and the old lady had bonded and so she was delighted to share her name with their daughter.

"That's an old lady's name!" he protested.

"Says who?" his grandmother barked via speaker phone. Killa reeled as if she were in the room ready to deliver one of her signature pinches.

"I mean...that's a wonderful name!" the kiss ass declared. "Hello there, Miss Deidra."

"Okay, we have to incubate her now," he doctor announced as a nurse came to collect the child. "She's healthy, so I don't expect her to be there long. A week, two tops."

"What about me? I have a pressing matter," Yolo began so professionally that no one in the world would phantom the brutal murders she had on her mind. Murda, Malice and that crooked cop were all about to die horribly for endangering her family.

"That will have to wait until tomorrow," the doctor replied firmly.

"I'll stay here with you," Killa offered to shut down the protest forming in her head.

"Okay," she smile and softened when she took his outstretched hand. Killa took a seat bedside where he would remain until the am.

Chapter 48

"Hang in there, Baby," Malice pleaded as she pressed a towel into Murda's bullet wound. Villain's bullet had broken his collar bone as it passed through.

"Ouch!" he protested from the pressure. "I can't move my arm."

"You need a doctor!" she said just as news of the shooting came on the TV.

"A Long Island wedding day was interrupted by gunfire. A prominent pastor passed away while preceding over the ceremony. Surveillance footage caught the gunmen, a man and a woman to be more precise escaping in a black SUV"

"You gotta burn the truck!" Murda said seeing their vehicle flash across the screen. "We got Killa and Yolo on our asses and now the police! What we gon' do?!"

Malice twisted her lips at the fear on his breath. It was the worse halitosis for a thug. She looked to him for guidance and instead here he was in a panic.

"Okay, I'll take care of it. You get some rest," she suggested. She held his hand and waited until he drifted off to sleep. As soon as he exhaled his first snore she made her move.

The couple of robbers couldn't use a bank for their booty so they kept several hundred grand in the closet. Malice didn't need any ID or withdrawal slips to make a full withdrawal. She simply snatched up the back pack and took it to the door. Next, she stuffed another bag with panties and bras followed by a few of her favorite outfits. She then grabbed her sexiest negligee too to help her cause.

"Peace out," she whispered to Murda and slipped out of the door. As soon as she was in the hall she made another call. "I need help."

"Where are you guys?" Phillipe asked so he could sell them out to Killa. He would trade their lives to keep his.

"I'm alone. I left him behind. I have money," Malice said, changing his plans once more.

"Is that right? Okay, meet me at..." he said and gave her an address out on The Island. A stash house he used to stash stuff he took from criminals. Money, dope and now the tender young thing with a sleepy eye.

****

Phillipe waited outside the Long Island home as Malice pulled up. Both had pistols locked and loaded for any bullshit. Both let out a sigh of relief seeing that the other one was alone.

"Is he dead?" the cop asked as a frazzled Malice stepped from the car. She'd left the SUV parked in front of the apartment for the police. They could have and Murda as far as she was concerned.

"Not yet," she shrugged. She had ten grand in her purse along with the negligee. Both as an offering while the bulk of the cash was still in the trunk.

"Well, come on in," he offered and turned. She followed him up the walk and into the modest, well-appointed home.

"Who stays here?" she wondered. It was a far cry from the Brooklyn Brownstones and tenements she was used to.

"You do, for now. We'll figured out what to do from here," he explained further by running his eyes slowly up and down her body. She blinked her eyes nervously when he reached them.

"Can I take a shower? It's been a crazy day," she asked and smiled softly. She understood where he wanted to take things and was down to go there.

"First door on the left," he replied pointing down the hall. He licked his lips lustfully as he watched her hips sway away.

Malice let out a deep sigh as the warm water caressed her weary body. It had indeed been a long day. It had begun bright and early when Murda rolled over on top of her and shoved his early morning piss hard on inside of her. She didn't get a chance to get wet as he dry humped to an orgasm. He busted a nut in her then rolled back off leaving her feeling like a rape victim without the violence. He'd neither knocked nor gotten her permission to enter.

"You gon' cook!" he demanded without the question mark.

"Sure," she agreed since she didn't have a choice. She'd accepted that she was merely a tool or one of his many accessories and etceteras, like his gun, chain or rims. She was his pussy that he used on demand like the local cable provider.

"Here," he said pulling out his dick to be sucked after lunch. He got another nut before they headed out to shoot up the wedding. She never could understand his fascination with Killa. Admiration is one thing but dick riding was on a whole other level and it disgusted her.

"That's why your dumb ass sitting there bleeding to death!' she huffed to herself. She washed her body on the outside although the inside contained semen and corruption.

She dried off and stepped into the negligee. She did a half turn in the full mirror to admire her ass cheeks. Protruding from French cut bottom. He breast looked like plump melons from the push up top.

"Hello?" Malice called as she stepped out into the hallway.

"In here," Phillipe called from a back bedroom. He wasn't quite sure how to make his move on her until he saw the negligee. It said all that was needed to be said so he began to strip.

Malice smiled at the handsome cop as he came out of his clothes. He had obviously worked out because a neat six pack rippled under a nice set of pecs. An average size dick came out next. It had a curve to it when erect just like the one she'd left behind. All and all it would do so she nodded in approval.

The cop knew what she liked from watching the AG sex tape so he dove straight between her legs. He sucked on her hot box like it was a mango from back home in Puerto Rico. Once she began to moan he flipped around into the 69 position and slid into her mouth. He stopped short of climaxing and changed positions again.

"On your stomach!" he directed as he flipped her over.

"Like this?" she purred and arched her back. Her plump pussy popped out and he leaned in to lick it again.

Once he'd worked up a good froth he dove inside and humped furiously. The sound of skin slapping echoed throughout the otherwise quiet house. Malice realized he was fucking for him and not for her. She let out a few moans to help him get off and he did.

"Shit!" he grunted and snatched out of her. He used his hand and the creamy lubricant she'd coated his dick with and skeeted on her back.

"Mmm, that was good!" she cheered, even though it was just okay. Still it was good enough to secure her spot.

"Yeah, it was. Now where's Murda?" he asked.

****

Murda awoke the next morning alone, confused and in pain. He twisted his face curiously at the empty spot Malice should have been in. Pain or no pain he wanted his morning nut, then a blunt, breakfast and a blow job.

"Malice! Where you at?" he called out. No reply came so he rolled out to find her. "OUCH!!!"

Murda grimaced from the pain then again when his search came up empty. It looked bad, but got worse when he looked out of the window. He hoped to see Malice coming out of the bodega with breakfast, but instead he saw the hot SUV still parked out in front of the building. A patrol car pulled up behind it and began to run its plates.

"Stupid ass bitch!" he spat. The plates wouldn't come back to him, but would match the crime scene. It was time to bounce before the block was crawling with cops. Yup, things got even worst when he went for the money. "FUCK!!!"

Murda grabbed his gun and phone and rushed out of the apartment. His injured arm hung limply by his side as he painfully descended the stairs. An involuntary tear escaped from the pain. He hit the sidewalk and busted a left away from the truck. The second car wasn't where it should have been so he turned a corner and found the third. Once he put some distance between himself and the building he pulled out his phone.

"It's murda!" Ja-Rule rapped signaling Murda's call. The ringtone was cute when they were cool but just sucked now. Malice would have sucked her teeth if not for the mouthful of dick between them. She continued sucking it and let it.

"Must...be...mmm...Murda?" Phillipe asked while on the receiving end of the blow job. She just nodded her head and kept on giving head.

"Fucking bitch ass bitch!" Murda cursed when he finally hung up. He'd noticed that she had become distant after the abortion, but didn't think she would leave him. He knew he needed help so he dialed the number to his newest asset.

"Yo!" Phillipe cheered when he took the call. The premise of talking to a dude while that dude's girl sucked his dick brought a smile to his face. She was doing pretty well on her own but he still reached down to guide her head.

"Yo, my bitch ran out on me! I need a spot to lay low until I get my bread," he pleaded.

"I got you, bro. I...hold on...ugh...argh...shit!" he grunted as Malice pushed him past the finish line. "Mmm. Okay. Go to my Brownstone."

"Okay. Okay," he grunted and set a new course. His wound was still bleeding and he needed a doctor.

The dirty cop made a call, but it wasn't a doctor who answered. No, it was quite the opposite.

Chapter 49

"Yeah?" Killa hissed when he took the crooked cop's crooked call. His hand gripped the wheel chair he was pushing Yolo in so tightly that his knuckles turned white.

"Look, bruh, I know it looks bad, but I didn't set it up. I'm with you! That's why I found them for you. Well, him. The girl is gone, but I know where Murda is. He's hurt and needs a doctor.""Mmh-mm. Okay. Sho-nuff," Killa adlibbed as the cop lied. He wrapped up the call as they reached the exit. Yolo had been cleared to go, but the baby had to stay a few days.

"What he say?" she wanted to know the second he clicked off the call.

"He found Murda. He's at his Brownstone in Brooklyn. Claims he needs a doctor, but has no idea where the girl is," Killa replied.

"I bet if he looks down at his dick he'll find the girl," Yolo shot back, twisting her lips into a *yeah right*.

"I bet," he agreed and helped her into the car. He buckled her in and turned to go back into the hospital.

"Where you going?" Yolo called out.

"To get a doctor," he smile mischievously. Yolo turned the radio on to keep her company until he returned. It wasn't long before he came back with a bag in hand.

"What's all this?" she inquired as he got in. He replied by handing it over so he could drive. Inside were a complete set of doctor's scrub along with gloves, boots, over-shoes, surgical cap, surgical mask, a visor and an apron. To her delight there was also a set of nurse's clothes underneath.

"You up for this?" he asked as he pulled onto the highway.

"I mean, I just had a whole person come out of my vagina, but other than that I'm cool," she quipped.

"Well, you should be use to that," Killa bragged and chuckled at his dick joke.

"Bruh, you straight and all but you are not, five pounds, two ounces!" she corrected.

****

"I'm here" Phillipe texted when he'd reached his Brownstone. He scanned the block for Murda but didn't see him. A moment later his trashcans rattled as the wounded man emerged. "You look like shit!"

"I feel like shit!" he grunted as he staggered towards him. He was so relieved to get some help that he would've hugged him if he had the strength. "I need water."

"Come on inside. The doctor's on his way," he said and unlocked the door. Murda looked around and saw being a crooked cop pays well. He was sweaty and bleeding so he hated to dirty up the place.

"Stretch out on the sofa. I'll get you some water," the cop said and went to retrieve it. The sofa was leather so it could be wiped clean. If not, he would use the money Malice took to replace it.

"Thanks," Murda said gratefully as the cop helped him sip the water. He plopped down once it was finished and went back to sleep. The next time he woke up would be his last.

Phillipe alternated between pacing and looking out the window. He would check the patient, his watch and then look back out the window before pacing some more. Finally, his phone rang ending the long wait.

"Where are you?" he fussed when he took Killa's call. He hated to sound impatient, but he was ready to get back out to The Island and inside young Malice.

"Look out the window," Killa replied. He waited until the man's face appeared before speaking again. "Look at your chest."

"I see," he said, seeing the infrared dot on his heart. "I thought... I mean... I found him... We..."

"Chill. Just a precaution. Where is he?" Killa as he advanced towards the front door. Yolo kept the gun pointed at his chest. One false move and she would blow his heart out of the back of it.

"He's sleep. Hurry up before he dies on his own," he urged. As if on cue Killa walked in dressed like a doctor. He had a doctor's bag in his hand, but it didn't contain anything that a doctor would carry. He'd stopped by the hardware store for the contents inside. "There he is!"

"Come in," he said into his phone as he smiled down at the sleeping man. A minute later Nurse Yolo walked in carrying a similar bag of her own. Hers had the smell of chemicals coming from it making the cop wonder what was inside.

"Hey, guys," Yolo cheered and sat the bag down gingerly.

"Um... Hey," Phillipe sighed. He was in the same room with two of the most dangerous people on the planet after double crossing them. "So, are we, um...?"

"Cool? No, but we're good for now," Killa cut in. "We want the girl too. Have your fun, but we'll be back in a week for her."

"One week," Yolo reiterated causing the cop's head to nod in understanding.

"A week. Yes, Ma'am, Sir," he vowed. He turned and rushed out and into his car. At least he had a week to spend up in the youngster and all her money. The double cross had now become a triple.

"Well, let's get to work," Yolo said once they were alone. She picked up her bag and set off throughout the house while Killa grabbed his and woke up his patient.

"Ugh!" Murda gasped and sputtered when Killa water boarded him with a pitcher of cold water. Once he got his bearings he was relieved to see the doctor standing over him. "Boy, am I glad to see you!"

"Hold that thought," Killa said from behind his mask. The mask hid his face and sinister smile as he removed items from his bag.

Murda was a thug, not a doctor, but still wondered at the hack saw, pliers, and vice-grips that he'd pulled out. They looked more like instruments from a mechanics bag than a doctor's. He watched as a hammer, blow torch, and finally plastic ties and duct tape came out of the bag. still wondered at the hack saw, pliers, and vice-grips that he'd pulled out. They looked more like instruments from a mechanics bag than a doctor's. He watched as a hammer, blow torch, and finally plastic ties and duct tape came out of the bag.

"Open up!" Killa ordered, drawing near with the vice-grips.

"I got shot in my shoulder," Murda protested, but compiled.

"Let's see here..." Killa contemplated as he picked a tooth. He settled on one front and center then snatched it out.

"The fuck?" Murda screamed and pulled his gun from beneath him. He raised it while Killa lowered his mask. If Murda wasn't so young he would've had a heart attack. "You!"

"Yup!" Killa smiled and waved as Murda innocuously pulled the trigger. "Took the clip out."

"Oh," he said since that explained it. "So, I guess you gon' kill me now?"

"Brutally," he chuckled as Yolo returned. "You're just in time. Finished?"

"Two more cameras to go, but it can wait," she replied and took a front row seat for the show.

"One question before we get started," Killa said with a curious frown. "What the fuck is your problem?"

"You gotta beat the man if you wanna be the man," Murda shrugged.

"Where did you get that dumb shit from?" Killa shot back. They never ceased to amaze him, the dumb mantras and stupid sayings people lived by.

Let your haters be your motivators, ball 'til you fall, fake it 'til you make it, and all the other assorted bullshit proverbs.

"On my block! That's what we live by," he stated proudly.

"Do we have any supplies left? We need to pay his block a visit," Killa turned to Yolo and asked.

"I used it all," she shrugged. "Wanna rupture the gas line? That should do it."

"Nah. Maybe just rent a Gatling gun. Can you rent a Gatling gun? I'll have to ask Bigs."

"He would know," she replied. Murda looked curiously back and forth at the two as they bantered about extinguishing his block. This was that Killa/Yolo shit he'd longed for. He smiled at just being able to see it firsthand.

"Aight, Bruh, time to go," Killa announced. He swung the hammer down causing it to lodge in Murda's forehead.

Killa and Yolo watch him writhe in pain for a moment. Killa then took the hatchet and hacked his arm off. Both killers ignored his screams as Killa literally took the man apart.

"Well, that was fun!" Yolo sang and clapped. She placed the last two cameras and they left.

Chapter 50

"You ready to go home, Miss Deidra?" Yolo sang as she was handed her healthy baby girl with a clean bill of health.

Killa had joined the family down in Belize while she'd stayed behind with their new baby.

The daughter locked eyes with her mother and cooed softly. Yolo took it as a yes and headed home to introduce her to the rest of the family. Their plane had landed an hour ago, so they would already be at home waiting when she arrived.

"Mommy!" Shyne cheered when Yolo walked in. She then rushed over to see her new sister while the boys played the back. "She's so pretty!"

"Let me see my namesake!" Grandma Deidra demanded, stretching her arms out to collect the child.

"Here you go, Grandma," Yolo said, passing the baby off. The two women locked eyes and had a moment at her calling her Grandma.

The boys finally came over to gawk at their new baby sister.

Yolo went over to Killa and took shelter under his arm. The proud couple looked on proudly at their family. It was all they'd both ever wanted. It was all Yolo had ever had.

"Still got some unfinished business," Killa reminded under his breath.

"So, let' finish it. I'm ready," she whispered back. "Make the call."

****

"Shit!" Phillipe fussed when *the* phone rang. It was the one reserved for his criminal activity. The one Killa used to reach him. His week was up and he was where he'd been the entire week.

"What's wrong?" Malice moaned and squeezed her tight vagina even tighter to help out with whatever was troubling him.

"Nothing," he ultimately decided. He'd contemplated taking the cock-eyed girl and the money and leaving the country, but he knew he would have to leave the entire planet to escape the wrath of Killa and Yolo.

He picked up his stroke and fucked the girl like there was no tomorrow. Actually, there wouldn't be for her. He then went ahead and bust a nut deep inside her since she was about to be aborted anyway.

"Be careful," Malice warned when he began skeeting inside of her. Although she wouldn't mind having a baby with him since Murda was no more. She'd personally helped Phillipe dump his body parts in dumpsters all over town. "You gon' get me pregnant!"

"You'll be okay," he assured her and pulled out. He took one last look at her fine frame and shook his head. "I gotta run into the city. I'm gonna take the money and put it in the bank with mine since we're together now."

"Okaaay!" Malice sang happily. She then let out a love sick sigh and rolled over for a nap.

Phillipe took a quick shower to wash the sex away. He then grabbed the bag of cash and headed out to his car. One he was in motion he returned the missed call.

"Yo," Killa replied. "Times up. I want the girl. Today!"

"I know, I know. Are you familiar with Deer Park? It's out on The Island. Suffolk County," the cop asked as he sped towards his Brooklyn Brownstone.

"Not really," he lied. Deer Park was actually two towns over from Wyandanch, but that was unneeded information so he kept it to himself.

"Long Island Expressway, then get off at..." The cop relayed the directions before giving up the exact address. "We good now?"

"Good as gold. You have my word, neither me nor Yolo will put a hand on you," he vowed while Yolo nodded in agreement.

"So, what you gon' shot me? Stab me?" he shot back skeptically.

"We won't shoot, stab, bludgeon, um..." he paused and looked to Yolo for help.

"Choke, smother, um...poison."

"Yeah, poison, electrocute, drown...," he promised. "Swear to God."

"I believe you," the cop sighed in relief. Now he had a couple hundred free grands and a new lease on life. Malice, on the other hand, was about to get fucked up.

****

Malice happily cooked lunch for when her baby returned. She wasn't much of a cook and she knew it. She also knew that she had some good pussy so planned on feeding him some of it too.

"Hey, Baby!" she sang from the kitchen when she heard the front door open. She poked her lip out and frowned when she heard the back door open too. "Phillipe? Bae?"

"Nope. Nope," Killa replied from the front while Yolo answered from the back.

Malice shot her in all directions looking for an escape. She didn't see one but did see the knife rack. She pulled the butcher knife and meat cleaver out to defend herself.

"That's not a knife!" Yolo giggled. She pulled her arm from behind her back and came out with a machete. "This is a knife!"

"Oh, so y'all gon' jump me? Give me a one!" she dared and glared at Yolo.

"Bitch, did you give my baby mom a one? Did Sin get a one, huh? Did you give us a one when you shot up our wedding?" Killa barked as he pulled his machete.

"Chill, Bae. Remember your blood pressure," Yolo warned lovingly. "I got her."

"Don't got her, get her!" he insisted and fell back. You know Killa so you know that he pulled out his phone to record the show.

"Me and you old lady," Malice giggled. Yolo was only in her early thirties, but Malice was still a kid.

"Old lady?" Yolo reeled from the insult. She shot a quick glance in the mirror to see if she looked old.

"That's right, old," Malice laughed and took a fighting stance with her knives. "And once I kill you I'ma put this good, young pussy on your man and keep him. Killa and Malice. Malice and..."

Yolo moved so fast that Killa was going to have to watch the replay in slow motion to catch it. The sharp blade glinted in the light as she swung. Malice was in midsentence when it caught her flush across the neck. Her crooked eye straightened out as her head came off and tumbled in the air.

"Well damn!" Killa exclaimed. He always did love that gangsta shit.

"Call me an old lady again," Yolo grumbled to the head as it rolled into a corner.

"Come on ol' lady, let's go home to our family," Killa said while taking her elbow and leading her away.

"That's right. Killa and Yolo!" she told the dead head on the way out. "*'Til Death Does Us!*"

The End

Epilogue

"The fuck?" Phillipe asked when *that* phone rang. He ignored it the first time, then answered it. "Sup yo? Our biz is done!"

"Almost," Killa corrected. "We still have to address the matter of your betrayal."

"Is that right?" the cop asked sticking his middle finger up defiantly.

"I can see you," Killa advised. "You're in the living room, wearing a red shirt and blue jeans."

"Huh?" he asked after looking down to confirm his attire. He spun around looking high and low. "You put...cameras in my house?"

"That ain't all!" Yolo giggled from his side.

"Wh-Wh-What about y-y-y-your word? Huh? You gave your word!"

"Not to shoot, stab, choke, bludgeon, drown or electrocute you," she reminded. "We never said anything about blowing you up!"

"We loaded your hose with semtex. Say goodbye," Killa cheered.

"Okay, bye-bye!" Yolo sang and pressed the button.

The screen went orange then black as the massive explosion rocked the Brooklyn block. The Brownstone crumbled to dust as the crooked cop got what he had coming.

Killa and Yolo high-fived at their latest victory. Yolo's vagina was still out of service from giving birth so he had to settle for a hand job while they made out. As usual he was fast asleep five minutes after getting off.

Yolo kissed his forehead and eased out of bed to wash her hands.

It had been a good day so she decided to make an entry into her diary. She now kept the book on the top shelf of their closet to keep her nosey daughter out of it. Or so she thought.

"That damn Shyne!" she fussed when she saw that it was missing. She marched down the hall and barged into her daughter's room.

Shyne was tossing and turning in her sleep with a smile on her face. The open diary lay on the bed next to her.

Yolo almost woke her but decided to let her enjoy her dream. You will to...

Yolo 6, still dreaming, is next